Luke watched her go. He could never not watch Laura, he realised. Whenever they were together his awareness of her was total: exactly where she was in the room, whom she was talking to, what kind of mood she was in. He read her body language – the tilt of her head, the slope of her shoulders – without being conscious that he was doing it. He knew that now, for instance, her unexpressive face and rather stiff journey towards the door meant that she was tired and unhappy.

'It's difficult,' Juliet said, interpreting his silence after they were left alone together. 'All these conflicting personalities.'

'What do you mean?' Luke switched his attention.

'Piers, I suppose. Philip's told me that Sheila's threatened to resign over him.'

He shrugged. 'That's not what bothers me,' he admitted. 'To be honest, Laura and I don't see eye to eye over this leukaemia business.'

'Ah. Have you talked it through?'

'Not properly.'

Juliet leaned towards the table so that he caught the full force of her gaze. 'Do it,' she advised. 'Do it now.'

Kate Fielding was born in Yorkshire and read English Literature at university before training as a teacher. She lives in Ilkley with her two daughters. She also writes books for children under her real name, Jenny Oldfield. Her series *Home Farm Twins* has recently been adapted for television by the BBC. Her two previous novels in the Ravensdale series, *Ravensdale* and *A Winter in Ravensdale*, are also available in Orion Paperbacks.

RAVENSDALE SPRING

Kate Fielding

ORION

An Orion paperback
First published in Great Britain by Orion in 1999
This paperback edition published in 1999
by Orion Books Ltd,
Orion House, 5 Upper St Martin's Lane,
London WC2H 9EA

A CIP catalogue record for this book
is available from the British Library.

Printed and bound in Great Britain by
Clays Ltd, St Ives plc

For my mother and father
who gave me Yorkshire
and much more

PROLOGUE

The land seemed to shift and disappear. Here, at the head of the Dale, so early in the morning that white mists still lay in the valleys and the far horizons vanished behind thin clouds, Dr Laura Grant felt keenly the limit of her skills.

She was on her way to Wingate, hoping to meet first with Rudi Grey to discuss her young leukaemia patients, Catherine Earle and Elliot Wood, and then to call in on Elliot in a side ward reserved especially for patients who had reached the terminal stage of their illness.

'Sorry, Mr Grey's been called to surgery,' his assistant told Laura as she knocked on the consultant's door. 'He said to join him for coffee at ten-thirty, if you have time.' So she went straight to the ward, stopping to chat in a corridor with a physiotherapist friend about the media attention the leukaemia cases were currently receiving, aware that she was putting off the moment when she must face Elliot's mother, Hannah.

'It's a pity the families have to take some of the flak,' the physio said. 'Apparently a couple of journalists tailed little Elliot's grandparents from the car park yesterday, to find out which ward he was in.'

Laura shook her head in dismay, then walked towards the paediatric unit, feeling guilty that she had delayed her visit.

Hannah was absent from Elliot's room when she arrived. The tiny patient was propped high on pillows inside a child's cot, surrounded by monitors and stand-by resuscitation equipment. A favourite soft toy had slipped sideways and caught on the cot bars. Laura leaned in and put it back on the boy's pillow, afraid to wake him. Years of training and practice work still hadn't prepared her for these moments that slipped out beyond the limits of medical knowledge into a hinterland of helplessness and confusion.

'It's all right, Dr Grant.' Hannah had halted in the doorway, cup of coffee in her hand. 'You won't disturb him. They've sedated him for the pain.'

Laura set a chair for Hannah to sit close to the bed. She could tell that the mother had slid beyond hope into a huge, aching void. Her eyes were dark and empty, her posture half-slumped, motionless. 'I went for a hot drink,' Hannah explained unnecessarily. 'But I don't really want it.' She offered it to Laura instead, who took it and put it to one side. 'I can't drink or eat with Elliot lying here like that. I even feel bad that I can get up and walk around when he can't, poor mite.'

'What have they told you?' Laura asked gently.

'That he hasn't got much longer, though his heart's still strong. Until three days ago he was sitting up and taking his meals, even playing with me and his grandad. We took him out into the grounds for a breath of fresh air. He sat on my knee in the sun and I made him a daisy-chain to go round his neck.' Hannah's full mouth fell half open as she remembered. 'Then, that night, Monday, he went downhill. His temperature shot up and he had trouble breathing. They said it was an infection that he couldn't shake off. Elliot showed them; he pulled back from that. But now he's in a lot of pain. His bones hurt, only he can't tell me, of course. He just looks at me and holds out his little arms to be picked up. I can't bear it, the way he looks at me and says my name. I'm glad they've let him sleep.'

Laura held back, standing behind Hannah's chair, looking down at Elliot's almost pure white skin. 'You can talk to him

2

whenever you feel like it,' she whispered. 'He won't wake, but he can probably hear what you say.'

Hannah nodded. 'I've been singing songs to him when there's been no one around to overhear. That's what he likes.' She turned to gaze at Laura. 'It's a funny thing; my heart's breaking, but I go on.'

Laura crouched to hold her hand.

'I buy myself a cup of coffee, I ring Mum to tell her to bring a pair of clean pyjamas, I ask the doctor questions. And all the time I'm thinking, how come I can still do this? Inside, there's nothing left. My Gary's gone . . . and Elliot's slipping away. They're my life, those two.'

Laura watched as tears slid unnoticed down Hannah's cheeks.

'I know you've done all you can. But the fact is, it's not enough. We brought him to see you too late. If I'd have had those bruises looked at sooner . . . Only, I . . . we thought it was nothing.'

'You mustn't see it like that.'

'Well, I wish it could be me lying there and not Elliot,' Hannah cried. 'What did he do to deserve this? What did any of us do?'

CHAPTER ONE

Nothing was solid, not even the hills. A clump of trees would appear, then the mist would swirl and envelop them. A bank of dark-grey cloud rolled across the flat ridge of Ravenscar and swept into the Dale. There would soon be rain.

Laura stopped her car. Her recently diagnosed ten-year-old leukaemia patient, Catherine Earle, was back home after two weeks in Wingate Hospital. The child was in early remission from the disease. The hospital and the family were optimistic.

But Laura needed to steel herself for this first home visit since Catherine's return.

'It's not the physician's job to take away hope.' Laura remembered the words of her med school tutor. Harold Vaughan had urged his students not to bombard their patients with hard facts that they couldn't process. 'Remember, the landscape of disease is bleak and forbidding,' he'd told them.

The land below echoed his admonition. Early spring, first light; cold and wind-swept.

It's not my job to take away hope. Laura filed the dictum back into its memory slot. Suppose I don't tell the Earles that of the thirteen hundred children who develop cancer in Britain each year only fifty per cent have a decent chance of survival? Suppose I remind them instead that after blood tests, X-rays, ultrasound and isotope scans, after the bone-marrow results and the two weeks of chemotherapy, Catherine's condition has stabilised? Let's put her among the lucky fifty per cent.

Am I giving them the sort of hope that I can justify? Am I doing what's best?

To cure, relieve and comfort are the goals of medicine. She reminded herself of Harold Vaughan's mantra as she faced the ordeal of visiting Catherine and her parents.

Laura drove on, passing Hawkshead Hall with its lodge standing empty by the stone gates. There was a glimpse of landscaped gardens, yew hedges, a Jacobean manor house with wide stone steps to a low doorway. Memories of Matthew.

Even now, on her way to what she knew would be a difficult interview, she had time to take in the sloping grounds, the canopy of beech trees to the west of the main house, the eighteenth-century landscaped garden and formal lake to the south. And now, as always when she came within sight of the Aires' family home, she recalled her first introduction to Matthew's mother, Maisie, and her own one-time hope that she and Matthew might have a future together in the Hall.

Before Luke, she told herself. In her early days at Ravensdale, when Matthew's kindness had helped to convince her that the move from London had been the right one. Before Luke, she had loved Matthew Aire.

With an effort she pulled her thoughts back to the here and now. Haresby Farm, where she was headed, still belonged to the ancient Hawkshead estate, but Maisie Aire took little interest. She left its management to her son. In turn, Matthew trusted the day-to-day running of the dairy farm to Peter and Sonia Earle.

To comfort. Of the three goals, Laura recognised that this was probably her strength. Being on the same side as her patients, getting them to trust her, came naturally.

'Don't lose your human face.' Vaughan had taken her aside during one of their early sessions in the anatomy lab. He'd flattered her by telling her that he'd singled her out for her evident compassion. 'Forget "we" and "they",' he'd said.

'Don't go in for this emotional-distancing lark. In the end, we're all in the same boat.'

At thirty-one, Laura was still young enough to feel the truth of her teacher's message, experienced enough to know how hard it was to hang on to. Not because she no longer cared, but because compassion came expensive in terms of a doctor's energy and resilience.

Like now. The country grew lonelier and the mists clung to the hollows in fields to either side of the narrow road. At the end of it, Sonia and Peter Earle had their daughter back home. But for how long no one could say.

Haresby Farm was stone-built and dated back to the seventeenth century. Because it was part of the Hawkshead estate, itself linked to the monks of Ravensdale Abbey, the house had certain elegant distinguishing features. The windows were built in Gothic style, there was a stone portico and a frieze of carved stone under the eaves. Its roof of thick sandstone slabs was mossy with age.

Laura parked by the side of the house, recalling the Earles' first visit to the surgery three weeks before.

Catherine was tired and listless, Sonia had said. Probably nothing, but it was better to be safe than sorry.

Laura had smiled at the fidgeting girl. Like her mother, Catherine was dark-haired and thin-faced. Both were slight and reticent in manner. It was the first time they'd visited the health centre since Laura had been made a partner almost two years earlier. She'd asked about other symptoms; nothing except a slight loss of appetite.

She took things one step at a time. No need to worry, Laura had said. They would do a couple of further checks, though the girl's temperature and blood pressure had shown nothing untoward. She'd asked about Catherine's diet, sleep patterns, possible anxieties at school. And she'd had one eye on the clock, aware of the next patient sitting in the waiting-room.

7

A week later a blood test had come back from the lab with the devastating result.

On the second appointment she'd asked both Peter and Sonia to come into the centre without Catherine. It had been the last week in March and they'd begun their session by chatting uneasily about the family's recently planned summer holiday in France.

'Always assuming these tests Catherine's been having don't stop us going away,' Peter had said. 'Our son, Adam, has a French pen-friend in Paris. The two families are getting together for a fortnight in Brittany.'

One more step; Laura had explained about the immature white blood cells found in the blood sample. A slow lurch out of normality.

'What does it mean?' Sonia's eyes had narrowed. 'Immature white cells?'

'They're the type of blood cells that fight infection. We call some lymphocytes, and some neutrophils.' Careful . . . careful. Laura had seen the flash of fear register behind the mother's guarded eyes. 'In Catherine's case it seems to be the neutrophils that are failing to mature. This means that the bone marrow works overtime to produce more cells, but these don't mature properly either, so soon the immature ones take over the system.'

Bone marrow had probably been the term that had done it. Sonia Earle's hand had flown to her mouth. Peter had frowned and looked out of the window.

'The immature cells are cancer cells.' Laura had said the words calmly and plainly. 'What the blood test shows is that Catherine has leukaemia.'

'Are you sure?' Peter Earle sat still.

'Positive. Catherine will need to go to hospital for further tests. There are two possible types of childhood leukaemia and a bone-marrow test will identify which kind she has. But

8

remember, cancer in children is very different from cancer in adults. The recovery rate is much better.'

Cancer. The biggest challenge.

'What do we tell her?' Sonia recovered first from the initial shock. 'We've left her at home with a sore throat and a temperature. She knows something's wrong.'

'That's largely up to you. At Catherine's age I'd say it was best to give her the facts, backed up by lots of love and reassurance.'

'Reassurance?' There was anger in Peter's echo. 'You say we should tell our daughter that she's got a fatal illness and at the same time urge her not to worry?'

'Leukaemia in children isn't necessarily fatal.' Laura stressed recent progress in treating the disease. 'We get long periods of remission when the patient has no symptoms and doesn't need any treatment. If we reach five years of full remission, we can talk about a cure.'

To cure, relieve and comfort.

Through the shock and confusion, Sonia Earle asked the ultimate, unanswerable question. 'If we get Catherine to hospital and they give her the chemotherapy and whatever else they need to do, she will be OK, won't she?'

The family had weathered the first few traumatic weeks by reading a 'yes' into Laura's response.

Sonia had been the practical one, arranging her work hours at a building society in Merton around hospital visits and care for their thirteen-year-old son Adam. When Laura had called in to see Catherine in the children's ward, she'd found Sonia discussing the detailed diagnosis with Rudi Grey, the oncologist, and taking in complex information about the cocktail of drugs needed to slow down the production of cancerous cells. The mother was with Catherine for every dose of radiotherapy, explaining that the buzzing sound made by the high-tech linear accelerator meant that electrons were hitting a target of tungsten to make the X-rays that would zap the cancer cells out of her central nervous system.

'She likes science fiction,' Sonia told Laura with a faint smile.

Peter seemed harder hit. He had gone along with medical advice without questioning, lavishing presents on his sick daughter. But when he was away from her bedside, he had given up all pretence of taking it in his stride.

Now they had her home.

The Earles' son, Adam, must have heard Laura's car pull up beside the house. He came out of the barn across the farmyard, saw who it was and veered off to pick up his bike by the gate. He left without a word, up the lane and across country, riding the rocky track into the wet mist.

Laura noted the deliberate shun. Serious illness in the family was no fun for anyone. Adam was probably feeling badly left out and, if he was anything like his father, would find it hard to say so. She knocked at the door, putting the boy's hostile reaction into context.

'Come in.' Peter opened the door. His bright voice and the smile on his regular, handsome face were brittle. 'I saw your car. Sonia's up in Catherine's room.'

'How's the patient? What sort of a night has she had?'

He ushered her through the big square kitchen with its wide open fireplace and heavy beams. There were get-well cards scattered across the table, just out of their envelopes. 'Catherine slept like a log. Sonia didn't get a wink. She was up every five minutes, going through to check on Catherine.'

'That's normal.' Laura followed him quietly upstairs.

'They sent her home with one of these tube things attached to her chest. For the ongoing drugs and blood samples and so on. Sonia's worried it's going to come out if Catherine turns awkwardly in her sleep.' Peter paused on the landing and glanced out of the window at Adam, cycling up the hill. He gave a short, suppressed sigh.

10

'It won't.' Laura reassured him about the Hickman line. 'These catheters are designed to stay in place for months. It shouldn't impede her in any way.'

Peter nodded and went on. 'It's Sonia I'm worried about. She's not getting any sleep.'

'What about you?' She could offer tranquillisers to the worried parents, if and when the time was right.

But Peter brushed her off. He climbed the broad stairs with a firm tread. He was brisk, pushing open the bedroom door with, 'You should see the presents and cards. It's like Christmas in here.'

Laura found Sonia plumping up Catherine's pillows. The patient was propped up in bed, surrounded by stuffed toys. They were pink and round and fluffy. 'Who are all these pigs?' she asked gravely.

'They haven't got names yet.' Catherine rearranged them in order of size, keeping the smallest in her hand. It had floppy arms and legs, and a logo on its middle in the shape of a red heart, with the words 'I luv you, Cathy'. She showed Laura. 'This one's from Daddy.'

'I like pigs myself,' Laura confessed. She found Catherine bright and matter-of-fact. 'Gloucester Old Spots are my favourites.'

The girl nodded. 'I'm going to call this one William,' she decided, letting Laura get on with the business of checking her catheter and taking her pulse. Two weeks in hospital had accustomed her to being prodded and poked.

'Good girl.' Laura realised that her battle to keep up morale would lie with Sonia and Peter Earle rather than with Catherine. 'You needn't stay in bed unless you want to,' she explained. 'If you feel like getting up and watching TV, that's fine.'

'Can I play outside?'

'For a little while. But you must take it easy.'

'Can I go to school?'

11

Laura glanced at Sonia. 'What do you think?'

'It's too soon. I've taken time off from work to look after her.' The mother's angular face, framed by the dark, bobbed hair, looked determined. 'I let school know that Catherine wouldn't be back for a few more weeks.'

'But I want to go.'

Sonia tutted. 'Trust you, Catherine. Anyone else would be thrilled.'

'Better do as your mum says.' Laura got up.

'If Catherine feels up to doing things, let her,' she reminded Sonia as they descended to the kitchen.

Sonia sat down heavily at the table, gathering the recent cards into a neat pile. Her slim fingers patted and shuffled them into position. 'I just want to wrap her in cotton-wool.'

'That's understandable.'

'I don't want her to catch an infection.'

'It's unlikely. Her blood count is nearly back to normal after her radiotherapy. That's why Rudi Grey discharged her. He's very happy with her. Look, if you're under too much pressure, I could arrange a home visit from Carole Fawcett, our medical social worker.'

'No thanks.' The refusal came quick and sharp. 'Peter would hate that.' She looked up at the sound of another car pulling up outside. 'That's Mr Aire. He knows Catherine's back home.'

Laura felt her heart jolt. She recognised the Range Rover from Hawkshead Hall, saw Matthew step down and head for the front door. She heard his quiet, low voice as he met and shook hands with Peter Earle.

'That's just like him to come and visit the first chance he gets. He's very good to the kids.' Sonia stood up, ready to greet their employer.

Matthew came in, stooping under the low lintel, carrying a card and a big box of chocolates for the invalid. His grey eyes

12

flickered as they rested on Laura, but he'd evidently seen her car and prepared himself. 'Hello, stranger. How are you?'

She smiled back. Once, she couldn't have imagined the day when she would stand on neutral territory and think with cold objectivity, this was the man I held in my arms and loved. Once. Now a stranger, saying a dispassionate hello. 'I'm fine, thanks.'

'How's Luke?'

'Fine too.' She passed Matthew in the hallway, checking her watch, seeing that she would just make it to the pre-surgery meeting at the centre. 'Give me a ring any time you need to,' she told Sonia and Peter Earle.

She got into her car and drove down the Dale. The mist was clearing, but she couldn't dismiss Matthew from her mind. She recalled their winter parting, Matthew's voice insisting that she couldn't just walk away: from Hawkshead Hall, from him. His hurt face, his struggle to hold on to her came back to her now and sat uneasily alongside today's superficial exchange at Haresby.

'I can't make you mean less to me,' he'd told her then, warning her that he wouldn't give up without a fight.

Yet aggression wasn't Matthew's style. Laura had loved him for his gentleness, which ran deep, and she hadn't expected him to pursue her after her final visit to the Hall. Not after it became public knowledge that she and Luke were together. Especially not then.

That must have been hardest of all for Matthew. 'It's Luke Altham we're talking about here,' he'd accused her, telling her how impossible it would be to watch her with someone else.

Overhead, the clouds thinned. Sun lit the limestone walls and trees cast long shadows over the way ahead. The road levelled and followed the bank of the River Raven into Hawkshead. Laura forced her mind back on to the business in hand, wondering what else she might do to help the Earles

13

through their crisis. Then she focused on the morning
meeting with Philip Maskell and Piers Chandler, the new
partner in the practice.

She wound through hairpin bends, between high stone
walls. Across the valley, Ravenscar rose in deep morning
shadow.

CHAPTER TWO

Laura glanced uncomfortably across the room at Piers Chandler. Beside her, Philip shuffled papers on his knee.

'I want to try out a new spread-sheet,' Piers told Sheila Knowles. 'The system of accounting we have in use at the moment belongs in the Ark.'

'"I grow old, I grow old,"' Philip muttered under his breath.

Laura gave him a quizzical look.

'Just a poem.'

Piers was six feet one inch of bristling progress. He knew every angle on fund-holding, basic practice allowances, particular fees, capitation and incentives. He waxed lyrical on state-of-the-art methods, which were way beyond Laura's and Philip's technological grasp. And he was upsetting their receptionist.

'I've only just got used to the present one,' Sheila complained. 'When I first came to work here nine years ago none of the patients' files were even computerised and we didn't have to give a second thought to what everything cost!' She glanced with a worried frown at Laura.

Come on, Philip, Laura thought. The sooner they moved on to the next agenda item, the better.

Philip stirred his coffee and rattled his spoon against the cup. Didn't the ineffectual man in the poem measure out his life in coffee-spoons? Laura wondered. She pictured him sliding all too easily into the chair that Gerald Scott had just vacated. A GP of the old school who'd lived in Hawkshead all

15

his life, Gerald had known most of his patients by their first names. He'd loathed computers and spread-sheets, whereas Piers Chandler seemed to have slipped from the womb computer-literate and spouting statistics.

'It'll be no problem,' Piers insisted. He ignored Sheila's flushed face and rattled on. 'I've asked around to find out the best program for what we want. We could get it up and running within the week, believe me.'

'Sorry I was late.' Laura leaned over to murmur to Philip. 'I had to drive up to Haresby to check on Catherine Earle.'

'How is she?' His question was personal rather than professional. Philip had known Peter and Sonia Earle since they were young.

'She's OK, considering.'

'Is it myeloid or lymphocytic; do they know yet?'

'Myeloid. I think Sonia realises it's the hard one to beat, but I'm not sure that Peter does.'

Philip shook his head. 'It's not something he would take on board. How's he coping?'

She shrugged. 'OK, apparently. He's angry, though.'

'Who with?'

'Everybody. He seems to be looking for someone to blame.' She remembered him at Wingate on the day of the lumbar puncture, demanding why it was so difficult to get his distraught wife a cup of tea.

'I don't see the problem.' Piers's voice cut across Philip and Laura's conversation. He was still hectoring the receptionist. 'If it's retraining we're talking about, we can easily sign you up for an evening class.'

Laura saw Sheila's face set hard as she spelled out her point of view. 'What I'm saying is, it isn't strictly necessary.'

'You mean, if it ain't broke, don't fix it?' For a few seconds Piers pretended to consider this. But he couldn't hide his condescension. 'In some cases I might agree. But when it comes to efficiency in submitting our claims for fees and expenses we have to be on the ball.'

Piers threw in colloquialisms to disguise his dogmatic assertions, Laura realised now. It was something she'd missed when she, Gerald and Philip had first interviewed him. And she'd paid too much attention to the traces of Geordie accent in his voice. It had made their new partner seem more approachable than in fact he was.

'Ready, everyone?' Philip chipped in at last with his usual opening to the eight-twenty meeting.

Laura watched Piers sit back hard in his chair, rocking it on to the two back legs, tapping a pencil against the edge of the table. Sheila sat stiffly next to Philip, whose posture mirrored hers. Trouble, she told herself. And it had been brewing since Piers Chandler had set foot through the door.

'I did a study a couple of years back on the links between childhood cancers and environmental factors,' Piers told Laura after what had turned out to be an edgy but uneventful eight-twenty.

After her disagreement with Piers over the new technology, Sheila had sat on the sidelines while Philip had brought everyone up to date about the usual shortage of beds in the psychogeriatric unit at Wingate and Laura had briefed them about her busy weekend on call. They'd both left the meeting promptly to get on with their work: Sheila to organise the patients already queuing in reception.

'Yes, I remember. It was down on your cv. Did you find anything useful?' Laura gulped the last of her coffee and glanced at her watch.

'I had it published.' Piers avoided a direct answer, but obviously wanted to engage Laura on his own wavelength. 'I didn't go for the usual antenatal or passive-smoking line. I was more interested in carcinogenic factors in diet, soil, water and so on. And I followed up a possible link between adults

17

who had worked in the manufacture of PVC and a higher incidence of cancer in their offspring.'

Laura was heading for the door, eager to be on time for her first appointment, resisting the allegiance. 'Causes of childhood cancers are notoriously difficult. But I haven't heard the PVC theory. What is it?'

'There's a gas: vinyl chloride. It's a known carcinogen.' Piers followed her out, explaining the details, ignoring the patients sitting in reception.

Laura was aware of Philip staying behind his desk and sighing.

Maybe Piers's singular lack of awareness of the effect he had on his colleagues would even out with the passage of time, she thought, as she settled in for her surgery. It was the keenness of the new boy, anxious to impress. After all, this was only his second month in the job. She compared Piers's attitude with her own early days in Ravensdale and, like Philip, she found herself sighing.

When Laura had arrived, she'd had a mountain of prejudice to climb; first, she was a woman, second she was young, and third she'd come to them from a London practice. All these factors mitigated against her as far as many of the patients in the Dale were concerned.

She'd worked conscientiously to find the right combination of calm manner and sound medical practice to bring round the Kit Braithwaites and Dick Metcalfes. It had been a matter of fine diplomacy and her hunch was that it would take Piers considerably longer than the fifteen months it had taken her.

If Piers had the staying power. And if the rest of the staff at the medical centre didn't mount a full-scale insurrection first.

Laura had just caught a glimpse through the door of Piers going behind Sheila's desk and commandeering her computer. She saw him point and gesture, obviously rubbishing something on screen to prove his earlier point about the spreadsheet. The entry into the consulting-room of Laura's first patient prevented her from witnessing the receptionist's response, but the flushed patches on Sheila's neck and throat didn't augur well.

During the next two hours Laura listened and prescribed, examined, referred, considered and counselled. She took a phone call about eighty-two-year-old Lucy Marlow, whose osteo-arthritis might force her to accept sheltered accommodation. And, though her list was full, she squeezed in Marjorie Brown with a case of acute lumbago, which she was able to relieve with an anti-inflammatory drug.

She was still behind her desk, checking her remaining appointments, when Hannah Wood sat down with the toddler; a heavy, pale-faced woman of twenty-three with long, straight brown hair and a round, expressionless face. Her sleeveless salmon-pink dress emphasised the pale plumpness of her arms as she wrapped them round her squirming son.

'How's Elliot doing?' Laura read the notes, which told her that the boy was an only child, with all the usual immunisations up to date. Looking at the toddler, she noted the strong physical resemblance between mother and son; the same grey eyes set wide apart, the same sturdiness.

'He's come down with something,' Hannah explained. 'I wasn't worried at first, but it's been going on for a few days now. I thought I'd better let you take a look.'

Laura smiled reassuringly and launched into the routine questions about appetite and sleep. 'Elliot's temperature is slightly higher than it should be,' she said after a glance at the thermometer. 'And he's a bit chesty. He's probably picked up some sort of virus.'

'Like flu?' Hannah Wood seemed relieved. She gathered the toddler in her arms and stood up. 'Thank you, Dr Grant. Sorry if I've made too much fuss. I wouldn't have brought him in, only Gary, my husband, said I should.'

'Quite right.' Laura studied the listless child. Elliot hadn't put up any of the usual resistance to being examined. 'You say he's been like this for a few days? Off his food? No energy? And he's been sleeping more than normal?'

Hannah gave her a blank look. Her light, still girlish voice tried to dismiss Laura's concerns. 'There's nothing else the matter with him, is there?'

'Probably not. Still, let's take another look at him, shall we?' Laura was about to propose that she should send the boy through to Joy for a blood sample when she rolled up the lightweight cotton trousers and discovered distinct bruising along the length of both shins.

'He's been falling over.' Hannah stared at the brown and blue marks.

'It's OK. I'm not thinking anything sinister,' Laura promised her.

Hannah seemed not to believe her. 'We haven't hit him. The bruises are from falling,' she insisted. 'I knew that's what you'd think: that we'd been hitting him too hard. I told Gary, but he said to come anyway.'

'Sit down again.' Laura had been mistaken. Hannah Wood's face hadn't been expressionless when she came in; it had been scared. It was like the fixed gaze of a rabbit caught in a car's headlights. 'Don't worry, Hannah. I'm not blaming you for Elliot's bruises, OK?'

Slowly she nodded and sat down. Elliot buried his face in her chest, his plump legs with their tell-tale marks dangling over her knees.

'I think we need to take a blood sample and do some tests,' Laura told her gently. She watched for any reaction other than the glazed, scared look in the wide grey eyes.

'We'll do it straight away, but we won't get the results for a week or two. When we do, I'll give you a ring. Meanwhile, you take Elliot home and look after him. Give him plenty to drink, but if he doesn't feel like eating, don't try to force him.'

'What for? Why do you need to do these tests?' Hannah

20

evidently hadn't taken in much of what Laura had said, but she'd heard the word, 'tests'.

Laura caught herself out in another mistake; she'd assumed that the boy's pale complexion was inherited. Hannah herself had a pasty look. But now that she looked again and combined it with the bruising, she thought that the pallor might be significant. And the proneness to infection. 'I just want to make sure that Elliot's problem is a straightforward virus. Better safe than sorry,' she explained, successfully disguising a niggling doubt.

And that was her third error. She'd underestimated Hannah Wood. Misled by the homely features and awkward manner, she had her down as a shy, unenquiring and passive girl. Someone she would automatically try to protect.

'Gary was talking to Peter Earle the other day,' Hannah told Laura. 'He worked for Peter when he first left school. He asked after Catherine.'

Laura sat on the edge of the desk, hands clasped in front of her, waiting. The suspicion escaped from the dark recesses and roared to the forefront of her mind.

'It turns out Catherine started just like this.' Hannah recounted the symptoms. 'She was tired, she wouldn't eat.'

Now they came to the core of it; the real reason why Hannah Wood had brought Elliot in.

'You suggested blood tests for Catherine, didn't you?' She looked up at Laura with her wide, hopeless stare. 'That was when they found out she had the cancer.'

CHAPTER THREE

'Are you on call?' Luke asked Laura, above the hiss of the shower and the sharp pin-points of water on his face. He kept the thermostat as high as he could bear.

It was the last Sunday in May. Luke had stayed over at Abbey Grange after a day spent shopping together in York. The sun and the dawn chorus had woken them.

'No. It's Philip's turn. For another whole twenty-four hours Hawkshead Medical Centre doesn't exist!'

'Then we should make the most of the day. What would you like to do?' Luke pulled the shower curtain to one side and made room for Laura. She brushed against him as she stepped in, her long dark hair catching against his shoulder and sticking to his wet skin. She smiled, then turned away, letting him run his hand down the length of her back.

She lifted her face to the jet. 'What sort of a question is that?'

'A sensible, straightforward question; honest!' He wrapped his arms around her, let the clean water collect in the angles of their crooked limbs and spill over. 'Let's do something special.'

'We could go for a walk up Black Gill.'

'Hmm.' He swayed her from side to side, holding her close. 'That sounds more vertical than the activity I had in mind . . . If not quite so energetic.' She made him ache with desire and disbelief, her body was so beautiful, with long, supple limbs and an incredible curve in the small of her back.

'Concentrate, Luke. We could see if we could get over the top into Swiredale.' With closed eyes and her head resting back on his shoulder, she described the route through the woods, past the deep pool and up the gorge to the limestone plateau of Ravenscar. Beyond that, the land dipped away again into a wider, more open valley.

'That's over ten miles,' Luke protested, reluctantly giving up the idea of making love to her again. 'Maybe it should be more of a stroll than a hike.'

'We've got all day. And it's beautiful up there. We can reach the top without seeing a single road and that means no day-trippers.' Laura slipped out of Luke's arms and reached for the soap.

Leaving her and putting on his trousers, Luke padded barefoot through the house, enjoying its sense of calm orderliness. Laura hadn't changed many things since she'd taken over the old place. The walls were plain, the furniture shone a rich dark brown. Turkish rugs covered stone flags and oak floors; there were small square windows with deep sills. Opening the kitchen door, he looked out on to a walled garden dwarfed by the scale of Ravenscar rising almost sheer from the narrow valley bottom.

He took a deep breath and tried to assess where he and Laura stood. They were easy together; pleasant, relaxed. For him this was rare and enjoyable. Unlike other women he'd known, Laura didn't crave attention or sulk when she didn't get it. She gave him space.

If anything, he found himself wanting to crowd her. He stared up at the clear sky. What was so special about Laura? It was a particular combination of smooth skin and smile, of shining dark hair and deep brown eyes, and a way she had of interpreting what he was about to say before he spoke. She seemed to know the way his mind worked. Perhaps he loved her. The word exploded his attempt to analyse the situation.

A bird held steady against the warm breeze. It was a kestrel, hovering over an unseen prey, backed by the hulking limestone crags that formed Black Gill. Then the wind caught it and wheeled the bird away, until it found another gentler current and hovered again.

'Ready?' Luke retreated from his own thoughts and feelings, went back inside and called into the bathroom.

Laura was out of the shower, but still wrapped in her towel. 'Five minutes,' she promised.

He made coffee, simply glad to be here in the morning, with the whole day ahead of them.

They swore not to talk about work on their weekend off. As a junior partner at Bootham and Wood's law firm in Merton, Luke specialised in criminal cases. But he was developing a growing reputation for fighting and winning environmental battles on behalf of the local community, and that was how he and Laura had met. Articulate and analytical, dedicated to his work, he'd had two significant long-term relationships with women.

The first had happened at university, when both he and the girl had looked to the security of a steady partnership as a defence against the tidal wave of new experiences thrown at them by student life. They'd weathered the storms and qualified for their respective careers, which then took them to opposite ends of the country. They didn't survive the distance or the process of growing up, as Sara had called it in her farewell phone call.

His second serious affair, years later, had been with a woman just separated from a fellow lawyer in Luke's firm. He'd known Maeve as Jeremy's wife; a small, fragile-featured woman of good taste and little common sense. Her helplessness at the break-up of her marriage had brought out a protectiveness in him, which he later grew to resent. Maeve's refusal to tackle life's practicalities like gas bills and divorce papers came to seem manipulative, yet oddly difficult to resist. A good sex life kept them together much longer than was right for either of them, until one day she came across another, more established and wealthier protector. And that had been that.

In the event, Luke had reached his mid-thirties unmarried, unlike Laura who was a few years younger with a failed marriage behind her.

At first, when she'd been involved with Matthew Aire, Luke had taken an honourable, strictly hands-off approach to Laura. He'd done his best to ignore her physical presence, which he characterised as serene, sexy and beautiful.

The surprise came when he'd realised that Laura didn't always want to do that. She'd been unhappy over Matthew's ex-wife and kids, and confided her problems to him. Luke had made a slight move in her direction, taken a rebuff. Then he'd waited. He'd still been there the next time.

It was not so much a pursuit as a quiet persistence. As doubts drove a wedge between Laura and Matthew, so Luke's support drew her to him. People might say it was Luke who had driven the wedge in, or that Laura had ditched Matthew for Luke. The truth, he knew, was always more complicated – and less conventional. Luke still had no idea where he and Laura were headed. He had his house on Tan Hill; a kind of warehouse for his few possessions to which he was wholly indifferent. And she had Abbey Grange, which she loved.

They set off in T-shirts and shorts, carrying sun-glasses and enough cash for a drink in a pub in Swiredale, should they get that far. By the time they'd crossed the field to the woods surrounding the Foss, Luke had described a manslaughter case he'd taken on earlier that week and Laura, without breaking patient confidentiality, had confessed her worries over a possible second case of leukaemia in the Dale.

'I thought we said no work!' Luke stopped by the deep, clear pool. Recent rain had brought a rush of water down the series of small waterfalls that fed the Foss. It splashed over the black rocks, shaking the small green ferns that clung to the scant soil.

'Sorry.' Laura kicked off her shoes and paddled into the pool. She'd told him that the family was still waiting for results, but Philip had indicated at an eight-twenty that bad news was probably on its way. 'It's just that two cases of leukaemia within such a short time is pretty unusual.'

'Because you're a small practice?' Luke sat on a boulder and watched her. He called it his favourite leisure pursuit.

'Relatively. Compared with a city list. But even in my old Camden practice with 13,000 patients it would have been rare to diagnose two similar cancers so close together.'

'Can you put it down to coincidence?' he asked. He'd heard voices coming through the wood and gestured to Laura to let her know.

'What else?' She frowned.

Bad luck, random chance; whatever you called it, Luke could see that the news for Hannah and Gary Wood, if it came through, would be terrible. And Laura would have to endure a second crisis of confidence about her own role. He'd seen it happen over the Catherine Earle case; a pensiveness and loss of optimism in her that had lasted for several days. He wished he could wipe out the action replay for her before it occurred.

'How is Catherine Earle?' Luke stood up as footsteps drew near.

'Holding her own. I saw her on Friday. She looks good. Peter and Sonia seem better too, now that the shock of the diagnosis and the strain of hospital are behind them.' Laura's shoes were back on and she was ready for the climb up the gill when Piers Chandler's voice called hello.

'Is there no escape?' he joked, striding ahead of Francesca and his two boys. 'We set off early so we could have this place to ourselves. And who do we find here?'

'Just what we were thinking.' Luke wondered what Piers had had to do to persuade Harry and Joe to come Sunday walking. At fourteen and twelve, he imagined the boys could drum up a dozen more exciting activities of their own.

He studied them during the awkward silence. Harry had his father's wavy blond hair and intense blue eyes. He was developing a hairstyle instead of the shapeless mop he'd arrived with at the start of the spring term. And a slouch to go with it. Almost overnight he seemed to Luke to have developed the symptoms of disaffected adolescence.

Two years younger, Joe was more like Francesca in appearance and still able to bear being seen in his parents' company.

'We thought we might go for a swim. Is it deep enough?' Piers swung a small rucksack from his shoulder.

'Easily. You can dive or jump from that ledge.' Luke pointed, wondering about the 'we'. Francesca didn't look either keen or ready. She made a shirt and shorts look like high fashion, with her long limbs, her swathe of auburn hair twisted back and pinned up, her wide, full mouth and green eyes. Though a similar physical type to Laura, the effect was the opposite; Francesca had 'Do not touch' written all over her, and her impact was contrived. Jumping off a slippery ledge through a waterfall and plunging into icy water didn't seem her style.

'You go ahead,' she told Piers, confirming Luke's opinion by spreading a striped towel on a rock and turning towards the sun.

'How about you?' Piers asked Luke and Laura. He was stripped off to his shorts, skirting the pool to reach the diving ledge.

'No thanks. We're heading for Swiredale.' Luke spoke for them both. Why did Piers's invitation smack of a holiday rep's enforced fun? He led Laura along the track with a clear sense of relief.

'By the way,' Piers called from the ledge. He was poised on the edge, looking perfect, sounding all wrong. 'I was giving some thought to the two leukaemia cases.' Laura turned sharply. 'One confirmed. One suspected,' she pointed out.

'Sure. I dug out a paper on the nuclear link for you to have a look at.'

She frowned. 'What nuclear link? This isn't Chernobyl, you know. Ravensdale doesn't have a power station on its doorstep.'

'The link between men who have worked at or near a nuclear installation and the increased cancer risk in their children,' Piers explained. 'The Radiological Institute has just produced new figures.'

'They fly in the face of a lot of other surveys that can find no link at all,' Laura reminded him. 'Anyway, what's the relevance?'

Piers raised his arms, preparing to dive. 'Ruthwell,' he said. Then he leaned forward, bent at the knees and leaped from the rock.

'What does he mean, Ruthwell?' Laura asked in an exasperated tone. 'It's nearly fifty miles from here!'

They climbed from ledge to ledge, crushing ferns and wild garlic underfoot. Soon they would come out of the gill on to the limestone pavement surrounding Ravensdale Tarn.

'Forty-five miles north-east.' Like Laura, Luke could make no sensible link between the Earles and the nuclear reprocessing plant on the east coast.

'We're a farming community. People stay put. They don't career about the country looking for work.'

'I realise that. But what's the Institute's theory?' Luke was curious, depite their determination to have a carefree morning. Public health issues were his thing.

'You don't want to know.'

'I do. Have they found some new evidence?'

'A new paper has just identified an increased risk of

28

childhood cancer in the offspring of workers in the nuclear industry. Satisfied?'

'Do they know why?'

She raised her eyebrows, obviously irritated by Piers for spoiling their morning.

'That means "no".'

'Anyway, the findings relate to all forms of cancer, not leukaemia in particular. And it's leukaemia we're talking about here.'

This time Luke stopped. 'You don't like Piers to be right, do you?'

'What makes you say that?' Laura was breathing hard. 'I haven't personalised the argument, have I?'

'You don't have to. It's obvious.' Luke had reached the flat stretch of rock which split into giant fissures; a geological feature caused by erosion of the porous limestone surface. To cross it, you had to risk jumping over chasms only a few centimetres wide, but many metres deep. He set off without looking back.

'I'm only saying that there are lies, damned lies and statistics.' Laura hurried to keep up, the fierce breeze whipping her hair from her face, in full sunlight after the dappled shade of the gill. 'This isn't about Piers.'

He relented and slowed his pace. 'What then?'

'I don't know. I suppose I don't want to look too hard at the causes of cancer in children. It's too – enormous.'

Suddenly Luke was sorry for pushing her. He reached out to hold her hand.

'And not my style,' she insisted, holding tight as they stepped over another fissure. 'I'm more hands-on and already having a hard time convincing myself that I'm any good.'

'No need,' he reassured her. 'But all credit to Piers for taking this on board. He's pretty sharp, isn't he?'

Laura leaped across the gap without looking down, keeping her eyes firmly on the stretch of smooth, brackish water that was Ravensdale Tarn. 'You'd like him to be right,' she told Luke. 'I recognise the look in your eye when you spot a good cause. There could be giant litigation, an international hue and cry.'

'That's not fair.' He stopped, regretting once more his apparent lack of support. What made him push at facts and figures when feelings grew difficult? 'Forget about Piers. We're both interested in finding out as much as is known about this cancer cluster notion. Yes?'

She nodded. The wind unsettled her, made her unsteady on her feet. She evidently wanted to be off the rocks, walking by the calm, smooth lake.

'So, let's read this paper and talk about it later.'

Again she nodded. 'One case confirmed,' she reminded him. 'One suspected. Nothing like a cluster.'

Slowly, one step at a time, they trod carefully across the deep chasms in the rock.

CHAPTER FOUR

The following morning Laura received a print-out of the white cell count on Elliot Wood's blood sample and a confirmation of the fact that he was in the second stage of acute myeloid leukaemia.

'Why?' Gary Wood made the only sound that he could shape. His jaw had worked, his eyes had closed.

'We don't know why.' Laura gave him and Hannah time. They sat in their living-room at Askby, in a bungalow that Gary had built, by a window overlooking the mill-race. Hannah clutched his hand in stunned silence.

'But why Elliot?'

Laura was silent. They would adjust, she knew. There would be a lurch into a new world where their child was ill, was to be tested and treated, was to fight for his life.

'Are you sure?' Gary's broad builder's hand covered Hannah's. Nothing in his twenty-five years as a local footballer, sometime farmer and now builder could have prepared him for this.

She nodded.

'We should have brought him in earlier.'

It seemed to Laura that he flew off at a tangent, seeking to lay the blame; on himself, on Hannah.

'Straight away, when we noticed the first bruise on his leg. I said we should have.'

'It wouldn't have made any difference. What matters now is that we get him to hospital, where they can look after him.'

31

'Will it hurt him?' Hannah spoke for the first time. She looked small and young next to her burly husband.

'The disease or the treatment?'

'Either.'

Here was where Laura could be positive. 'On the whole, no. There's no surgery involved initially, so think of that as a good thing at least. The machine that gives the radiotherapy may look a bit frightening, but it's painless. Chemotherapy is where we inject drugs to fight the cancer cells. It might make Elliot feel tired and sick, but he'll soon get over it.'

'He's so little.' Hannah stared out of the window.

Gary dropped his head.

'We'll get him into the children's unit at Wingate,' Laura promised. 'The specialist, Mr Grey, is the doctor who's been treating Catherine Earle. He's very good.'

Brown water swirled through the mill-race. Two mallards swam in quiet circles on the pond upstream. Laura watched while Gary cried and Hannah comforted. In spite of all her training and experience, here she was, face to face with her own helplessness once more.

Laura glanced up at Ravenscar. Never take it for granted, she told herself. Notice the way it rises sheer out of the valley and casts its shadow over the town, recognise the rocky ridge where dark land meets wind-whipped clouds, backlit by the sun.

She needed its solidity today and the feeling of being dwarfed by the landscape. To be insignificant, a mere temporary mortal, was a relief.

'Problems?' Luke asked as she walked into his house on Tan Hill and upstairs to find him in the attic room with a view. Cello music slid around the white walls and down the sloping ceiling.

'No more than usual.' She kissed him.

'Problems,' he confirmed. 'Any developments over Piers?'

'No. Just the same. Still dashing in where angels fear to tread. Francesca's made an appointment to come and see me, though. I'm wondering what that's about. God, what a day!'

She stared uneasily out of the window, recalling the effort she demanded of her facial muscles as she tried not to allow her expression to alter whenever she relayed a blood test result, gave a diagnosis. Philip was good at that; his gaze was always steady, even when the news was bad. Maybe it got easier as you grew older: shattering people's lives.

'The results finally came through for the Woods' little boy,' she told Luke. 'I went to see them.'

'How did they take it?' He turned down the music.

'Badly. I know they've been expecting it since they first compared notes with the Earles. I'm going over to Askby to see them again first thing tomorrow.'

'Come here.' Luke put his arms round her.

She rested her head against his shoulder and closed her eyes. The notes of the cello plunged and sobbed.

'I'm so sorry,' he murmured into her hair.

'Don't talk, please.' She wanted to drift, be released from the day.

Luke tilted her head and kissed her face. He stroked his fingers across her eyelids. 'I love you.'

The world altered. The shadows lifted. Laura opened her eyes and saw the blurred outline of his cheek, the dark eyebrows over soft grey eyes, smudged out of focus by their closeness. She breathed him in, kissed him, as the sun fell on them and slowly the music died.

CHAPTER FIVE

Francesca Chandler had made an appointment at the surgery and she intended to keep it.

She walked up the gently sloping ramp, pushed open the door into the medical centre, knowing that Piers was safely out of the way. She'd checked his diary, arranged her visit to see Laura to coincide with a regular fundholders' meeting in Wingate.

Though she was punctual as ever, she doubted that Laura would be running to time. She expected instead an awkward wait in reception, where she would be neither fish nor fowl: not an ordinary patient, but there again not one of them, the medical team.

'Hello.' Sheila greeted her in friendly fashion, looking over the top of her glasses and ticking the book. 'Take a seat. Laura shouldn't be long.'

Friendly, but not too friendly. In fact, there was a definite hint of keep-your-distance in the way the receptionist had handled the situation.

Francesca sat on one of the low chairs, unable to resist analysing the response of Piers's colleagues towards her. Doctor's wife was how even she identified herself. Thrusting, ambitious doctor with suitably glamorous wife: tall and pale-skinned with green eyes and long, red-gold hair; self-conscious, not at ease. She smiled to herself and picked up a magazine. How right they were.

Even to come here for her appointment Francesca had spent

time in front of the mirror, checking details of clothes, make-up and jewellery. She'd made sure that the cool turquoise of her dress had complemented her bright lapis lazuli necklace, and that both set off the colour of her eyes.

Once upon a time she'd expected to grow out of this boring attention to appearance. She would emerge one day from the shell of careful presentation, like chrysalis to butterfly in reverse, like prince becoming frog. People must take her as they found her. But the years had gone by and she worried more, not less, about whether or not they approved of her.

That was partly why the move to Ravensdale had proved so difficult. It had meant leaving the few good friends she'd kept over the years; women who had known her since the early days. They had insecurities in common about the state of their marriages, the progress of their children at school and memories of one another that stretched back to their teenage years. They made allowances, went some way to understanding the tensions of living with Piers.

And, of course, it had been because of Piers that they'd had to move away. Opportunity, a fresh start: those were the overworn words he'd used and as usual there had been no argument, for what reasonable wife could refuse her husband such a step up? Except that reason only went so far for her, leaving untouched layers of regret and fear that Francesca fought hard to ignore.

'I hate needles,' she told Laura as, finally, she was sent into the consulting-room. She sat upright on the chair by the desk and offered her arm. 'Silly, isn't it? Especially being married to Piers.'

'I don't like them myself.' Laura checked her computer screen.

'Yellow fever and hepatitis boosters,' Francesca informed her. 'We went to Kenya on safari earlier this year.'

Laura concentrated on preparing the injection. 'You could

35

do with making an appointment for a smear test to keep you up to date,' she suggested.

Francesca gave an exaggerated shudder. 'I'm a terrible physical coward, that's my problem. Piers tells me off about it. I say there's only one thing worse for your health than being a doctor and that's being married to one.'

Talking too much. Talking nonsense as Laura worked. Francesa heard her own quiet, clipped voice with its underlying huskiness; a voice that she disliked when she heard her recorded message on the answer-machine at home. So much so that she must persuade Harry to replace it with the anonymous male voice that came with the machine when it was installed.

'I suppose it makes you aware of what can go wrong with the human body,' Laura said quietly.

Francesca glanced at her. 'Yes. Without having any of the knowledge to put it right. Which makes me neurotic every time one of the boys so much as sneezes.'

She winced as the needle went in, then took the swab of cotton-wool from Laura. 'Piers has the opposite reaction. Instead of being cowed by the body's vulnerability, he pummels it into shape.'

'What about Harry and Joe?'

'More like me, I'm afraid.' Was she beginning to relax, Francesca wondered. This was unexpected. 'In fact, Joe's off-colour at the moment. He's got another sore throat. Harry's through that stage, thank heavens. I don't see him for dust these days. He's off after school during these light evenings. I suppose that's good. It means he's settled down and made friends, which I never thought he would. He hated leaving his old school. So did Joe, as a matter of fact.'

'Has Harry made new friends in Merton or in Hawkshead?' Laura ditched the spent needle in the disposal unit.

'Neither really. He spends a lot of time with Adam Earle. Haresby Farm is way out in the middle of nowhere. Not that

36

Harry ever asks for a lift. This spring bank holiday he went off on his bike first thing and I didn't see him until it was beginning to get dark again.'

'I'm sure Sonia Earle won't mind. She'll be pleased that Adam has someone to hang around with. They have a lot on their plates at the moment.' Laura seemed in no hurry to move Francesca on.

Francesca dabbed at her arm and considered her next sentence. 'To be honest, it's a relief to me that Harry's had the holiday to find his feet and get used to his new surroundings. I was finding it more and more difficult to get him actually to go to school.' As she confessed her worries to Laura, Francesca couldn't help thinking how closely Harry's reactions to the move had mirrored her own hidden ones. Her son's angry outbursts had centred on the fact that he was being forced to give up his friends and his membership of the school soccer team without even being consulted. Yet she'd failed to stand up for the boy during Piers's impatient dismissal of his complaints. She'd let him down and Harry had turned against her too.

'How old is he again?'

'Fourteen. His exam courses start in September and I'm desperately hoping that he'll calm down before then.' She sighed and went on dabbing with the cotton-wool long after it was necessary.

'Is Piers worried about him too?'

'I haven't told him.' Francesca pressed her lips together and shook her head.

To her own surprise, still thinking about Harry, she began to cry. Trying not to had only made it worse. Her thick hair fell forward across her pale cheeks, her hand shook as she took the proffered tissue.

'I'm sorry.' With a contortion of her face she sat up and pushed her hair back behind her shoulders.

'OK now?'

She nodded, then broke down again.

'How about you? Have you found the move to Hawkshead a strain too?'

Francesca cried silently as Laura put her finger on the core of the problem. Yes! she wanted to cry. I hate the upheaval, the strangeness, the doomed attempt to make myself acceptable all over again. I'm defeated by the fact that Piers neither notices nor cares! 'Don't be kind to me, Laura,' she said quietly. 'It makes it worse.'

'How are you sleeping?'

'Not well. And I'm so apathetic. I find it hard to get a sense of direction. The days are just drifting by. That's not like me.' She was saying much more than she intended. Admissions of weakness were dribbling out along with the tears.

'What does Piers say? Is he worried about you?'

'Nothing. No. Sorry about this outburst.'

Laura ignored the apology. 'So you're not sleeping and you'd say you were having unusual mood swings. In a way it's not surprising. Moving house is counted as a significant life event. You have to rebuild your social life from scratch for a start.'

'You think I'm depressed?' Knowing that it was true, Francesca made a half-successful effort to pull herself together and so defy the diagnosis.

'Do you?'

She avoided Laura's probing gaze and shrugged. 'Don't say anything to Piers.'

'I won't.'

'Only, he has enough to cope with. He's the one who has to deal with the pressures of a new job. Not that he lets anyone know that it's a strain.' Playing the loyal wife, Francesca was aware that she was digging herself in deeper. Piers wouldn't thank her for telling Laura anything about their domestic situation, so she frowned at the less than perfect picture she'd painted. 'In fact, strain isn't the right word. Piers loves a

38

challenge and that's how he regards getting to grips with this situation.'

She made it sound like climbing a mountain: more effort than enjoyment.

'Don't worry. I won't say anything,' Laura promised again.

And that was the outcome Francesca preferred. She left the surgery without treatment for her mild clinical depression, with Laura's promise of confidentiality.

'How was your day?' Piers would ask when he came home that evening.

'Fine.' She would be busy in the garden, or reorganising furniture in the lounge. The question would be flicked aside.

He would go upstairs, change, come down again and describe the latest dinosaur GP from the sticks to emerge into the light of their fundholders' meeting. He would make her smile. She would say nothing.

'Do you think Joe would mind if I backed out of that cricket match I'd arranged to take him to see?' Piers might say. 'Only I've got so much work to catch up on.'

'No, I'm sure it'd be OK.'

Or, 'I have to stay up late to sort out these figures for our eight-twenty tomorrow morning. You don't mind, do you?'

'No.'

'I'll follow you up shortly.'

She would go to bed, stare at the ceiling, not say a word. Just as she'd visited Laura at the surgery and not told her about the real reason for her visit. Silence. Denial. It was her usual route. But soon there would come a time when these defences would not be enough.

CHAPTER SIX

'There are seventy-five companies involved in the nuclear power industry, employing over 80,000 people,' Luke told Laura, Philip and Philip's wife, Juliet. They'd met after work at the Falcon. Though it was midweek, the long evenings brought people up the Dale and the bar was crowded. The local corner consisting of the old brigade of Kit, Harry and Dick was full, as were the tables in the flagged yard. The landlord, Brian Lawson, and his wife, Alison, were working at full stretch.

Luke had done his research after Laura and he had discussed Piers's theory on their Sunday walk. He realised that Laura probably wished he'd never started to delve in to the topic of Ruthwell, that for her it had been intended as a way of letting off steam against Piers. Evidently she hadn't reckoned with Luke's own campaigning zeal.

'I can't help it,' he'd told her as he'd armed himself with the relevant papers and magazines. 'Call it a weakness. If I spot a possible cover-up, I have to ferret away at it until I get some answers.'

'It's what makes you a good lawyer,' she'd conceded.

'But difficult to live with.' Immediately he'd wanted to retract that remark. It had seemed to call up for them both an unwelcome image of Laura's ex-husband, Tom Elliot, a journalist and another tireless campaigner for the underdog. But Luke had said it and the reminder lay uneasily between them.

'That's a whole bunch of people who may produce children who are genetically susceptible to developing cancer,' he insisted now.

'And a whole lot more who would be panicked by the idea if it were to gain credence,' Philip pointed out. 'I can see your lawyer's brain ticking over, Luke. You're thinking of the potential litigation if it could be proved that the industry was involved in some sort of massive cover-up.'

'Actually, I'm not. That's what Laura thinks too and I can't seem to convince her that I've no particular axe to grind.'

He looked from one to the other. Laura had clammed up and he saw again that he was pushing her into an area where she'd prefer not to be. She sat running her forefinger around the rim of her glass, her face slightly flushed and half hidden by her long dark hair. He could back down right now, let it drop. And Laura would be happy. But his digging, ferreting habit was too strong. 'Would someone like to tell me what's going on over this leukaemia business?' he insisted.

'Nothing.' Philip shrugged and glanced at Laura.

'Piers is what's going on.' Juliet spoke for the first time. She'd been silently listening and observing; a role that came naturally to her. Luke thought of Philip's wife as a quiet centre to his more turbulent frenetic life: one of those attractive middle-aged women whose stylishly cut hair never seemed to grow, whose skin always had an outdoors feel and whose voice was never raised. Now her glance towards the door warned them that the new partner himself had just walked in with Francesca, Harry and Joe. 'He's treading on people's toes.'

'He has different priorities,' Luke said, watching Francesca object to the crowded room, then decide to wait outside with the boys. As yet, the Chandlers hadn't spotted their group.

'No one's denying that the cancer cluster theories are possible; just that this isn't the time or the place.' Laura was still annoyed with him, as the group adjusted to welcoming

41

Piers among them. 'The families involved are having a hard time coping as it is.'

Now that the newcomer had seen them he deviated *en route* to the bar. 'Small town,' he joked. 'One decent pub and that's it.'

'We're not complaining.' Alison Lawson swept glasses off a nearby table. 'Mind you, there's little chance of keeping your affairs to yourself in a place this size.'

'I'll remember that.' Piers offered to buy drinks, but Philip stepped in and went with him to order, as if willing at least to rebuild the bridge that had collapsed over the unresolved tensions in the surgery.

'They'll be there all night,' Juliet warned, as the two of them settled at the bar.

'Trading statistics,' Laura agreed. After a while she said she would go outside to warn Francesca that Piers and Philip were talking shop.

Luke watched her go. He could never not watch Laura, he realised. Whenever they were together his awareness of her was total: exactly where she was in the room, whom she was talking to, what kind of mood she was in. He read her body language – the tilt of her head, the slope of her shoulders – without being conscious that he was doing it. He knew that now, for instance, her unexpressive face and rather stiff journey towards the door meant that she was tired and unhappy.

'It's difficult,' Juliet said, interpreting his silence after they were left alone together. 'All these conflicting personalities.'

'What do you mean?' Luke switched his attention.

'Piers, I suppose. Philip's told me that Sheila's threatened to resign over him.'

He shrugged. 'That's not what bothers me,' he admitted. 'To be honest, Laura and I don't see eye to eye over this leukaemia business.'

'Ah. Have you talked it through?'

'Not properly.'

Juliet leaned towards the table so that he caught the full force of her gaze. 'Do it,' she advised. 'Do it now.'

Outside the pub, Francesca told Luke that Laura had decided to walk home to Abbey Grange. 'She fancied the fresh air, I think.' She gave him a brittle smile. 'Actually, I was just on my way in to ask Piers what had happened to the drinks for the boys.'

Harry and Joe had retreated to their car to slouch in the back seat, windows open, music blaring.

'He's deep in discussion with Philip,' Luke told her.

'Then he's probably forgotten.' Francesca appeared to change her mind about seeking him out. Her mouth turned down and she seemed to sulk.

'Would you like me to remind him?'

She shook her head. 'No. You catch up with Laura. I think she took the riverside path past the medical centre.'

'OK. But tell Piers I'm interested in following up the Ruthwell thing. I'll talk to him about it as soon as I dig up anything significant.'

Francesca promised to do this and he hurried on. Juliet had been right: it was more important for Laura and him to sort out their differences. If he walked fast across the playing field and joined the path Laura was following on the bend in the fast-running river, just past the medical centre, he would probably catch her up.

But when he reached the point where he expected to see her there was still no sign. Beeches and oaks arched from the bank over the clear water, finding a footing in unlikely rocky ground, their gnarled roots stretching across the footpath. In one place, close to the ruins of Ravensdale Abbey, the river narrowed between dark, pitted rocks. It ran deep through unseen caverns in swift currents that would drag a swimmer to his death. Despite the warning signs, Devil's Leap claimed at least one life every summer.

Perhaps Laura had left the path and gone down to the water's edge. He wouldn't necessarily see her if she'd stepped down between bushes of elder and willow on to the stretch of bare rocks where the water surged by. Telling himself casually that it was worth a look, but drawn at some deeper level to the dangerous spot, he decided to investigate.

'Don't do it,' a man's voice said; not to Luke, but to someone already down by Devil's Leap.

Luke stopped, moved to one side and stood where he could see the two figures by the water.

Laura was looking at the current swirling by just inches from her rocky ledge. Matthew Aire was the man who was urging her not to jump. And now Luke spotted his Range Rover parked further down the leafy track.

'I wasn't going to,' she replied without turning to look. She threw in a twig and watched it surge away. 'Hello, Matthew.'

Luke felt as if his world were being taken from beneath him like the green twig sucked under by the current. Matthew Aire had said three simple words to Laura and she had replied as if she were expecting him.

'You were looking as if you thought you might jump in just to see what it was like.' Matthew joined her by the edge.

'Water rushing by has that effect. It partly terrifies me, partly fascinates me, you should know that.'

DANGER. THESE CURRENTS ARE TREACHEROUS AND HAVE CLAIMED LIVES IN THE PAST. From his hidden vantage point the quaint wording of the warning notice stuck in Luke's mind. He watched Laura test the wet green moss underfoot.

Matthew caught her arm. 'I mean it, Laura, you're too close.'

She let herself be led back from the edge. She didn't ask Matthew to let her go. Instead, the two of them began to walk arm in arm away from Luke and Devil's Leap towards the abbey.

Luke lost the sound of their voices in the roar of the swift water. He saw them reach the new wooden footbridge built alongside the monks' ancient stepping-stones. Across the bridge, Abbey Grange stood solid and square in the last rays of the evening sun.

Was she inviting Matthew in for coffee? Luke felt the blood pound in his head. They'd stopped half-way over the narrow bridge and were looking down at the water again. Finally Matthew let go of her arm and walked away.

Luke waited. He heard Matthew drive off in his car. He waited longer, until he could force his world to stop sliding and tugging out of shape. 'It means nothing.' That was the phrase he hung on to. Except for the lack of surprise in Laura's voice when she'd first spoken. Apart for the fact that she'd let Matthew hold her arm.

He retraced his steps to the village to pick up his car, giving himself time to regain control before he drove over to Abbey Grange and tried to behave as if nothing had happened.

'I just saw Matthew Aire when I was on my way home.' Laura greeted Luke too quickly, without her usual gladness. 'He'd been working up at Haresby.'

'With Peter Earle?' He knew that Matthew was the Earles' boss, and must be helping out.

'Yes. It's for moral support as much as anything.'

'How was Peter?' Luke forced himself not to react.

'Pretty bad, apparently.' There was a pause, then Laura went on, 'Matthew passed on some information that might be significant. Peter reminded him that Ruthwell is the common factor between the Earles and the Woods.'

'How come?' Luke was finding it hard to concentrate.

'It seems that ten years ago both he and Gary Wood worked on a farm near the power plant.'

Suddenly Luke's mind snapped into focus. 'Are you sure?'

She nodded, 'I did know that they'd worked together, but not where. Peter was the foreman. It was the job he had before he came to Haresby, so Matthew still has the address somewhere. He kept references from the employer; an Alan Greenwood of Morefield Farm.

'The story is that Gary had just left school and couldn't get work in Ravensdale. His family knew the Earles and got in touch to see if Peter could give Gary a job at Morefield. A couple of years later Peter applied for this job at Haresby and, not long after that, Gary gave up farming altogether, went to college and eventually set up as a builder in the Dale.'

'So the connection's there, staring us in the face' – something he would never have dreamed of. Excited by the discovery, Luke saw a range of new possibilities. If there had been an unreported leak of irradiated material from the power plant into the ground during the period when Peter and Gary had both worked at Morefield Farm, or if the local water supply had been contaminated . . .

'But it's still a tiny sample,' Laura warned. 'And it could be a coincidence. You can't base a scientific conclusion on two isolated cases.'

Luke frowned. He was trying not to let the image of Laura standing with Matthew by Devil's Leap interfere with his thoughts.

'. . . Luke?' Laura was waiting for a reply to a question he hadn't even heard.

'Sorry. What?'

'I was asking you not to push this Ruthwell connection too far. I don't think it's a good idea.'

Not a good idea as far as he and Laura went, he knew. He could capitulate here and now, give up before he really got started. But it was Matthew catching Laura's arm and walking her back to the Grange that he fixed on instead. 'It's an interesting theory though.' He blinked and turned his head. 'And God knows where it might lead.'

CHAPTER SEVEN

'Hello, Philip. Come through to the study. I can tell from your face that this isn't a social call.'

Francesca heard Piers open the front door. It was late on Thursday evening. She wondered whether the visit was to do with the installation of new technology at the surgery. Piers had described his colleagues' resistance with more than a tinge of scorn and she guessed there was bad feeling about it.

'What might it mean?' She'd attempted to cut through the arrogance, frightened, not for the first time, that Piers had opened up a gap between himself and the other doctors that couldn't be bridged.

'Nothing.' He'd shrugged it off. 'No need to dash to the estate agents to put the house back on the market just yet.'

And now Philip had caught him in sweat-shirt and jeans, with a day's growth of stubble. She could tell from his voice that Piers was annoyed by that.

'Joe, tell Harry to stop kicking that football around in the front garden while Daddy's in his study.' Francesca went to make coffee. Down the long hall she could still hear Philip's reply.

'Sorry, am I looking businesslike?' He stepped into the wide Victorian hallway. The walls were lined with framed architectural prints of great Renaissance buildings, which Francesca had brought back from Italy. They matched the polished terracotta, black and white tiles, which led to broad stairs, turning at a right-angle under a long stained-glass window of red and blue.

'Just a tad.' Piers led the way into his study at the front of the house.

Francesca picked up a tray and followed them into the room, which she'd decorated with lavish swags of Pre-Raphaelite fabric around heavy curtain poles behind Piers's rosewood desk. On the other side was a cream sofa stacked with fat cushions and, on the floor, Turkish rugs in deep-red and cream. The rich effect was well-judged and gave her satisfaction.

She smiled at them both. 'Coffee?'

As Philip sank into the sofa, she sensed his resolution sigh and escape with the slight rush of air that his body created against the feather cushions. What had been planned as a straight talk with Piers was obviously already receding.

Piers took his cup and the intiative all at once, enlisting Francesca and catching her unawares. 'Philip, I've been thinking about the conversation you, I and Laura had last week,' he began without prompting. 'I'm sorry if I jumped down your throats. I told Francesca after I'd come home and had a chance to think about it that I'd probably been a bit too pushy. Didn't I?'

She nodded. Rewriting history had become Piers's speciality and he left her no room to disagree without being brutally disloyal – which wasn't her style, as he very well knew. Better to settle down and watch the performance. She sat by the window, one eye on Harry arguing with Joe outside.

'What I mean is you and Sheila are probably right to resent my initial manner. A case of a new broom sweeping too clean for their liking; I can understand that.' He drew his own chair from behind the desk, pulling it close to Philip's end of the sofa. 'You want me to pull back a bit on the new software?'

Clever, Francesca knew. The expression 'taking the wind out of your opponent's sails' came to mind. Philip looked

49

nonplussed by the brittle, tactical edge to Piers's apology. Yes, she thought, my husband is brilliant at keeping one step ahead in whatever game is being played.

'Laura and I think it would be best,' Philip agreed.

'Fine. I'll go easy. Obviously there are changes to be made, but softly, softly.'

In the front garden Francesca noticed Harry give Joe a shove and carry on thudding his football between the legs of a wrought-iron bench. A nearby bed of blue irises would soon suffer from the shots that went wide.

Piers saw it too. It irritated him, but he ignored it. Instead, he asked Francesca for more coffee, then steered the conversation towards details of administration at work, telling Philip what needed to be put on the agenda for future meetings.

She went down to the kitchen, refilled the cups and returned to find the two men playing reverse roles: Piers looking for all the world as if he were the senior partner, Philip reduced to passive, boxed-in subordinate. She felt sorry for the older man, recognising only too well how he'd been wrong-footed, since this had long been Piers's speciality in their relationship too. She stood, coffee-cup in hand, watching Philip stare out of the window at Harry playing the joyless game on the lawn.

'Laura, Francesca Chandler would like to see you. She says it's important.'

Francesca heard Sheila announce her arrival over the intercom, uncertain of what to do next.

It was midday, the day after Philip had come to their house. Obviously Laura wouldn't be expecting to see anyone out of surgery hours. But she wouldn't refuse.

Francesca stood quietly by the plate-glass screen. What she'd put off for too long had to be faced.

'Laura says to go straight through,' Sheila told her after a brief conversation on the phone.

She passed the low tables stacked with magazines, the rack of information leaflets, went behind the screen that divided the waiting area from the consulting-rooms and caught sight of her reflection in her pale-yellow dress, arms bare, hair swept up, in the window of Laura's room. Laura put her paperwork to one side and looked up.

A dozen times, at the beginning, Francesca had tried to broach the subject with Piers. Forcing herself to the point had been like staring into the deepest, widest canyon and she'd always retreated into silence. Lately she'd given up even trying. It was bound to be easier to tell a stranger.

'Is it all right for us to talk?' She sat on the edge of the seat, legs crossed, tilting forward.

'Sure. Go ahead. You've saved me from having to fill out yet more dreadful forms.'

'I know I should have made an appointment . . . In fact, I did . . . for the hepatitis jab. But I didn't mention what it was I'd really come to see you about.'

Laura's gaze was steady. 'What was that?'

She'd shaped the words, the whole sentence a hundred times as she drove over from Merton. 'The fact is, I'm pregnant.'

It was out, it was real. It wasn't just inside her head.

'Are you sure?'

She nodded. 'About sixteen weeks.' She had to take a deep breath, then continued, 'The point is, Piers doesn't know.'

'Why is that?'

'It wasn't planned. It may sound stupid for someone in my situation, but this whole thing is a terrible accident.'

Laura didn't react for what seemed a long time. 'How old are you? Thirty-six. Not so old for a third pregnancy. How old is Joe?'

'That's not the point. A baby is the last thing Piers would want.'

'How about you? Do you want it?'

Francesca had prepared herself for interrogation, but still couldn't answer this inevitable question.

'Unplanned babies can sometimes be very welcome, once you both get used to the idea,' Laura pointed out.

'Not in our case. Everything must be tailored to fit.' Inadvertently she gave away another glimpse of her life with Piers.

There was a further pause as Laura checked the file.

Francesca felt her mouth tremble. She bowed her head and hid her face with her hand.

'Take your time,' came the soft, kind advice.

'You can't imagine what it's like!' she sobbed. 'It's been tormenting me ever since I knew. I can't think, can't sleep, can't eat.'

'But why? What makes it so bad?'

She took her hand away, letting Laura see her misery. 'Everything that makes women feel good about being pregnant makes me feel desperate. Mainly because it's another life inside me, someone else to be responsible for and I'm already loaded down with responsibility. I can't cope with them as it is. Oh yes, I know how it looks: nice house, beautiful children, successful husband.'

'No one's life is that straightforward.' Laura tucked a tissue into Francesca's clenched hand.

'How can I explain? With Piers I'm living on a knife-edge. Fine if I can gain his approval, but if not . . .' She shrugged helplessly.

'And that's what puts you under stress?'

Francesca nodded. 'I feel as if I always have to get things right. And this!' She spread both hands upwards on the desk. 'Piers would say I was so pathetic for letting it happen, for thinking I needn't take my pill because the stress of moving house meant that I'd stopped menstruating. To him that would be unbelievably stupid.'

'I hardly need say it takes two.'

'But he would see it as my respnsibility!' With an effort she sat upright and pushed her hair back from her face. She knew it must be smeared and blotched. 'I'm sorry, I must look terrible.'

'Are you OK?'

'No. I'm desperate.' She drew breath and attempted a smile – meaningless, empty. 'Will you help me, Laura?'

Laura stared blankly at Francesca.

'Help me to have an abortion,' she said in the same dead, flat voice she'd used earlier. 'Will you arrange it for me, please?'

CHAPTER EIGHT

Laura said goodbye to the last of the mothers who had come to her Friday morning mother-and-baby clinic. She shouldn't have been surprised that rumour and hearsay could so quickly take hold, but she was.

'Everyone's talking about this Ruthwell scare,' Sheila had told her earlier that morning. 'Word got around the Falcon on Wednesday night and within twenty-four hours the jury had been out and was back to deliver their verdict.'

'Which was?' Laura had hardly needed to ask.

'That because Peter and Gary both worked on the land next to the nuclear site their kids now have cancer.'

'Oh, God! Imagine how those two fathers must feel.'

Gloomily she'd walked through reception and into the eight-twenty. Instinct told her to steer the meeting away from the leukaemia cases and she was relieved when Philip too had nothing new to report. She'd noticed that even Piers avoided the topic that was on everyone's mind, and instead conceded a minor point over the installation of the new software that was making Sheila's life so fraught.

But her relief was short-lived.

'About the Ruthwell connection.' Piers put his head round Laura's door as her clinic drew to a close. 'Last night Luke and I looked up some more figures.'

'Later.' Laura shook her head. Since Francesca's shock revelation the day before she doubted she could even look Piers directly in the eye. What's more, she was struggling to come to terms with Luke's decision to carry on working on the Ruthwell theory. 'Right now I have my hands full.'

Luckily for her, Philip squeezed past Piers into her office and Piers retreated. Laura asked Philip to shut the door. 'Three mothers came to my clinic just now and asked me about the cancer risk in Ravensdale,' she told him.

'For crying out loud.' Philip's reaction was unequivocal.

'I know. Two were in tears, including Alison Lawson. Her toddler is roughly the same age as Elliot Wood. She and Hannah came to antenatal clinics together.'

'You reassured them?'

'As best I could. You've no idea how a scare like this takes hold. Alison seemed to think that it was proved beyond a shadow of a doubt, not only that Ruthwell was to blame, but that anyone within a fifty-mile radius could be contaminated.' Laura spoke forcefully, leaning across the desk in her exasperation. It was escalating, just as she'd feared.

'One in ten thousand,' Philip reminded her. 'A nice round figure. That's the risk for children whose fathers actually work in the radiation industry.' He told her he'd made it his business to read the Radiological Institute's latest report. 'And there's still no evidence that there's a direct link. Some studies put it down instead to a highly mobile workforce within the industry. Population mix is supposed to expose children to an unknown infective agent that causes the cancer.'

'Try telling that to a weeping mother whose teething child refuses to sleep and who bruises his leg against a cot rail.'

He grunted an acknowledgement. 'But you can keep a lid on the panic. They trust you.'

Laura drew back and stood up straight. 'I know.' That wasn't the problem. It was more a case of whether she could trust Piers and Luke to handle things sensitively; to put the needs of the cancer victims and their families before their rapidly growing campaign.

*

A Saturday on call took Laura out to see an emphysema patient in Merton. While she was at the geriatric unit, the care assistant asked her to look at a resident who'd been complaining of chest pains. The problem was musculo-skeletal and didn't need a referral, she decided.

She was driving back to Hawkshead, past the old lead-mine workings at Ginnersby and looking forward to lunch in Merton with Luke, hoping to patch up differences between them that been developing lately, when she got a call from Sonia Earle.

'Adam's had an accident. He's hit his head. Do you think I should take him to Casualty?'

'No. Stay where you are. I'll be there in ten minutes.' Putting her foot down harder, Laura turned towards Haresby.

When she arrived the boy was sitting in the kitchen, pale-faced and sullen. There was a cut an inch long over his right eyebrow and a lump the size of an egg.

'Don't ask,' Sonia warned, sighing as she cleared away an ice-pack and let Laura draw near. 'He says he fell off his bike!'

Laura examined the wound. It was superficial and clean; no grazing of the skin. It also looked from the clotting of the blood as if it had been done a considerable time before. Adam sat stiffly, hands gripping the chair, eyes averted. 'Does it still hurt?'

'Not much.'

'No headache or stiff neck? You don't feel sick?'

'No.'

'And you didn't hit the back of your head when you fell?'

Adam sighed and gave a minimal negative.

'Good.' Laura checked the pupil of the injured eye and asked the boy to follow the direction of her forefinger as she moved it to and fro. She stood back, satisfied that there was no concussion. 'So where did you come off your bike?'

'Up on the moor.' Adam delivered the information through clenched teeth.

'It must be a mountain bike, then. How many gears?'

'Twenty-one.'

'Good mountain-biking country up there, I suppose.' Laura thought it through. 'Were you alone?'

'Yes.' This time the answer was sharper, accompanied by a resentful glance.

Sonia frowned and sniffed sceptically.

'I was,' Adam insisted.

Laura couldn't decide whether the surliness was endemic to a thirteen-year-old boy, or particular to the situation. Adam's slouch, the gawkiness of wrists and ankles, the glowering expression were typical. But his anger seemed to have a definite focus.

'Normally he would go around with Harry, Dr Chandler's boy. There would be someone there with him. I don't like him to drift off by himself.'

'Quite right,' Laura agreed. 'Listen, Adam, this could easily have been much worse. Imagine what would have happened if you'd knocked yourself unconscious and there'd been no one around to fetch help.'

'Mum's just making a meal of it.' Adam stood up. 'I don't need stitches, do I?'

'No. It'll heal by itself. No other cuts and bruises?' If not, why not? Laura wondered. A fall from a bike usually meant sprained muscles, contusions at least.

'Look, I'm OK. I told her I didn't need a doctor.' Adam sidled out of the room before he was asked any more questions.

Sonia looked at Laura and sighed. 'Sometimes I think he's had a personality transplant when I wasn't looking. Maybe it's because we've been so busy worrying about his sister. Adam hasn't had much of a look-in these last weeks.'

For a while they discussed Catherine's treatment and the lessening likelihood that Rudi Grey would now have to start the search for a bone-marrow match in the build-up to a

57

transplant for the girl, who was out in the Land Rover with her father.

'As you know, we thought maybe in two or three months' time her blood count would be good enough.' Sonia's dark eyes were bright and intense. 'But in fact, Mr Grey thinks it might not be necessary at all.'

'Good. But I'm still a bit worried about Adam's cut.' Laura watched the boy slope off across the yard. Slinging a leg over the crossbar of his bike, he pedalled away down the hill. 'It didn't look like a fall to me; more like he'd been hit from above by something sharp.'

The remark sent Sonia off on a breathless justification of Adam's story. 'I can easily see how he came to fall. He's so reckless on that bike. He never sticks to the official tracks; always has to be riding across country, showing off in front of Harry Chandler's gang.'

'But Harry wasn't there today.' Laura paused. 'Adam couldn't have been involved in a fight, could he?' It might explain why the boy had been so niggardly with his replies.

His mother brushed the suggestion aside. 'Who with? He's never been that sort. No, I think you've got it wrong there.'

The subject happened to crop up again with Sheila Knowles, who called Laura out later that afternoon to see her mother. Jean Inglesby was visiting Fellside, the Knowleses' converted barn on the high, narrow road across Ravenscar, and her poor balance had resulted in a fall.

Although Jean was shaken and disorientated, there was no serious damage. This meant that once Laura had ordered her to bed for a rest, she could relax over a cup of tea with Sheila and listen to her free-flowing bulletin on life in the Dale.

'Mark's been at a loose end over spring bank holiday so he's doing a bit of work for Dick Metcalfe at Hawk Fell,' she reported. Mark was her son, half-way through his GCSE course at Hawkshead Comprehensive. 'Dick may not pay the best wages in the world for casual farmwork but, to be honest, I'm glad Mark's got something to keep him out of harm's way.'

'You make it sound as though he's been hanging around with some disreputable types. Has there been any trouble?' Laura was curious.

'From what I can winkle out of Mark, some of the lads from his class have been ganging up on the younger boys.'

'Fighting?' She thought immediately of Adam Earle.

'Apparently they pick on someone who's a bit of a loner, pretend to befriend the poor kid, then give him a hard time – making fun, daring him to do stupid things.'

'Sounds nasty.' Laura realised that Adam's current home situation might make such a group pick him out as a potential victim.

'Yes, and if the kid resists there are threats. It's the kind of situation that can easily lead to fights.'

'How many against one?'

Sheila thought there were three or four in the gang. 'Mark wouldn't give me any names, but I did hear something on the grapevine.' Suddenly her smooth delivery faltered. She stirred the tea and poured, her gaze fixed on the steaming cups. 'It's been a bit awkward, as a matter of fact, finding out who one of the boys might be, but without any definite proof.'

'Can you tell me?'

'You won't like it, Laura. Apparently this nonsense started up after Easter: scuffles in the boys' toilets between lessons, some of the Year Tens deciding to bunk off on a regular basis. It only takes one ringleader to send a whole bunch of them off the rails – and the name I keep on hearing over and over is Harry Chandler!'

CHAPTER NINE

Laura felt edgy as she drove the mile and a half out of Wingate to the hospital to visit Elliot Wood. She had bumped into Piers on her way out of the surgery and allowed herself to get into another debate about new versus old technology and its benefits for the patient. As usual, he had had the last word and the exchange had re-awakened her misgivings about the way they were handling the current cancer scare.

She'd been seeing more of Piers than she wanted to outside work hours recently. He'd visited Luke's house, when Laura was there, to exchange information about the various surveys on the nuclear industry and she found that dogmatic assertions littered every aspect of his conversation. Luke said again that Piers was unusually sharp and quick on the uptake, and that she should look at the content, not the manner. But for her the two were inextricably linked. She increasingly resented his overbearing manner and the way his theory was beginning to cause friction between her and Luke.

In fact, she found that the way something was said could often outweigh the content: Matthew finding her by Devil's Leap, saying simply, 'Don't do it.' Luke tearing enthusiastically into conversations with Piers about the Ruthwell link, ignoring both its implications for her patients and the fact that she might want a break from all that after a hard day in the surgery.

She found Gary and Hannah Wood in the children's ward, playing with Elliot on his toy-scattered bed.

'Mr Grey's been called away on an emergency,' Hannah explained. She picked up the little boy and perched him on her arm, stroking his soft bare thigh.

'That's what they call it,' Gary scoffed, taking a bright plastic clock from the bed and offering it to his son.

'The nurse said it couldn't be helped.' Hannah jiggled Elliot as he began to murmur and reach out for his dad. Then she found a dummy and slipped it into his mouth. 'She said, if Mr Grey didn't make it back in time, you would be able to look up Elliot's notes and explain things to us, Dr Grant.'

'What I want to know is, what could be more of an emergency than this?' The young builder's short, almost black hair was uncombed, his checked blue shirt rolled to the elbow. 'I broke off work to come and see him. We've been waiting all week to find out how Elliot's getting on and now the boss-man has palmed us off on to you.'

'I'm sorry about that.' Laura held out her hand to the little boy, but he turned his face and pressed it against Hannah's chest.

'How do you think it makes us feel?' Gary flung the rejected toy down on the bed. 'About this size!' He held up his forefinger and thumb to measure the couple's self-esteem. 'It's always the same with these specialists; they ponce about and don't tell you anything.'

'Gary, if you'd just pipe down and let Dr Grant get a word in edgeways, maybe we'll find out what we want to know.' Hannah sounded weary.

'Let me fetch the notes from the nurses' station.' Laura slipped away, hoping to give them space. But when she came back she found that the young father's mood had worsened. His voice was raised as he railed against Rudi Grey's absence. Other visitors in the ward looked over in consternation and Elliot had begun to cry in earnest.

Laura held up the case notes to Gary and gestured towards

an empty side room. 'Try and settle Elliot down for a nap,' she told Hannah. 'Join us in there.'

His anger still simmering, Gary followed her. He glanced round the pale-grey room, at the single stripped bed and resuscitation equipment fixed to the wall. 'They're nice as pie to your face,' he told Laura. 'In the beginning they explain what the problem is; white blood cells, blood counts, Metho-trexate-this, Actinomycin-what-have-you, and the magic cure they've got lined up. They can't do enough. You go home thinking that's OK; they really know their stuff. Then you come in here and look at other kiddies on the ward and you can see they're getting poorlier by the day.'

'Not always. Concentrate on the positive side; the ones who stabilise and achieve remission.' Laura tried to follow the staccato switches from one thought to another, aware that fear stoked Gary's anger.

He brushed aside her remark. 'That's when you begin to think that maybe they don't know what they're doing, only they don't let on. When it comes down to it, they can't even decide why it happens; why Elliot's got leukaemia and millions of other kids haven't. Well, I might not know much, but I do know that finding out the reason has got to be step number one.'

He turned and walked to the door, gazed out through the small window panel at Hannah soothing their son and putting him into bed. 'You know something else?' he said to Laura, shoulders hunched, his back towards her. 'I don't think they sodding care.'

'They do. We do.' She went to stand close behind him. 'You have to believe that.'

'Yes, and you can say it and be lying through your teeth. What's it mean – you care? Prove it.'

Laura paused. Her response seemed to her to be banal and unrelated. 'I could have chosen another career.'

'Yeah?'

62

'That's not meant to be flippant. I was good at maths . . . and languages for that matter. But I wanted to do something really worthwhile. Most of us feel like that when we start. Some lose it, I admit. Some hide it, because you can't wear your heart on your sleeve all the time. But honestly, Gary, we wouldn't do the hours we do and live our lives like this if we didn't care.'

He nodded grudgingly. 'And will caring cure Elliot?'

'That's a different thing. Caring means we'll do all we possibly can. Is that enough?' Through the small window she could see Hannah making her way across the ward.

He closed his eyes and drew a deep breath. 'Maybe. Let's hope so.'

Opening the file and reading the latest blood test results, Laura saw that the MR scan had located metastases in Elliot's descending colon.

'We hope radiotherapy will reduce the size of the secondary tumours,' Rudi Grey had explained to the silent parents. He'd dealt with his emergency and come down to the ward to find Laura giving the Woods the bad news. 'Meanwhile the chemotherapy will tackle the production of more cancerous cells.'

Laura had stayed in the side ward with them and watched Hannah gather herself together slowly. She had allowed herself to cry for a few minutes only, then she'd drawn on her emotional reserves. Gary, on the other hand, seemed to have sunk even lower. The specialist's talk of an eventual colostomy had provoked no response.

'I'll get back to work then,' he told Hannah, as she stood with Laura in the hospital car park.

'Do you have to?' In the daylight Hannah's face looked drained. She'd gone back to Elliot's bed and kissed her sleeping child goodbye, but the action had almost broken her. She struggled once again to keep back the tears.

Gary looked at his watch. 'It's only three. The job I've started won't wait.'

'What time will you be back?'

'I don't know when I'll get finished, do I?'

It seemed to Laura that Gary was playing up for her benefit. 'I'll see you soon,' she told them, thinking it best to leave the Woods to it.

Gary Wood ignored her. 'And don't make any supper. I'm meeting Pete Earle at the Falcon straight after work.'

'How am I going to get back in to see Elliot tonight?' Hannah protested.

'Can't you ask your dad?'

Hannah gave a shallow, painful sigh, then nodded. 'What do you want to see Pete Earle for?'

'You know. It's this nuclear fall-out stuff he's been reading up about. I want him to explain it to me.' He turned away, looking for his pick-up truck across the crowded car park.

'Oh, Gary.' Hannah sighed his name in a mixture of pain and exasperation.

'"Oh, Gary" what?' He turned on her, his temper exploding. 'You're not going to get on at me for trying to find out what's at the bottom of this leukaemia business, are you? Anyone in their right mind would want to know!'

She hung her head and took two or three steps in the opposite direction. 'What's the point?'

'What's the point?' he repeated incredulously. 'I can't believe you said that. Our lives get ripped apart and we're supposed to take it without asking any questions?'

'Gary, don't!' Hannah glanced in embarrassment at Laura as her husband created a scene.

A driver wheeled a patient out to a waiting ambulance and two visitors walked in clutching bunches of flowers.

'Don't what?' He picked up every word and flung it back. 'Don't rock the boat, just do as we're told? I'm only asking

Peter what he's found out from the Ruthwell Report, for God's sake!'

'And you think you'll understand it?'

He stormed off towards his truck with Hannah in pursuit. Laura kept her distance.

'You really think you'll have the first clue what these scientists are talking about?' Hannah taunted. 'I tell you, Gary, they've been looking into these so-called cancer clusters for years and getting nowhere fast. And these are the experts, going round and round in little circles, saying yes, you run a risk if you work anywhere near one of these nuclear reactors, then no you don't, there's no need to worry.'

'What would you know?' He tried to climb into his cab, but Hannah's hand on his arm stopped him.

'More than you think. I watched a film on TV.'

'So that's it. You know everything?'

'I never said that. That's just the point. No one knows!' She refused to let him go, her long brown hair falling across her face as he tried to wrench his arm free. 'But I do know one thing; you smoked like a chimney when I was pregnant with Elliot!'

'So?'

Laura approached them, not sure how to intervene. She saw Gary shove Hannah away, jump in the truck and slam the door.

'I told you not to smoke. All the books say you should stop when you're pregnant. It never made any difference to you though, Gary!' Hannah screamed above the roar of the pick-up's engine. 'Forget Ruthwell. If you want to point the finger at someone, take a look at what you did to Elliot with those filthy fags!'

'I shouldn't have said that.' Laura had driven Hannah home to her bungalow in Askby after Gary had gone off in a rage. She'd hidden her head in her hands and sobbed all the way out of Wingate, until Laura had reached the open road. Then she'd calmed down and stared out with a puzzled frown at the newly green trees as if asking how they could possibly have come into leaf without her noticing.

'I haven't thought about anything except Elliot for weeks,' she told Laura when she was home. 'Elliot's tests, the clothes Elliot needs for hospital, the toys I can take in. Gary and me, we've never found time to talk about anything properly. And now I've gone and blamed him.'

'Don't take it to heart. I'm sure Gary won't when he's calmed down.' Laura knew she had to be back in Hawkshead in time for evening surgery. As far as she could judge, Hannah should be able to cope now. With her plump face and figure, her crumpled blouse and straight brown hair parted down the middle, she seemed to have unexpected strength. 'Will you ring your father to arrange a lift for tonight?'

Hannah nodded. 'Thank you, Dr Grant.'

'And call me any time you need to. Or anyone at the medical centre. We're all there to help.'

Hannah smiled briefly and followed Laura to the door. 'I was wrong to blame Gary, wasn't I?'

'I can understand how it happened.'

'But it wasn't right. I don't really think it was his cigarettes that's given Elliot leukaemia, do you?'

Laura shook her head. The Woods' bungalow had a newly laid paved drive. The strip of garden to either side was still piled with hardcore and sand. She saw how hard Gary had worked on the house. 'You'll never know the reason,' she insisted. 'It may be partly genetic, partly to do with the environment. You have to add in things like diet, the water we drink, the soil we grow our food in to the equation. Even the rock our houses are built on contains some natural radon gas.' She shrugged helplessly. 'Certainly, smoking tobacco is only one of a whole range of factors.'

'And what do you think about the Ruthwell business?'

Hannah appeared reluctant to let her go. She stood on the doorstep, staring down at a child's yellow plastic tractor upturned on the drive. 'Do you think it's a load of far-fetched rubbish?'

Did she? Coming up against the direct question, Laura had to decide. Hannah was hanging on her answer, trusting her judgement.

Why had she been so sceptical up till now? Was it really because the sample was far too small to build a cancer cluster on? Was it because Ruthwell was Piers's pet theory and she wanted him to be wrong, as Luke had said? Or was it for fear of the vast implications? Ought she not to confront the possibility?

'Is it?' Hannah persisted, her eyes still red from crying.

'It's no more rubbish than any other theory,' Laura confessed. 'And I don't see how we can stop Gary and Peter from looking into it if that's what they want to do.'

CHAPTER TEN

It was early morning and Luke was out by the river near
Devil's Leap, thinking of the night before, realising that among
the changes that had come about since he'd seen Laura and
Matthew together there was a loss of simplicity and ease in
their love-making. Now, he acknowledged, there was a part of
him that wanted to cling at all costs and, equally, another
that resented the need. And again, since the picture that he
couldn't erase of Matthew and Laura walking arm in arm had
lodged in his brain, he was distracted by images of Laura in
bed with Matthew, by Laura's voice whispering not his name,
but Matthew's. Matthew Aire – the words hammered away
inside his head and robbed him of all peace of mind.

Luke had shown up unexpectedly at Abbey Grange the
night before to find Laura tired but restless. The wise thing
would have been to stop for a drink, then go back home. But
he'd stayed and they'd quickly gone to bed to avoid having to
talk things through. They'd made love and it had been less
total than before. Quickly seeking the refuge of sleep, Luke had
woken at first light with a head full of jagged, paranoid
dreams. He'd dressed and come outside.

Abbey Grange was visible in the bend of the River Raven, its
stones nearly as ancient and mossy as the landscape it nestled
in. Deep foundations mingled with the roots of old oaks and
chestnuts, thick walls overlooked the curving, fast-flowing
current.

Aware that Laura might be watching him from the

bedroom window, he climbed down the slope out of sight, picking his way where the river had gouged out the earth and left arches of twisted, exposed root.

He stepped out on to the dangerous domed rock where Laura and Matthew had stood. A hundred yards downstream, where the river widened and slowed, was the spot from which he and two school friends had used to fish with home-made nets and rods. There was a flat rock mid-stream: Fisher Rock. It was an island surrounded by ripples of silver water and he stepped from stone to stone towards it now.

It rescued him from the confusion of his doubts about Laura and about the impending Ruthwell scare. He stooped to dip his hand into the cool water. Yes, he could understand the angry reaction of Peter Earle and Gary Wood, their desire to get to the bottom of something that was actually unfathomable. It was like the aftermath of the Lockerbie disaster, or a parent's long fight to uncover the secrets surrounding the violent death of a child in a far-off country. Someone, somewhere must be accountable.

And yes, he shared Laura's concern for the Earles and the Woods, who were already under unimaginable strain. As far as he could see, it was only the men who were set on proving a link between their children's cancers and the Ruthwell plant, while the mothers quietly got on with the task of looking after Catherine and Elliot. He wondered about the different, seemingly gender-based reactions, echoed by himself and Laura.

A surge of fresh resentment broke through. It didn't seem to occur to Laura that her open opposition to his and Piers's course of action was hurtful to him, that he needed to have her on their side. Did she think he was immune to doubt? Swirling his hand through the stream, he frowned and shook his head.

In any case, he was committed to investigate further. He

took his hand out of the water, abandoned Fisher Rock and turned towards Abbey Grange.

'Do you want to come and meet Jim Conroy later today?' he asked Laura when he got back.

'Who?' She was flying round the house getting ready to go to work.

As always, Luke followed her every move, recognising that she looked perfect in a cool white top and dark trousers. 'Jim Conroy. A medical journalist with a special angle on nuclear reactors. I thought he might prove useful.' He'd gone ahead and contacted him via Piers, who knew Conroy from way back.

'Where are you meeting him?'

'At Haresby Farm. At seven this evening.'

'I don't know. Maybe.' She finished loading the dishwasher and was ready to leave.

Luke interpreted her blank look and lack of interest as another rebuff. It dug deep beneath his skin. 'Come to the meeting tonight, please,' he urged.

'Luke, don't you know that stuff like this spreads through a small community like wildfire? Once it catches hold of people's imaginations, there's no stopping it, especially when young kids are involved.'

'So we do nothing?' This wasn't the time or the place to be thrashing this out, he knew. A snatched few seconds, sending them further into opposite camps.

She stared back angrily. 'The mothers at the clinic are already in bits about it. They're convinced there's a major cancer cluster about to be uncovered in the area.'

'Maybe there is.'

'And maybe not.' Laura picked up her bag. 'And I wouldn't go running to tell a journalist and make a big thing of it, create a whole media circus, before I was sure of my facts.'

Luke followed her out into the hall. 'That's your problem,' he insisted. 'You and journalists.'

'You mean, me and my ex-husband?' She stopped. 'So I'm prejudiced against all media people, is that it?'

'Maybe. And as you're so concerned about the Earles, perhaps you should remember that this isn't just something that Piers and I have drummed up. It's Peter Earle who's pushing us, saying that the official reports into childhood cancer are all biased in favour of the nuclear industry. He told me on the phone that he wants to get in touch with an independent body or individual to dig beneath the surface. That's when Piers came up with Conroy and why we're holding tonight's meeting at Haresby Farm. Peter's the one who set it up!'

Would Laura come? Luke got through the day with the question nagging at him. Reason told him that they should be able to differ over the Ruthwell issue without it affecting their relationship, but if he looked hard at it he knew that he was giving Laura a bad time about her stance on the cancer cluster theory because of the picture embedded in his consciousness of Matthew Aire taking her arm and leading her away from Devil's Leap.

Here, in his office, he realised that it was even possible that his own willingness to step in was less to do with his well-known public-spiritedness than with a mean need to counter-act the jealousy that was quietly working its poisonous way through his system. But he was committed, he told himself. Whenever an idea was too twisted and tortuous to pin down, the commitment phrase was one he brought into play: a matter of principle, of standing up for what was right.

On his way to Haresby Farm that evening, just after Luke had spotted Harry Chandler secretly sloping away from the house on his bike, he gave a thought to Laura's concerns about the media circus. There had been plenty of repercussions in the Dale just after Laura had arrived, when a company called Frontier Stone had tried to open a quarry on

Ravenscar. TV people, journalists camping out in backyards, himself fronting the opposition and talking to camera. And what good had it done? It had been the Aires, the owners of the land, who had backed out of the sale to Frontier for personal reasons, not media pressure, that had stopped the quarry.

But that wasn't the point as far as Ruthwell was concerned. As he drove through the gates into the Earles' farmyard, Luke at last pinned down a clear reason to go ahead and support Jim Conroy's work. On the one hand, Laura was saying they should drop the possible Ruthwell link in order to calm local fears. But what he would say – and presumably Peter, Piers and Jim would too – was that what they needed was more information to produce the same effect: openness was fundamental.

Relieved, he parked in the farmyard and went in to join the others.

'OK, so the information that comes out won't necessarily be comforting,' Jim Conroy was warning the Earles, Piers and Philip, who had obviously decided to be in on the meeting. The journalist was a slightly overweight man in his mid-thirties, prematurely bald, with a grey beard. There was no sign of Laura, Luke noticed. 'Maybe what we have here is two cancers linked to nuclear fall-out from the power plant.'

'And that might be something that this community has to face,' Piers took up the argument. He looked keen and sharp, his fair hair newly cut, giving his face an extra eager edge. 'What we mustn't do is patronise these people, as we would if we withheld the facts.'

'Explain that one to me,' Philip put in as Luke sat down at the kitchen table beside him.

'Concealment of the facts would be saying they're not capable of dealing with big issues.'

'"These people"?' Sonia Earle echoed quietly. 'We may be a

72

backwater here in Ravensdale, but we're not from a different planet.'

'What I mean is that by protecting the community we're taking away responsibility,' Piers continued. 'Whereas if we help Peter to dig deep, we're . . . empowering you!'

Philip stood up in the silence that developed. For a second, Luke thought that he was about to walk out on the meeting, then he realised he was giving up his seat to Laura who had just arrived.

As ever, Luke's whole awareness shifted to focus on her. She was across the table from him, hair loose over her shoulders, now wearing a short-sleeved, pale-blue shirt. She smiled briefly at him, then tuned in to the debate.

'Maybe we're all a bit too close to the issue.' Piers was refusing to give an inch. 'Laura, we're looking to you for a bit more objectivity.'

Laura sighed, glancing at Luke. 'As for objectivity, I can only say that I haven't had much other than Ruthwell on my mind for the past few days, and the only clear idea I can come up with is that if we give publicity to this situation here in the Dale it becomes a bit like the cancer cells themselves, multiplying out of control.'

Cancer. Luke pictured the mad riot of reproduction in a body unable to defend itself, a fatal growth. It defied the spring and summer, the early scent of hyacinths and the late fall of May blossom from the trees on the Earles' lawn.

'Peter?' Piers swung the focus towards the person in the room who really mattered.

'I agree with this empowering idea,' he told them. 'That's why I went to the library in the first place.'

'And what about you, Sonia?' Philip asked.

'If Peter wants to press ahead, I'm willing.' She sat on the edge, hands crossed on her lap in a posture of hard-won self-control. 'I'm not so sure about the Woods, though.' She turned to Laura.

73

'I've just come from there,' Laura confirmed, looking deeply unhappy. 'Things are different for them. Elliot's diagnosis is more recent for a start and the cancer may be more advanced. Gary and Hannah are also younger than you and Peter. Elliot is their only child.'

'Has something happened?' Philip picked up the hesitations in Laura's account and leaned across for a private word.

Luke took time out from the ongoing flow of information between Piers and Jim Conroy, and tuned in to her quiet reply.

'Hannah and Gary had a row, ostensibly about this Ruthwell thing, but to tell you the truth it's too many pressures piling one on top of the other. It turns out that Gary couldn't cope. He's packed his bag and left home.'

The news stunned Luke and he sat back in his seat. He hoped that the Woods' split wouldn't last long, that tempers would cool and they would pull together in the struggle to save their son's life. But he couldn't have much faith in the possibility, not when he studied Laura's sombre face, her averted gaze. His heart sank as he realised that the woman he loved was placing responsibility for this latest disaster squarely at the door of the instigators of the Ruthwell campaign.

CHAPTER ELEVEN

It was more than a week since Francesca had gone to Laura to talk about her pregnancy. Each day since then she'd tried to put the problem to one side, waiting for the doctors to make the necessary arrangements and get back in touch with her. Life goes on, she told herself, then realised with a terrible pang of conscience that for one small unborn being that was exactly what it didn't do. Life . . . it ended before it had begun.

Sickened by her decision, yet unable to see another way out, her already shaky self-esteem plummeted. Each morning, as she struggled out of a troubled and broken sleep, she found it more and more difficult to face the day. Small things required great effort, routines that she'd held on to all her adult life grew meaningless. It was now almost more than she could do to look in the mirror, comb her hair and put on her make-up.

She would stare blankly at her own face, seeing only shadows and hollows, the defects and the damage. Her normally self-critical gaze became coldly self-destructive: why bother to style her hair, shape her eyebrows, put on her lipstick? Why bother to leave the house and present a face to the world?

Yet now she must. She sat opposite Laura in her consulting-room, waiting to hear the details of her abortion.

'I don't need to point out that termination at this stage is a significant procedure,' Laura began.

Francesca nodded before the sentence ended. 'I don't want

you to enter the pregnancy on my file,' she insisted. 'Piers has access to that, doesn't he?'

'Yes, and I know you have a right to confidentiality. But it does create a dilemma.' Laura studied the screen displaying her patient's case notes. 'If I don't document the pregnancy and the termination, it leaves a big hole in your medical history.' She sighed and turned away from the monitor with a significant enquiring stare.

'Whatever. I still don't want Piers to know.' Francesca felt the pressure of Laura's steady gaze. 'And I won't change my mind.'

'Sorry.' Laura looked down at the letter from the clinic which she'd called Francesca in to discuss. 'I don't mean to seem unsympathetic. And I do have the consent of a second doctor. All the forms are signed . . .'

'So we can go ahead?'

A brief nod from Laura wrecked Francesca's fragile composure. She felt her lip tremble, the hot sensation of tears welling up.

Laura handed her a tissue without comment as Francesca retreated behind her hand, her whole body shaking.

'I don't normally cry like this.' Was it relief or fear? Or a mixture of both. The sight of the forms laid out neatly on the desk made her shudder.

'It's OK,' Laura said gently. 'Give yourself a break. Now might not be the time for a stiff upper lip.'

Perversely, Francesca found that permission to break down made her do the opposite. She drew herself together and sat upright in her chair. 'I'm fine as long as we don't mention Piers,' she insisted. 'This is something I have to do myself.'

Laura fiddled with a consent form. 'It's all lined up, so unless you want to ask me anything or discuss it further, I just need your signature for me to go ahead and make an actual appointment at the clinic.'

Francesca accepted a pen and turned the form towards her. She heard Laura's voice continue as if from a distance.

'We have to move pretty fast at this stage, so I'll try and fix a time for next week, Friday at the latest.'

Francesca's trembling hand formed a signature that didn't look quite right.

'Francesca, I have to ask,' Laura said, reaching out to retrieve the signed consent form. 'Are you absolutely sure you don't want this baby?'

Baby. Unborn child. Person. Francesca let her eyes flicker up towards Laura with an expression of profound shock. She refused to let go of the form. 'This isn't to do with what I want.'

'You mean, it's what Piers would want?' Laura conveyed doubt in her tone and answering gaze. 'But how can you be sure unless you ask him?'

'You don't understand.' No one did. You lived with a person for years before you learned the rules of their particular game. They put up disguises, played tricks, but from the inside you knew the way their mind worked. Piers did not in any circumstances want to increase the size of their family.

The knowledge left Francesca marooned on a miserable island of rejection. Her husband didn't want another child. It made her angry, it hurt her deeply. She nursed the wound in customary silence.

'No, I don't. Are you saying that left to yourself, you might actually want the pregnancy to go ahead?'

Francesca drew breath; half sigh, half sob. Pregnancy. Termination. Procedure. Those were the clinical words that let her off the hook, made it easy for her. 'I've made up my mind,' she insisted.

'But . . .?'

'It was when you used the word "baby". That felt different. I know you're used to dealing with unwanted pregnancies. This is probably nothing to you.'

Laura shook her head. 'Believe me . . .that's not true.'

'I've never been one of those women who support abortion on demand.' Francesca had few certainties in her life, but first and foremost was that having Harry and Joe had been the uncontested high points of her life.

Yet she felt she hadn't lived up to the role of mother as well as she would have liked. Over the years she had been indecisive, made some wrong decisions about how to handle the growing boys' misbehaviour. Piers had called her weak and taken over the discipline role. She'd stood by and watched them cry when he punished them with a withdrawal of affection, a cool determination to make them see the error of their ways. 'They're only children!' she would remind him. 'You have to make allowances!'

She wanted to tell Laura her feelings about this without knowing how to put it into words. 'I don't think I have the right. It's the child whose rights are important.'

'That principle's fine until you come up against the reality yourself.'

'But it stays a principle. Deep down, I know I shouldn't be doing this to him.' She meant to the child whose rights she was denying, who was becoming more real to her by the second. 'But that's not the point!' she wailed. 'It's as if I have to put myself and even the baby to one side. It's not to do with what I want.'

Laura stood up from the desk: a gesture of frustration. 'Why not? I can't think of anything more fundamentally a woman's own decision than whether or not to give birth.'

Francesca lowered her head and stared at her pale hands clutching the crushed paper tissue. 'Because I can't just think about myself. I'm Piers's wife. We have two children.'

'And you think that another baby would destroy the family?'

'I know it sounds perverse and hard to grasp.' She closed her eyes and tilted back her head. She was falling down a well of loneliness. It was dark and narrow, and if she reached out her hands to break her fall her fingertips would find no purchase. 'But believe me, Laura, if I went ahead and had this baby it would break us all apart.'

Francesca stood up, then thrust the hated form across the desk. She'd said too much, hadn't been able to convey the complexities, only her overwhelming sense of defeat. It was useless. Turning quickly, raising a hand to hide her tears, she rushed from the room.

CHAPTER TWELVE

Laura waved at Sonia Earle as, the following Saturday, she stepped out of the passenger side of Luke's car.

'Is this an official visit?' Sonia asked.

'It's another weekend on call, if that's what you mean.' Laura glanced down at her sleeveless cotton top and trousers. Her long dark hair was pulled loosely back and secured into a rough pony-tail. 'But I'm hardly looking official, am I?'

'You're looking wonderful, as always,' Sonia said warmly. 'You don't really want to see Catherine on your day off.'

Laura saw her patient breeze out of the farmhouse, the inevitable stuffed pig under her arm. The girl, who had already achieved her wish of going back to school, came grinning towards them.

'I'll see Catherine whenever she wants!' Laura smiled back. 'Official or unofficial.' The three linked arms and walked around the side of the house, while Peter met Luke on the doorstep and went in to talk about Ruthwell.

'Would you like to hear a true pig story?' Catherine drew Laura towards a rope-swing, bestowed the toy into her keeping and climbed on.

'I'd love to,' Laura laughed.

'Well, this really happened. There was once a tornado in Lincolnshire.'

'No!' Laura feigned amazement.

'Yes. We have tornadoes in England, didn't you know? And one hit a pig farm near Lincoln. And the wind was so strong it lifted the pigs off their feet and blew them through the air!' Catherine swung to and fro, letting the breeze blow her dark fringe back from her face.

'No!' Laura said again. This time she meant it.

'Like this!' Catherine jumped from the swing, seized her toy pig and threw him high.

Sonia reached out and caught him.

'Why are you laughing? It's sad. The pigs died.' Seeing her father at the open kitchen window, she ran across. 'Daddy, tell them the real life story about the tornado and the pigs. They won't believe me!'

As her daughter skirted round to the front of the house, Sonia shrugged at Laura. 'Is this really just a friendly visit?' she checked.

'Yes. I heard Luke say he wanted to come up to talk to Peter and I asked if I could tag along.' She glanced at the open moorland behind the farm, at the banks of bright-yellow gorse bushes and the sharp ridge of land beyond. 'I love it up here.'

'In spring and summer,' Sonia conceded. 'You should try living up here in winter.' She gave Laura a second, more penetrating look. 'You're sure there's no news? Nothing from the hospital?'

'Believe me.' Laura moved to convince her. 'It was actually Adam that I wanted to mention.' She'd decided to suggest to Sonia that they get in touch with the boys' teachers. If there was bullying going on, it probably occurred both in and out of school.

'Adam?' Sonia's head went to one side. 'What about him?'

'I might be quite wrong about this and, if I am, you can tell me to mind my own business, but I'm guessing Adam is going through a hard time.'

'We all are.' There was a momentary chink in Sonia's cheerful armour.

'I know.' Laura touched Sonia's hand. 'But Adam might feel

81

that he's floating on the outside of all this, not knowing where he fits in.'

Sonia closed her eyes and drew a deep breath. 'Please don't tell me any more bad news. I know you think Adam was involved in a fight and I've been worrying about it ever since you mentioned it.'

'It's connected with that. I thought maybe you ought to follow it up.'

'And I know he's been impossible. For instance, an hour ago he gave me a hard time, then went off on his bike without a word. But it's just a phase. When we get Catherine through this we can all relax and Adam will be back to normal.'

'You think he's OK at school?' Laura linked arms again with Sonia and they walked round the lawn.

Sonia stopped by a pink azalea bush just coming into flower. 'To be honest, I don't know. Are you here to tell me he's not?'

'No. But it might be advisable to give his tutor a ring. The school knows about Catherine's illness, so they should be keeping an eye on Adam for you.' Laura could see that she'd firmed up the uneasy doubts. 'Remember there's always counselling for him if we find he needs it.'

'It's my fault.' Sonia sighed. Her grey eyes narrowed and closed again, her lip trembled. 'I've put so much energy into willing Catherine to get well.'

'It's not your fault. You're being magnificent. And Peter. You both are.'

'I don't feel magnificent.' Sonia heard the approach of another car and looked down the narrow road. 'Peter's asked Jim Conroy to meet him and Luke again. I expect that's him now.'

Laura recognised the stocky, bearded figure getting out of the car, which he had parked on the grass verge by the farm gate.

'You'd think he was harmless to look at him,' Sonia

murmured, taking in Jim's shambling walk, his broad, even-featured face.

'No journalist is harmless,' Laura joked, then held back to avoid Conroy as he went in to join Luke and Peter. 'I should know. I was married to one.'

'Really?'

'In London. Tom was an investigative journalist. He occupied the high moral ground.' She explained her ex-husband's careless, exploitative eagerness to track down a worthy cause. 'They're the worst sort.'

'I'll bear that in mind.' Sonia asked Laura to come into the house. 'I need your support when those three get going,' she confided.

So Laura gave in and soon they were all seated around the big kitchen table, papers spread out.

'What you have to realise is that the latest papers on the subject all point towards there being no causal link between childhood cancer clusters and nuclear fall-out,' Jim reminded them. 'To put it in another context, only 0.1 per cent of our sources of exposure to radiation can be put down to the production of nuclear energy. On the other hand, cosmic rays produce ten per cent of our exposure, medical X-rays twelve per cent. We ingest another twelve per cent in our food, fourteen per cent through environmental gamma rays and a staggering fifty-one per cent through radon and thoron, which are naturally produced gases given off by the rocks beneath our feet!'

Peter Earle sat back in his chair. Evidently, these were not the figures he wanted to hear. Laura, on the other hand, felt they justified her sceptical point of view.

'What's more, all the studies relate to parents who have actually worked in the nuclear industry, not to those who may have been exposed to radiation by accidental seepage or disposal of waste.'

'Which is the category you and Gary come into,' Luke

noted. 'The farm you both worked on was on land in the immediate vicinity of Ruthwell, but your cases wouldn't alter the current statistics because the papers only study nuclear workers themselves.'

'We might as well give in before we start, then.' Peter shoved away the papers. 'What you're telling me is that we don't have a cat in hell's chance of proving anything.'

'No. Jim's saying it's going to be an uphill fight,' Luke insisted. 'On top of the statistical difficulties, if we do come up with a convincing case about the link between Ruthwell and the two instances of leukaemia in Ravensdale we're bound to hit a wall of official denial.'

'Why?' Sonia sat on the edge of the group, listening out for Catherine, who had gone upstairs to watch TV.

'Because the industry stance is that there is no link and the government supports that stance through absence of other evidence.' Luke spread his hands. 'Look at all the money and effort the nuclear people put into advertising their energy as clean. Think of all the jobs tied up in it, the lack of viable alternative energy sources.'

'We want you to know what you're taking on.' Jim was talking directly to Peter.

Laura studied the faces; the patient, watchful expression of the journalist, Luke's clear grey eyes fixed on Peter, giving nothing away. It was the Luke she'd first known: the public man, the astute lawyer, difficult to reconcile with the gentle, generous lover whom she alone of the people gathered here knew anything about.

Catherine's father and mother looked at each other across the table; Sonia hesitant and afraid, Peter growing more defiant.

'You can't tell me it's coincidence!' he said at last. 'What are the chances of Catherine and Elliot going down with the same thing? Millions to one!'

'Agreed.' Luke nodded. 'Both Jim and I are willing to look

hard at this for you. Piers Chandler has a fair amount of specialist knowledge behind him and Laura here is looking after the individual patients. Between us we'll give you all the support we can.'

He'd counted her in automatically, though he knew her doubts. He ought not to have done, yet he obviously needed her support. Laura frowned and cleared her throat.

Peter glanced again at Sonia, allowing her a token say. 'What do you think?'

'I'm not sure.' She shook her head. 'And, at the end of the day, what are we after?'

'Yes, you must think about that,' Laura murmured. Again she wondered why the Earles and the Woods should put themselves through this. Especially Hannah Wood, who was now having to cope alone. She was afraid for them all if they took on the kind of opposition that Luke had described.

This appeared an easy question for Peter to deal with. 'It's all the rest I find so difficult,' he confessed. 'The diagnosis, the hospital visits, the tubes and drips ... I want proof.' He slammed the table with the flat of his hand. 'Evidence that there is a link. They can deny it as much as they like but, in the end, they're going to have to sit up and listen to us.'

On Sunday morning Laura and Luke slept in. Laura woke to find that the clear sky had clouded over and the church bells of St Michael's and All Angels across the river in the abbey grounds were calling the dwindling faithful to prayer.

She slipped out of bed to make tea and it was while she was in the kitchen, looking out beyond the garden at Black Gill and Ravenscar, that the telephone rang.

She picked it up, expecting an emergency call-out. 'Laura Grant.'

There was silence at the other end.

'Hello?'

'Bitch!' One word. A deep, muffled voice.

Laura pulled the phone away from her ear, then put it back quickly. 'Who is this?'

'Bitch!' The same word repeated. A click. A disengaged tone.

Shaken, she punched in the digits to identify the caller.

A recorded message told her that the number had been withheld.

Her first thought was that it must be a joke. Her second that it could be Gary Wood.

'Why Gary Wood?' Luke had come downstairs at the sound of the ringing phone. He stood in the kitchen doorway, still bleary-eyed, while she told him about the call.

'I don't know. Call it an instinct.'

She hadn't recognised the voice, but Gary flew into her mind. The last time she'd seen him had been in the hospital car park, when he'd argued with Hannah and stormed off. It could have seemed to him then that Laura was siding with his wife. 'He doesn't like doctors at the moment,' she told Luke with a shrug. 'And to be honest, I can't think of anyone else.'

'It's probably a total nutcase.' He was ready to dismiss it, grumbling at the interruption to their peaceful morning.

So Laura too let it drop. But when Luke said later that he had to go home to Merton to catch up on paperwork the phone call was still on her mind.

She decided to use the rest of her morning to pay a visit to Hannah Wood to discover more about Gary's state of mind. Then she would drive over to meet Luke for lunch.

At eleven o'clock she pulled up on the newly laid drive outside the Woods' bungalow.

Hannah must have heard her car and came out to greet her. She was pale and quiet, but composed, dressed in a loose-fitting salmon-pink dress, her hair down around her bare shoulders. She explained to Laura that she had half an hour before her father arrived to take her to Wingate: 'Mum's at the hospital with Elliot now,' she told her. 'She's been there overnight. I don't like to leave him with no one to keep him company.'

'How are you?' Laura walked into the house, noticing the toy tractor tipped on to its side and other signs of neglect. There was a pile of unopened mail on the hall table, a pair of trainers flung into a corner. 'Is there anything I can do?'

'No, thank you. You heard about Gary?'

'That he's left home? Yes, you told me.'

'Did I?' Hannah went into the living-room and cast about aimlessly for items to go into the bag she was taking into hospital. 'Do you know, he hasn't been to see Elliot since he walked out of here?'

'No, I didn't know that.' Laura felt herself wince. 'That must be dreadful for you.'

'I mean, it's not that Gary doesn't care; because he does. But we had this awful row. It was me getting on at him for smoking after I fell pregnant; you heard me, remember? I said I was sorry, but he wouldn't let it drop.' She sagged forward, puzzled by the open bag and a child's T-shirt which she held in her hand.

'I expect he's frightened about Elliot.' Laura took the T-shirt and put it in the bag. 'He's taking it out on you.'

'On me and everyone else,' Hannah told her.

'Including us doctors?'

'He's got it into his head that you don't know what you're doing.' An embarrassed smile flitted across her lips. 'And he thinks that you put me up to all this stuff about smoking just to send us off the real track.'

'And what's the real track?' It was as Laura had expected. Fear turned to anger. Anger turned to blame.

'You know Gary believes Elliot's leukaemia has to do with him working near Ruthwell? He can't stop thinking about it. He reckons he knows more than all of you put together.'

Laura shrugged. 'Listen, would you like me to talk to him? Do you know where he's staying?'

'He hasn't been in touch, but I've heard he's drinking and letting people down over work. They say he's renting the lodge at the Hall.'

'The Aires' lodge?' Laura knew that it was empty and that Matthew would be willing to let it cheaply to someone in need.

'Would you really talk to him for me?' Hannah grasped Laura's offer. Her eyes filled up as she met her gaze for the first time that day. 'Tell him Elliot's asking for his daddy, Dr Grant. Say I need him here at home with me.'

CHAPTER THIRTEEN

Hawkshead Hall stood on the gentle side of the valley, across the river from the village clustered at the foot of steeply rising Ravenscar. It had been built in the early seventeenth century, out of stone stolen from the already rapidly decaying Ravensdale Abbey, secular sign that Papal power was gone for good from the heart of England's stern northern lands. Rambling, mullioned, its low, main porticoed entrance approached by broad stone steps, the Hall had been Laura's favourite building since she had first come to the Dale.

Even now, as it came into view, she appreciated the house's solidity. She'd connected Matthew with that sense of permanence, she realised. Life with him would have been steady, uneventful, reliable. She would have been enveloped by his quiet, strong, protective love. Whereas Luke ... She swept round a bend, swishing through water at the roadside ... Luke presented her with a challenge. He had layers of contradiction: gentle and loving, yet fiercely idealistic and averse to compromise. Luke's love was more demanding, more passionate. It aroused her and felt dangerous when he refused to make concessions: over the Ruthwell scare, for instance. This kept her alert, constantly wondering whether his principles got in the way of her love for him, or made him more desirable still.

Everything shifted and disappeared, like the land beneath a morning mist.

And now she must concentrate on the lodge at the gate; a diminutive nineteenth-century replica of the Hall's original

Jacobean style, on Gary Wood's red pick-up truck parked outside and on the curtains still closed at midday.

Laura knocked and waited. From inside she could hear a door bang and slow steps come down the hallway.

Gary Wood opened the door just enough to peer through the gap. 'Yes?'

'Can we talk?' She felt her heartbeat quicken.

Gary looked unshaven and grim, blocking her entrance. 'What about?'

'Elliot.'

He turned his head to one side, did battle with his own thoughts, then opened the door. 'Come in.'

'Thanks. It's not bad news, but I wanted to bring you the latest.'

Gary led Laura through into a tiny living-room. Newspapers and ashtrays lay scattered across the chairs and table, so they stood awkwardly in the middle of the floor. 'Get it over with,' he told her. 'Has the hospital fixed a date for his operation?'

'Mr Grey thinks late August, maybe early September.' Laura got used to the mess in the darkened room. She took in the empty cans and bottles, a sleeping-bag thrust roughly behind a cushion on the settee. 'It'll depend on Elliot's blood count being good enough after this present course of chemotherapy.'

Gary listened. 'And how is he?'

'Doing well so far.' Laura noticed Gary's jaw clenched tight, the tense sinews in his strong neck, and took a calculated risk. 'Hannah says he's missing you.'

His face showed no reaction, but he swayed dangerously.

She put out a hand to steady him. 'What can I do?'

'You can mind your own bloody business.' He turned and walked out into the narrow corridor, wheeled back again, then hit his fist sideways against the wall. 'You can't do a sodding thing. Unless you can wave a magic wand!'

'I didn't mean Elliot.' Laura tried to hold her nerve in the face of Gary's unpredictable response. She knew that she was no physical match for the tall, muscular builder. 'I meant, can I do anything to help you? Are you sleeping? Are you able to work?'

'Am I drinking? Am I taking it out on my wife?' he retorted. 'Say it if that's what you meant.'

'It wasn't. Listen, Gary, I came to let you know how Elliot is. And to see if I could help patch things up between you and Hannah. She really needs you.'

'She told you to say that, did she?'

'No. But she said she wants you to come home.'

'So I can get her pregnant and blow smoke in her face all over again?'

'She doesn't really blame you.'

'Yes she does. What do you know?' Suddenly the pent-up tension exploded. Gary came at Laura, making her retreat against the window. 'You know how it feels to be told your kid has cancer, do you?'

'No.' She leaned back, aware of the stale smell of alcohol and tobacco on his breath.

'Well, I'll tell you. It feels like bloody hell. It works away at you until the only thing you want to do is to bump yourself off. No, better still; bump yourself and your kid and everyone else off and get it over and done with!'

Laura struggled as he grabbed her arm and pushed her back against the drawn curtain. She overbalanced and pulled at the musty fabric to steady herself.

'You think about it so much, you're ready to do it. Every time you walk into that hospital and see his little face, all you can think is you wish it would end. You feel even worse when you walk out again and leave him there.'

'I know, I know!' She twisted her wrist, trying to pull away from him.

'That's it; you don't! That's what I'm telling you.' He tore at

91

the curtain in his exasperation, half pulling it from its hooks. 'All you know is what it says in the bloody textbooks!'

He wrenched Laura's arm so hard that her hand rapped against the window. She heard the pane crack and saw that he'd kicked at a chair and sent newspapers sliding to the floor. 'Please!' she gasped, pathetic in her own defence. 'Gary, please!'

Something – the speaking of his name, the cracking glass – brought him to his senses. He let her arm drop and backed off, breathing heavily.

Laura clutched her wrist. She heard a car heading down the long drive from the Hall.

Gary Wood heard it too. His shoulders heaved as he fought to breathe evenly, and he stared over her shoulder out of the window at the approaching Range Rover. Quickly he turned and made off down the corridor, out of the front door, leaving it wide open. Within seconds, he'd started his truck and was driving recklessly towards Hawkshead.

'Laura?' Matthew's voice called from outside the lodge. He stepped in through the open door. 'Are you all right?'

Trembling, her wrist still burning from Gary's fierce grasp, she pushed her hair back from her face and stood up straight.

'I saw your car. Where are you?' Footsteps came down the corridor.

'In here.' She closed her eyes to block out what had just happened. When she opened them again, Matthew stood in the doorway.

'Where's Gary?' He looked around at the mess in the room.

Ludicrously, Laura tried to tidy up. She hitched the torn curtain on to the sill and stooped to pick up the newspapers. 'He had to go.'

Matthew too bent down and took hold of her injured hand. The wrist was red, the skin on the knuckles scraped off. 'Did he do this?'

'It's OK. It's nothing.'

'Did Gary do it?'

'He lost control. He's under a lot of strain.' Laura pulled her hand away and cradled it. Then Matthew drew her towards him and held her.

She sank against him. For an instant, she remembered how it felt to be in his arms, then knew that nothing was the same as before. Quietly she drew back, not wanting to hurt him, intent on finding another, safer level.

'You won't throw Gary out, will you?' She eased her scuffed fingers and rested her wrist against her other hand.

'Give me one good reason why not.' Matthew glanced around the wrecked room.

'He's clinically depressed. Push him one more step and he's over the edge.'

'Typical Laura.' Matthew smiled briefly. 'The guy attacks you and you stick up for him.' He went to examine the cracked window-pane, squeezing between her and the upturned chair. The air was still electric.

Laura recognised the outline of his shoulders, the dipped, shy tilt of his dark head. As if she could ever forget. 'He didn't do any real damage,' she protested.

Matthew turned. 'I'm worried about you. We should tell the police in case he tries something like this again.'

'He won't. Gary Wood is much more of a danger to himself than he is to anyone else, believe me.' Laura sounded more confident than she felt. She wondered whether to let Matthew know about the abusive phone call earlier that morning.

'Laura?' He moved towards her again with a protective gesture, his voice soft and low.

She put up a hand to stop him, panicked into confiding in Matthew rather than let him hold her again. 'OK, there's more. But you're still not to do anything about it. I've had a nuisance call. Just one, early today. Nothing very bad.'

'Gary Wood?'

'I don't know. It could be. It's one possibility.'

'Does Luke know?'

'He was there when it happened.' Laura watched Matthew's expression stay resolutely the same as he worked it out; early Sunday morning and Luke had been at Abbey Grange. That meant he must have slept there. She knew the concealed dismay she would have felt to discover that Abigail, Matthew's ex-wife, had stayed overnight at Hawkshead Hall. Laura and Matthew had no ties now, yet the dead promises between them stood up and rattled their dry bones.

'What did he say?'

'Not much. He thought it was probably a random call.'

'Not linked to the Ruthwell business, then?'

Laura frowned. It was the first time this had occurred to her. 'How, "linked"?'

'It's no secret that you and Luke are backing this protest group that's trying to prove some conspiracy theory.'

She opened her eyes wide in astonishment. 'Is that what they're saying?' Jim Conroy's investigation had barely got off the ground. There'd been two short meetings at Haresby Farm. And already people were calling them a protest group?

'You know Hawkshead.'

'I know that they've got it all wrong! Luke's agreed to act for the Earles and the Woods if there's any legal move to be made. But I'm not part of any group. Anyway, what you're saying is that people think that I am and that this phone call could be linked in with that?'

He nodded. 'Ruthwell's less than fifty miles from here. And a lot of jobs are bound up in the nuclear industry. Has Luke stopped to consider that?'

Laura shook her head. 'Leave Luke out of this.'

Matthew smiled bitterly. 'I only wish I could.'

'Matthew, I didn't leave you for Luke!'

He stared at her. 'No?'

'No,' Laura insisted, shaken, unsure. 'I left you because our relationship wasn't right for me.'

Matthew dropped his gaze and backed towards the door. 'It was right for me,' he said.

As he climbed into his Land Rover she wanted to run after him and remonstrate, but felt weighed down and tired out by what had passed. Instead she watched him drive off, aware that his parting words had closed tight around her heart.

CHAPTER FOURTEEN

'I hear you went to see Laura last week.' Piers wandered into the kitchen at the end of an afternoon that had been overcast and cool.

Francesca steadied herself to receive a light kiss on the cheek before he carried on into the conservatory. She was still waiting for a firm date, leading a double life. For Piers and the boys she had to seem normal, nagging Joe and Harry to do their homework, organising trips to the supermarket, preparing meals around Piers's erratic schedule. Inside, her head was bursting with doubts, her heart withering under the pangs of conscience, the hammer blows of downright fear. And now there was another problem flaring up and threatening to consume her; one that she would definitely have to discuss with Piers.

'What was that about?' he asked casually, picking up the newspaper from the low glass table.

'Booster jabs and it was weeks ago,' she lied.

He opened the Sport section and flicked through. 'Philip must have got it wrong.'

She began to make a pot of tea. Let it drop! Say nothing.

'Only, he mentioned he'd seen you at the medical centre late last week.'

'Oh, that. It must have been when I called in to see you about something. You were in Wingate at a meeting.' She tensed under the lie and spilled boiling water across the tiled surface. She mopped it up without any sign of irritation, controlling every minute reaction.

'You never mentioned it. Was it about Harry?'

'I don't remember. I expect so.'

Piers came back into the kitchen. 'You make it sound like it wasn't important.'

'It probably wasn't.' She poured the tea, handed him his mug, sighed when he caught her hand.

'What's going on? Look, I know you. You're making out this is something trivial.'

'It was. I can't even remember,' she protested.

He pressed harder. 'Getting information out of you these days is like squeezing blood out of a stone.'

'That's because there's nothing to tell. I must have been passing by and just decided to drop in. I probably told you what it was about when you came home in the evening in any case. It's gone out of my mind completely.'

He let go of her hand at last. There was an anxious look in his eyes. 'If it's Harry you're worried about, don't you think I ought to know?'

'Well, yes.' She hesitated. 'I am concerned about the way Harry's been behaving; he's made it plain he couldn't care less about anything, he's not doing a scrap of work as far as I can see and, on top of that, he seems to have been building up a lot of aggression against Joe since we came to Ravensdale.'

'So we have to tackle it. I can see it's getting you down and, to be honest, me too. I didn't predict problems with the kids when we moved. We've never had any trouble with either of them before. So why now?'

'Lots of reasons.' Francesca suddenly felt so exhausted that she had to sit down. She leaned her elbows on the table and massaged her temples.

'Tell me.' Piers's tone lost its sharp edge. He stood behind her and stooped forward protectively.

97

'There wasn't anything definite last week; just a general uneasy feeling.'

'But this week?' He sat down opposite, as if to prepare himself.

Francesca drew a deep breath. By putting Harry's head in the noose, it was as if she was saving hers. 'I got a phone call out of the blue this morning. The head teacher rang me to say they've excluded him.'

Piers looked stunned. He drew his brows tight. 'For how long?'

'Two weeks minimum. They're going to discuss him at a governors' meeting before they decide what action to take long-term. They say he's been bullying the smaller kids.' Francesca watched the news alter Piers's entire physique. He seemed narrower, less robust and looked every day of his thirty-eight years. 'And truanting,' she added.

'Where is he?' Piers stood up as if to storm through the house to find him.

'Out. I don't know where.' Harry had been sent home from school straight after the head teacher's phone call. She'd driven over to Hawkshead to collect him and brought him back. He'd slammed upstairs to his room, stayed there for a couple of hours, then slipped out of the house behind her back.

'What did he say?'

'Nothing. I couldn't get a word out of him.' The drive home had been totally silent, resentful on both sides.

'I wonder where he gets that from!' Piers flashed angrily, striding up the steps out of the kitchen along the hallway.

Francesca slumped in her chair. 'Joe's in his room. He doesn't know yet,' she called softly.

'What did the Head say?' Piers came back down.

'Only what I told you. And that teachers had found him disruptive in class.'

'So, reading between the lines, it doesn't look like they

minded so much about his unofficial absences – it made life easier for them than when he was actually in the place! And they didn't bother to draw our attention to it until it was too late. That's brilliant!'

'It's not their fault.'

'It's ours?' He rounded on her. 'What are we supposed to do when he's so secretive? We're not bloody mind-readers!'

'We've known . . . I've known there was a problem.' She felt empty and tired beyond belief. She wanted to be angry like Piers.

'And you didn't see fit to talk it through with me? I expect you hoped it would just go away if you didn't mention it.'

Now it was her turn to be accusatory. 'If you like. Problems do have a way of growing bigger when you and I try to discuss them.'

'Are you serious? You're saying we never agree?' Piers stopped.

Francesca sighed and stood up. Piers could switch within seconds from blame to being seriously floored and vulnerable. 'What I mean is you always want to rush headlong at the solution you choose, whereas I might want to go more steadily, look at different ways of handling it.' It was her fault, but not in the way he might think. She realised all over again that she'd been too submissive, too admiring of Piers's dynamism when they had first married. It was this pattern that had trapped her and made her uncertain how to handle the big decisions in their lives.

'What do you mean – go steadily?' he demanded, anger bouncing him back on to the offensive. 'Oh yes, I see. You mean, do nothing!'

'Piers, please. Let's not have a row. What are we going to do about Harry?'

'This time we have to do something, do we? This isn't a go-steady problem?' He was striding up and down the room again, not caring about Joe overhearing their raised voices.

'I'll tell you the first thing we're going to do.' He reached for his car keys. 'We're going to drive over to Bridge House to see Philip.'

'What on earth for?' She was staggered. 'Shouldn't we be out looking for Harry and trying to talk some sense into him?'

'No. Philip knows Ravensdale better than I do,' Piers insisted. 'I want to know what impact he thinks Harry's problem at school will have on my standing in the Dale.'

'On *your* standing . . .?'

'Yes!' His voice rose to a shout. 'I suppose it's too much to expect your support on this?'

He slammed out of the house and Francesca leaned on the table, her head hanging. It had all gone wrong. Her carefully constructed role as wife and mother had collapsed in ruins: rubble and dust, broken slabs of life, holes gaping where walls and roofs had once stood. There was a hollowness inside her, an explosion tearing her apart: a war zone, not a life.

CHAPTER FIFTEEN

It was that time of year when the days were at their longest. Light wrapped itself around the darkness and almost met edge to edge, so that night was squeezed to no more than six starlit hours.

Luke lay awake beside Laura early on Saturday morning. Almost a week after Gary Wood's assault, which she'd told him about in her usual understated way, her hand had healed, but the news in Hawkshead was that Gary had gone further off the rails. He was drinking every night in the Falcon and failing to show up for work next morning. There was still sympathy for him among the pub stalwarts, but the client who had employed him to build a garage extension had given up and gone elsewhere.

In the past five days Laura had received two more abusive phone calls.

'Bitch.'

She'd described the flat, toneless threats and her own response: indignant, frustrated, scared.

'Bloody interfering bitch.' The voice hadn't let up.

She'd slammed down the phone both times, shaking with anger.

Luke stirred now and found she was awake.

'What time is it?'

'Five-thirty. Go back to sleep.' He stroked her cheek with his fingertips.

She kissed the palm of his hand, lying in the crook of his

arm, curled in towards him. A lock of her hair was caught under his elbow, so he leaned across and released it. He brushed the soft skin of her neck with his hand, then ran it over her breasts. Her small, sharp intake of breath invited him on, so that soon he was kissing her, her arms were bringing him closer and he wanted her.

'You know what you do to me?' he murmured into the silky mass of her dark hair. 'Just looking at you drives me crazy. I love the smooth skin on the inside of your arm, the way you look at me when you catch me eating you with my eyes . . .'

Laura kissed his face, his mouth. 'Tell me,' she whispered. 'Let me hear you say it.'

'I want every inch of you. I want never to let you out of my sight.' It was true. She made him ache, she scared him with her beauty and the way she loved him, head against the pillow now and gazing at him with half-closed eyes, arms spread wide.

When they'd made love he knew she would slip out of bed, happy to have him watch her as she went to the shower, smiling down at him when she came back to get dressed.

'It's daylight,' she said softly, wrapped in her white towel, rubbing her damp hair. 'Come and see.'

A clear dawn sky invited them out into the garden. Swallows darted silently at the eastern wall of the house, swerved at the last split second and winged upwards.

A blaze of red tulips spilled their petals on to the path. Luke watched Laura scoop them up from the gravel, a handful of velvet, weightless and soft. She scattered them on the wet lawn.

The swallows darted and soared.

They walked together under the beech trees towards Devil's Leap, and came out into the clearing with Black Gill and Ravenscar behind them, the abbey ruins in the sheltered bend of the river beyond. The early sun filtered through tall, empty arches, on to crumbling walls, casting long shadows on the uneven ground.

Here, where the river narrowed between the grey, pitted rocks and the water ran with dangerous force, was where Luke had seen Laura and Matthew deep in conversation. She stood on the edge now.

He watched the water swirl and rush, heard its roar. Rain during the week had swollen the river to a foaming brown torrent.

'You mean as much to Matthew Aire as ever, don't you?' he said quietly.

Laura started, then glanced at him. 'Did you see us?'

Luke nodded. 'He still loves you.'

'Yes.'

'What about you?'

'I left him, didn't I?'

'That's not what I asked.' He knew from her early confidences how the sharp fragments of Matthew's past – his ex-wife, his two children – had worked their way under their skin, how they'd distressed and undermined them both. She said she'd hoped afterwards that they could still be friends. From this alone Luke knew that she still cared about him. And from the way she'd let Matthew take her arm.

'I saw him again at the lodge,' she confessed. Her pace towards the footpath was slow. 'When Gary lost control, Matthew came along and helped me. I should have told you.'

'He's not giving you up without a fight.' Why couldn't she say that she no longer loved Matthew? That she loved him instead? He wanted it to be simple, or to hear her say that it was.

Then he hated himself. Jealousy made him stupid, dullwitted, childish. It still flashed images into his mind of Laura in bed with Matthew, inflamed a lethal cocktail of resentment and insecurity, so that he walked on without her, bitterly regretting having started the dangerous multiplication of unwanted emotions.

Laura sighed. The current dragged a small green branch through the narrow gap and raced with it downstream to the slow bend by the Abbey.

Luke considered his own lack of ties, living on a hill in a back street in Merton, unattached to his surroundings, though the house on Tan Hill had one beautiful room: the light, uncluttered attic with a dormer window looking out on to the moors. By comparison he'd come to Laura unburdened by past complications.

He remembered how in the early days she'd wanted to go slowly, find her balance once more after Matthew. 'You hardly know anything about me,' she'd told Luke in his empty attic room.

'What is there to know?' he'd said.

But recently it had become more complex than that. His heart was full of her, her brown eyes and black hair, her grace and compassion, her slender, smooth body. And now there was a question hanging between them. He had walked ahead and waited for her to catch up. 'Where does it leave us, Laura?'

'I don't know!'

Closing his eyes, he turned and made his way back to the house.

'I'm at the medical centre.' Fuelled by a sense of guilt, Luke rang Laura. It was eight o'clock, Piers's weekend on call and the building was empty. Magazines stacked on the low tables in reception, information leaflets tucked into racks, gave the place a manageable, orderly air that it lacked during the week.

'And I've gone back to bed. Why aren't you with me?' Laura sounded wistful.

'I just wanted to let you know where I was. I kind of ended up here and now that I am, I want to glance at that other recent paper on radiation workers that Piers has given me.' He made himself sound busy and bright. 'It's a wonderful morning. Why not get up and join me here in an hour or so?'

'Great. Maybe we could go on up Ravenscar, over the top. I fancy another day walking off our worries and cares.' Laura promised to bring her boots and rang off.

Still worried, and willing to use the Ruthwell figures as a refuge from his confusion over Laura, Luke turned to the paper on the desk in front of him. It was a reprint from a specialist magazine of a study carried out by a team of occupational epidemiologists and a cancer research group sponsored by a radiological institute in Glasgow. He read the title: 'A Linkage Study of Cancer to Ionising Radiation'.

Here it was, dry and formal, the paper that Piers was convinced would back the cancer cluster theory. 'Peter Earle has already seen it,' he'd told Luke. 'In fact, it was Peter who dug it out of the journal in the first place. He's been reading everything he can lay his hands on, but this one seems especially relevant.'

'Objectives: To test the hypothesis that childhood cancer can be caused by parents' exposure to ionising radiation.' Luke dug into the opening paragraphs on the design of the study and the breadth of the sample chosen.

For half an hour he read attentively. He learned that this study, unlike previous similar ones, was not confined to families in the Registry for Radiation Workers, but also included those living in the immediate vicinity of nuclear installations. It was a broad sample and used data from Scotland, Cumbria and Oxford. In total, more than 50,000 children with cancer were under observation.

Slowly he absorbed the facts and figures, wondering how Peter had made sense of terms such as preconception doses of 100mSv and relative risk measures of 1.77(1.05 to 3.03). However, there was no doubt in his own mind about the clearly stated conclusions.

An increased incidence of childhood leukaemia and non-Hodgkin lymphoma was found among children of families living within a ten-mile radius of the nuclear installations included in the study. However, no link between incidence of cancer and level of dose of radiation was found.

The observed increased incidence is small, rising from an average risk of 6.5 per 10,000 among the average population to 11.4 per 10,000 for offspring included in the study. Because incidence of the disease was unrelated to dose of parental preconception irradiation, the results of this study cannot support the hypothesis that parental preconception irradiation is a cause of childhood cancer. The conclusion is therefore that these findings of increased risk may be due to chance or to other unidentified oncogenic infective agents.

Chance? Other agents? Luke reread the conclusion. He was puzzled. The study seemed to demolish the causal link which the Woods and Earles were looking for. Why did Piers see this paper as helpful to their cause?

He was still puzzling over the contradictory findings when Laura arrived.

'What is the incidence of childhood cancer round here?' he asked, determined to put his early-morning doubts to one side. She was dressed in walking boots, light trousers and T-shirt, her hair twisted back and up, and secured with a silver clasp. 'Not high, surely?'

They did some rapid calculations, then realised that Piers's new cross-referencing computerised system included the facility for them to look up the exact figure. Laura switched on the computer and tapped the keys.

The screen gave them names, ages, dates going back to the early sixties. Reading them with Laura's reluctant consent, Luke experienced the same feeling that faded inscriptions on gravestones produced: a mixture of respect, trepidation and sadness. He noticed that Ravensdale over the last thirty years had fallen well below the current recovery rate of fifty per cent for children with cancer. Here it was more like twenty-five per cent, the last child having died under Gerald Scott's care three years earlier.

He read the name: Louise Edwards. Louise had been thirteen years old when she died of non-Hodgkin lymphoma, the third daughter of Frank and Julia Edwards who lived at The Millstones in the old lead-mining village of Ginnersby.

Laura switched files to find the family's case notes, then they studied details of the relentless progress of Louise's illness. Like Catherine and Elliot, Louise had been a patient of Rudi Grey in Wingate. She'd achieved two lengthy periods of remission, before the final bout set in around two years after the disease was first diagnosed.

Switching sub-files, Laura pointed out that the other two Edwards girls had suffered only the usual childhood ailments, but that the mother, Julia, had been treated for depression after her daughter's death. Julia's case history was interesting; her health was patchy, disrupted by periodic bouts of stress-related illness and hypertension. She'd retired early from a high-pressure career . . . Luke read on with sudden interest.

Julia Edwards had qualified with an M.Sc. in Chemistry and worked for many years as a research scientist, latterly in a government health body that studied the flammable properties of household fabrics, but before that in the nuclear power industry. Her last job before moving to Ginnersby eleven years earlier had been at the Ruthwell power plant.

CHAPTER SIXTEEN

Laura and Luke postponed their escape on to the wilds of Ravenscar. Instead, Laura went straight to see Philip at Bridge House.

'Before you say anything more about the Edwards case, let me tell you something else.' Philip had taken her out into the garden where they wouldn't be interrupted.

'You're not going to tell me something that makes the whole picture look even worse?'

Philip nodded. 'Another possible case.'

Laura grimaced and held back the deep protest she felt welling up inside.

'Though I should stress that there are no results yet.'

'Who?'

'The Lawsons' baby, Emma.'

'You delivered her at home,' she recalled. 'Pre-eclampsia, premature labour; it was touch and go.'

'That's right. The baby's six months old now and thriving, or so we thought.' Philip poked at a mossy stone with the tip of his shoe, turned it, then picked it up and threw it down the bank into the river.

'And Alison Lawson's not one to make a fuss?' Laura prompted. She knew the family from the Falcon fairly well.

'That's right. Well, she brought the baby into surgery yesterday afternoon because she was off-colour, as Alison put it: a raised temperature, poor appetite, listlessness. And because of the bruising on her arms.' Philip thrust his hands deep into his pockets and walked on down the slope.

'You told her it needn't be significant?' Laura realised how much she wanted this not to be a new case of leukaemia. 'It's much more likely to be a mild viral infection.'

'I did my best to calm her down. But you're right, these mothers are in a state of hysteria about the whole business. I said that babies can thrash about in their cots at this age. It was quite possible that Emma had banged her arm against the side bars.'

'And is that what you really think?' Laura caught up with Philip at the river's edge.

'I don't know. I've sent off blood samples to the lab, tried my best to reassure Alison. Meanwhile, we just have to keep our fingers crossed.' He sounded subdued and asked Laura to remind him about the Edwards case.

She and Luke had reread a section of the Glasgow report that highlighted the fact that children of mothers who had worked in the nuclear industry ran an even higher risk of developing leukaemia than those of fathers. The incidence was still small and the sample lower, but the researchers had made it a strong conclusion.

'Let me have a look at it on Monday. Meanwhile, I have an advance copy of Jim Conroy's article here which I must read.'

'Some weekend off, eh?' Laura sympathised. 'Me too. I was supposed to be going out for a walk with Luke.'

At that moment Juliet came out of the house and called to tell her that Piers had tracked her down to Bridge House and wanted a word. 'You can use the phone in Philip's study,' she suggested, as Laura ran up the slope.

She went into the house, almost glad of the distraction.

'Laura? Thank heavens.'

'How did you know I was here?'

'I spoke to Luke at the medical centre. Listen, I'm arranging to send a patient from Oxtop over to Wingate Hospital and I'm held up here until they collect him. Meanwhile I've an emergency of my own.' Piers paused for breath. 'Did you know we've got trouble with Harry at the moment?'

Laura admitted that she'd heard as much.

'Well, he's pushed as far as he can at school and managed to get himself excluded. He refused to talk about it when we tracked him down late last night, but now apparently it's all blown up while I've been out on call. Francesca rang me, but I can't get there. Honestly, Laura, I wouldn't ask you to step in if I weren't seriously worried.'

'What do you want me to do?' Laura tried to imagine the scene at the Chandlers' house.

'Can you get over there right away?'

'Yes.' She glanced at the clock.

'Fran sounded desperate. Thanks, Laura. Tell her I'll be there as soon as I can.'

There was nothing for it except to call Luke, then drive swiftly to Merton. How desperate did a woman have to be before she would let a comparative stranger intervene in a family dispute?

As Laura negotiated the bends in the narrow road she prepared herself for the situation ahead.

Once at Merton, she had to slow down and thread her way through the traffic. Saturday was market day. The main street was lined with stalls and parked cars: slow going. Laura looked at her watch; it had been twenty minutes since she'd received Piers's call. But here was the house, set back from the road behind a neat laurel hedge, double-fronted and sedate.

The front door was closed, so Laura parked her car on the street and walked down the side, still apprehensive about intruding. Round the back of the house she found an open door and heard the sound of raised voices.

'Never, never speak to me like that again!' It was Francesca, standing alone in the kitchen, shouting along the corridor.

'What? What did I say?' Harry's voice yelled back.

'It's not what, it's how. And don't ever so much as touch Joe, you hear!' Francesca hurled herself up a short flight of steps and out of sight.

Harry must have slammed a door in his mother's face. From the back step Laura heard Francesca beat her fist against it.

'You think you can get away with this, but you can't!' Francesca ran back to the kitchen, grabbed the phone, then changed her mind and rushed back to scream at Harry.

Laura glimpsed her distraught, pale face, distorted almost out of recognition. Long strands of hair were streaked across her wet cheeks. She was hammering at the glass panel of the door that Harry had slammed shut, rattling the pane, quite beside herself.

Laura acted before Francesca put her fist through the glass. She went in quickly, up the steps and along the corridor, seizing Francesca's wrist to stop her from harming herself.

Francesca gasped, then struggled. Laura held tight, shocked by Francesca but even more so by the blank stare on Harry's face from inside the front room. He was tauntingly close to the door, looking out with half-closed, dead eyes; an expression that conveyed complete disgust.

Laura felt Francesca give up the struggle. She let her head drop so that her tangle of red hair fell forward to hide her face, then she allowed herself to be led away from the door to sit down in the kitchen.

'Where's Joe?' Laura was very worried.

'In his room.' Francesca winced as the lounge door opened and slammed shut.

Laura watched Harry wrench at the front door. It opened with a wild swing, then he vanished without a backward glance. 'Is Joe OK?'

'Harry kicked him. Joe was on the floor and Harry was kicking him.' Francesca sobbed, head in hands. 'He said it was because Joe wouldn't come out of the bathroom and he wanted to use it!'

'Shall I check on how he is?'

Francesca glanced up. 'Where's Piers? Did he send you?'

Laura nodded. 'Try to calm down. Tell me which is Joe's room.'

'I had to ring Piers. I found Harry attacking Joe and I didn't know what to do. But then it got worse. Harry overheard. He turned on me.' She grasped Laura's hands.

'Did he kick you?' Immediately Laura felt concerned about a possible miscarriage.

'No. But he said such dreadful things: that he hated me and always had, ever since he could remember. Vicious things about me and Piers.' Francesca's mouth drooped, her bottom lip trembled. Then she leaped from her chair and rushed along the corridor. 'Oh my God, I've left Joe!' Stumbling, sobbing, she ran upstairs and out of sight.

Laura found her in a bedroom, arms around her son, who was leaning against the wall on his bed.

'Let me take a look,' she said gently. Prising Francesca away, she asked Joe where it hurt. Though he was pale and shocked, he sat up without too much difficulty and, when Laura eased up his T-shirt, she was relieved to see only superficial bruising to one side of his ribs. Asking him to move his arms and torso, she satisfied herself that nothing was broken.

'You might be stiff tomorrow,' Laura warned him.

He stared back at her, sitting on the edge of the bed, waiting to be told what to do.

'Poor baby,' Francesca murmured. 'Daddy will soon be here.'

'Is it all right for you to lie down here for a bit while your mum and I go downstairs and have a talk?' Laura asked.

Joe nodded, so Laura lifted the duvet and watched him crawl underneath. He curled on his side like a much younger child, hugging his bruised ribs.

'I'm sure the damage is slight,' Laura told Francesca when

they were back in the kitchen. The door still stood open, letting in bright sunlight. 'Piers might want an X-ray, just to be sure. He could also suggest tranquillisers for you.'

'If he does, I won't take them.' Francesca sat at the table and looked at her with dazed, tearful eyes. 'Do you always stay calm, Laura?'

The question startled her. 'Not always. Professionally, yes, I hope so.'

'Professionally!' A hollow laugh turned to a groan. 'You sound like Piers. Doctors must never lose their cool. But with you I've noticed it's more than that. Stronger. More like serenity.'

'You think so?' Laura gave a grateful smile.

'I mean it. And it doesn't make you seem distant either. Not like Piers.'

'Francesca ...' Allowing her to pursue this would put Laura in a difficult position.

'No, let me say it. I need to ... Piers and I ... He shouldn't have asked you to come here today.'

Laura tried to follow her jagged train of thought.

'I shouldn't have rung him at Oxtop. I should have coped. But this problem with Harry is more than I can handle.' Francesca pressed her temples with her fingertips.

Laura sat quietly. No, she wasn't always calm, not even in her professional capacity. She hated violence and loss of control. Being helpless caused her deep frustration. In any other situation, if Francesca had been a friend, she would have put her arm round her and comforted her.

'Now is when I can least deal with Harry's behaviour!' Francesca looked up in agony. 'Oh, Laura. What am I going to do?'

Laura heard a key turn in the front-door lock.

Francesca didn't appear to register the small metallic sound. 'I came to you about the pregnancy because I felt you'd understand. But I realise now that you don't want me to go ahead with the termination . . .'

Laura saw Piers open the door and step inside.

'But it's settled!' Francesca's sobbing voice rose. 'Everything's fixed. Laura, tell me there's no going back. I have to go ahead and have this abortion!'

In the sudden silence which followed, Laura looked from one shocked face to the other. Then a fresh storm broke. Piers shouted and Francesca sat defiantly at the kitchen table while recriminations rained down.

'You can't do this to me – to us!' Piers's initial shock turned to anger as he kicked a chair aside, swept a bowl of roses to the floor.

Francesca gripped the edge of the table, shoulders hunched.

'You have to talk,' Laura insisted, aware of Joe lying in bed upstairs, hearing the crash as the bowl hit the tiles.

But the humiliation of having a witness to the whole mess only increased Piers's rage. 'What's the matter?' he taunted his sullen wife. 'Afraid of another pregnancy ruining your figure? Don't want to get up in the middle of the night for a crying baby? Would it spoil your social life? What social life, you ask? Yes, that's it: you're punishing me for moving you away from your precious friends!'

'Piers –' Laura stepped forward. 'There's been a fight. Harry hurt Joe. Joe's upstairs listening to this.'

Francesca stood up and, with trembling hands, began to pick up fragments of broken bowl. 'You see,' she whispered, collecting the pieces in the palm of one hand, 'I can't inflict this on another child. It's bad enough as it is.'

CHAPTER SEVENTEEN

The further Francesca fell, the less hold she seemed to have on the outside world. Routines that would normally rescue her were impossible to sustain; roles through which she would identify herself had become meaningless.

Wife and mother. She knew she was bad at being both: she was a shallow, inhibited woman unable to express her needs, a conservative parent who had imprisoned both boys within a rigid moral framework, which they would inevitably reject. First Harry, then Joe. It was just a matter of time.

She didn't blame Harry for his rebellion at school, knew it was a demonstration to her and Piers that they had got it badly wrong. Looking ahead a couple of years she had imagined an identical pattern for Joe: sullen silences, unaccounted-for absences from family meals, a refusal to come on holiday with them. And her heart had been squeezed until she could no longer sit in the house after the row with Piers had fizzled and died. She'd got up from the sofa and walked out into the deserted midnight streets without caring where she went or knowing what she was going to do.

She ached; wanted to cry out in the hope that if someone could hear what she was going through they would rescue her from the bottomless pit she was falling into. At the same time the street lamps, parked cars and privet hedges reminded her that such thoughts were excessive and therefore ridiculous. Not even a full-blown depressive wrapped in her own misery, she told herself, but a half-hearted one aware of the self-centredness and absurdity of her condition.

She'd walked for an hour through the streets of Merton. The lights were out, the curtains all drawn when she finally returned home.

Piers had gone to bed. He'd heard about the baby, ranted while Laura had been there, then retreated into a hurt silence. His accusations had been predictable: that she should have told him earlier (yes, she should); that a decision to have an abortion should be a joint one (of course this was true); that it was stupid of her to have stopped taking her pill (silence from her). If she'd asked his advice on the matter he would have told her the medical fact that menstruation can reassert itself at any time after a stressful episode and that the woman then immediately becomes fertile once more.

'Stop talking about me as if I'm a biological machine,' she'd pleaded.

'You are. I am. We all are.'

'And nothing else?'

'Obviously, other things come into it.'

'Such as?' Feelings, the quality of relationships, the ability to communicate, she'd thought, but had not been brave enough to say.

Piers had shrugged dismissively. 'Random chance. Genetic predisposition. You're probably particularly fertile.'

This had been after the ranting phase, which Francesca suspected even at the time was for Laura's benefit. He'd soon retreated into scorn, after that into the silence that had driven her out of the house.

Then he had demonstrated that he was perfectly capable of normal behaviour in spite of the blow she'd delivered. He had washed and cleared the coffee-cups while she'd been out, locked the windows and doors, and gone to bed as usual.

It was this that she couldn't bear. I could be dying in a corner and Piers would still keep a hold on what's locked and what isn't, she thought. Burning with resentment, she had thrown clothes into a bag at two in the morning. Let him take charge, she told herself furiously. He's competent and rational. Let him look after the boys; see how time-consuming and complicated it is; what fine judgement is needed to keep them healthy and happy. Catching herself out in this, she realised that in any case Harry and Joe would be better off without her.

The impulse to run grew stronger by the minute. If she fled she could avoid the moment when she had to step through the clinic door. She pictured a heavy revolving one, her entering, carrying an infant wrapped in white, its round face framed by lace; the image of a baby dressed for its christening. The door would turn. She would come out empty-handed. Fear shook her from head to toe.

She must leave Piers. It was the only way to find breathing space. To do it now, in the middle of the night, was vital. Having flung the clothes noisily into the case, she became meticulous in her movements. Piers must not wake up. But what about the sound of the car starting up? She was outside in the back garden, suitcase in hand, staring up at the moon. You could hear a cat breathe, a spider spin its web in the nearby hedge.

Risk it. What could he do even if he woke now? She was in her car, turning the ignition key. The engine roared. Even if the bedroom light went on and he came to the window she would already be out on the road, heading over the humped bridge towards the High Street. She would be gone.

The light didn't come on. Piers slept through her leaving him without a note, without a clue about where she was going.

WINGATE – 17 MILES. It was as good a place as any, since she couldn't face family or friends, so she pointed the car in that direction.

She would arrive there in Sunday's small hours and cruise the streets as dawn broke, then find a hotel overlooking the park, where no one would bother a single woman with little luggage. There were any number of them in the old spa town and she needn't be choosy. If it was comfortless and anonymous she wouldn't care. In fact, so much the better. It was only a space to contain her while she fell.

No one would care. Her husband would scarcely bother to look for her, playing down her disappearance even to Harry and Joe. She would be alone. Later, there would be time for her to make her decision.

CHAPTER EIGHTEEN

Jim Conroy's piece was destined for publication in a small journal sponsored by a European cancer research organisation, but, like everyone else, Luke knew that this was the prelude to much wider media interest. He reread the article on the Sunday morning after Laura and he had discussed details of the Edwards leukaemia case, and before he was due to meet Piers, Philip, Peter Earle and Gary Wood in the Falcon that lunch-time.

Conroy's investigation had been thorough. He'd dated the length of time during which Peter and Gary had both been employed at Morefield Farm near Ruthwell and linked the period with various scares over leakage from the nuclear reactor: all officially denied, but giving rise to local and national coverage at the time.

Then he went on to identify the type of leukaemia common to both Hawkshead patients currently undergoing treatment, and tied them to a similar case within the practice four years earlier. Conroy reported the subsequent death of that patient, who wasn't named. It was clear to Luke that the journalist referred to Louise Edwards and that he had dug very deep indeed for his information.

Luke picked up the copy of the article from Laura's study desk and went to find her. 'What do you think of paying a visit to Julia and Frank Edwards up in Ginnersby?' he asked.

She looked up from where she was sitting on the kitchen floor reading the Sunday papers. The back door was open

119

behind her, and Luke could see the garden and the river beyond. 'I've thought about it. But will they want to be dragged in?'

He tapped the rolled-up article. 'They already are. Conroy mentions Louise's case.'

Laura winced. 'It's going to be very painful for them if it all gets churned up again.'

'That's why we should go to see them now.' There were a dozen things Luke would rather be doing, but curiosity and determination combined pushed him to organise the visit.

'You go if you must.'

Once again he felt a spurt of resentment at Laura's resistance to the campaign. Surely she could see it was disloyalty to him, as well as to the principle they were all fighting for. 'Julia Edwards could be very useful to us,' he pointed out. 'She has lots of inside information.'

But Laura insisted that she would prefer to stay at home and perhaps meet him and some of the other campaigners in the pub for lunch. He left for Ginnersby alone.

Yet it was only a few nights ago that tenderness and intimacy had soothed his fears: Laura and he making love – a moment of complete yet passing safety.

Now he had to take refuge in the spectacular view from the top of Hawk Fell: the ridge of Ravenscar dipping away into Swiredale under a blustery, cloud-torn sky.

As Luke pulled up outside the remote house, he saw Julia Edwards weeding her garden. She came towards him, trowel in hand.

He noted the orderly rows of young beans and brassicas. Julia was dressed for gardening in a sweat-shirt, trousers and trainers, with thick gloves to protect her hands and a blue patterned scarf tied bandanna-style around her short grey hair.

She looked apprehensively in his direction. 'Are you another journalist?' she asked quietly.

'No, but it is about the interview you gave.' He introduced himself quickly.

Taking off her gloves, Julia nodded. 'Jim Conroy warned us to expect other visitors.'

Luke smiled. 'It happens when a case receives publicity, I'm afraid.'

Julia raised her eyebrows. 'Don't worry, I'm prepared. And I was impressed by Jim's methods. He didn't find out about us via the doctors here, but from records of past employees at Ruthwell. He matched up my name against census information in Merton Library. He turned up on our doorstep last weekend.'

'I'm relieved,' Luke admitted. 'The article could have caused an uneasy feeling in the village over access to confidential information, yet Jim's research had followed ethical lines. He must have been on to the connection between Louise's case and these two new ones long before us. I take it you didn't mind co-operating for the article?'

'Yes and no.' She asked Luke to sit on a garden seat that looked out over the rugged hilltop down into the next dale. A cool wind tugged at them. 'Talking about what happened to Louise isn't easy at the best of times.'

Luke let a silence develop. He gazed down at the grey remains of an old smelt mill: a rough green track leading to crumbling gable-ends, a tall chimney and tunnel entrances to a warren of underground lead-workings. Beyond the mine the countryside was still scarred by tippings and by deep vertical grooves in the hills where streams had been dammed to uncover valuable veins of ore.

'Three years.' Julia sighed. 'A drop in the ocean.' She turned her strong, direct gaze towards Luke. 'Some days I still go into Louise's room and expect to see her there. And, yes, Frank and I spend a lot of time wondering "Why Louise? Why this family?". That doesn't ease with the passage of time. So when Jim Conroy came along he wasn't digging up dead stuff and distressing us all over again, if that's what you were worried about.'

'It was,' Luke confessed. 'And you don't mind that he's trying to establish this link between Ruthwell and a supposed cancer cluster in Hawkshead?'

'Which makes me and my job responsible for Louise's illness?' she prompted. 'Of course I mind. It crucifies me, just as it does the Earles and the Woods from what I hear. Only, it's still new to them. I've been living with it for over four years.' Julia spoke unemotionally, but there was effort behind her self-control, more disturbing to Luke than if she had broken down and cried.

'You suspected this from the start?'

'I'm a chemist,' she reminded him. 'I knew the risks created by ionising radiation when I was a student.'

'Yet you took the Ruthwell job?'

'Paternal preconception irradiation does not carry a significant increased risk for children of workers in the nuclear industry. For mothers, the numbers are too small for reliable estimates of the risk, if any, to be made.' She quoted the official jargon.

Luke nodded. 'Is that what you really think?' Her answer meant a lot to him. With the evidence mounting to the contrary and the unwelcome media attention about to descend on their quiet dale, he needed to know where the Edwards stood.

'No.' Julia's reply came slowly, weighed down by grief. 'I know that our daughter would be alive today if she hadn't had a mother who'd worked at Ruthwell.'

The meeting in the pub broke up on an uneasy note. In fact, Luke thought afterwards, the whole session had been far more difficult than he'd imagined.

'Look at the families in Leeds who lived on the doorstep of that asbestos factory in the 1950s,' Peter Earle had pointed out. 'They got justice in the end. And now nobody lets kids play on a heap of asbestos dust, like they did.'

'Asbestos is different,' Laura said to Luke and Philip, as they stood outside the Falcon. 'You can't see radiation, or measure the sources of exposure to it.'

'No. And they proved the link between asbestos and lung cancer without a shadow of a doubt,' Philip agreed.

'Which is precisely what we're attempting to do in this case,' Luke pointed out.

'I thought Piers was below par today.' Luke had noticed the doctor's uncharacteristically subdued contribution to the debate. They'd left him inside still chatting with Jim and Peter.

'Yep.' Laura smiled apologetically.

'Meaning you know why, but you can't tell me? Well, I'll have to tease it out of him myself. Would you like a lift home?'

'No thanks. I'll walk.' Laura set off across the village square towards the footpath that led to the river.

As Luke said goodbye to Philip, dug into his pocket for his keys and headed up the side of the pub for the car park, he bumped into Piers leaving by the back door. Caught off guard, Piers was minus his usual bright shield of brisk competence. He seemed distracted, momentarily hesitant.

'Had enough for one day?' Luke tried to ease the awkwardness, gesturing towards the table inside where Jim and Peter were still ensconced.

'Yes. I have to get back home.' Piers looked at his watch, pulling himself together. 'I've been longer than I planned. The boys are there by themselves.'

At fourteen and twelve, Luke didn't suppose this would be a problem. But it obviously was to Piers. 'What's Francesca up to?' he asked.

It was as if Piers had been hit. His face registered shock, then anger. He tried to cover up the reaction and failed. 'What sort of question . . . I'm sorry, Luke. It's not your fault. I've just found out Francesca's pregnant.'

Luke took this in slowly, then offered uncertain congratulations. 'That's great.'

'No. We had this . . . this situation with Harry yesterday. It all came out when Laura was there and I learned Francesca had kept it from me. Until then I had no idea.'

'I'm sorry.' Luke was conscious of how inadequate he sounded. 'But I'm sure you'll soon sort things out.'

'You think so? The big question is, will she or won't she go ahead with the abortion Laura arranged for her?' Piers thrust his hands into his pockets and stared out across the roofs of the houses straggling up towards Town Head.

'This probably isn't something that Francesca would want you to discuss with me.' Luke backed off, anxious to get away.

But Piers was obviously still struggling to come to terms with his wife's secrecy. 'She was convinced I wouldn't want the baby so she never even bothered to tell me. Can you believe that? Laura knew. Get that? Francesca discusses it with Laura, but she won't talk to me!'

'That's pretty tough.' Luke walked Piers towards his car. 'But why are the boys by themselves?'

Piers leaned on the roof of the car. He hung his head and stared at the key in his hand. 'Francesca's gone. Last night. Packed her case, didn't leave a forwarding address. She's left home without saying a word.'

CHAPTER NINETEEN

The footpath which Laura took after leaving the Falcon took her towards the riverside walk across Hawkshead's playing field, past the single-storey, recently built medical centre where she spent her working life. It was a sympathetically designed group of buildings constructed of local stone, with large windows and a glass section in the roof, which cast plenty of light into the open-plan reception and waiting area. Carefully tended evergreen shrubs edged the car park and the entrance, which overlooked the river and Ravenscar beyond, was adorned with a stone drinking trough rescued from the village square during an unwise council move to create more parking space there. Now the trough served as a plant container and sported a bed of scarlet impatiens, just coming into flower.

On this Sunday lunch-time the centre was deserted, though tomorrow Laura would arrive for the eight-twenty and plunge once more into the fray. They were expecting the blood-test results on the Lawsons' baby girl from the hospital lab and Monday was the day she would fix a date for Francesca's abortion. The irony struck Laura forcefully: one family praying for life, another agonising about a termination.

Laura was so deep in thought that she didn't notice Gary Wood until it was too late to avoid him.

He came unsteadily out of the entrance to the surgery, obviously drunk. He swayed across Laura's path, his eyes unfocused, his face unshaven.

'Gary, it's Sunday. Everything's closed up.' She indicated the locked door behind him. 'I expected to see you at the meeting. Where were you?'

'Where were you?' he mimicked, curling his lip. 'What's it to you?'

Trying to keep her distance and being careful not to react, Laura decided not to mention her own doubts about the meeting. 'Everyone's pleased with the article Jim Conroy's written. Luke says it's bound to produce an official response. Then the pressure group can start lobbying the industry for full disclosure of the facts.'

Gary swore at her, his words slurred.

Laura stepped off the path on to the grass. If she walked on quietly, perhaps he would leave her alone. Then she realised that the path ahead led away from civilisation under the beech trees to Devil's Leap.

'You know what, you're a stuck-up bitch!' Gary followed her down to the riverside. 'Lobbying this and disclosure that!'

Laura stopped in her tracks and tried to double back. But she only got as far as the entrance to the surgery before he overtook her and lurched across her path once more. 'Gary, please!'

'This is what you mean by caring, is it? Walking away from me when I want to talk to you.'

'I'll discuss things when you're in a better frame of mind.' She thought about running away across the playing field, but felt it would look absurd.

'When I'm not pissed?' He stood in her way and brought his face close to hers. His skin was sallow and greasy, the rims of his eyes red. 'You'll wait a long time then.'

'OK.' She took a breath to steady herself. 'What did you want to talk about if it wasn't what went on at the meeting?'

'I want to know what you get off on.' He stayed close, breathing a mixture of hostility and insinuation over her. 'Come on, I'm trying to work you out.'

126

Laura found herself backing towards the stone trough at the entrance to the building. If need be, she could use her key to slip inside and phone for help.

He saw what she intended and swung ahead of her, boxing her into a corner in the entrance porch. 'Helping people. Sister of Mercy. That's your thing. Well, help me. I'm willing.'

Laura felt him close in. She looked up and met his gaze, staring coldly at him. 'You've got me wrong, Gary. I'm just a GP, remember.'

'Doctor, doctor, I'm in trouble!' He let his head drop and his mood swung from belligerence to mocking self-pity, but he didn't shift position. 'I am.'

'I know.' She sighed. Pleas for help came in different ways, some less attractive than others. 'Look, Gary, back off and let's get things straight.'

He slumped against the wall, letting her escape to the safety of the path. 'You know what I think? This stuff that Peter's got on the go . . . It's crap. It is, isn't it? We'd be better off banging our heads against this wall.' He knocked the back of his head hard on the stone.

Laura narrowed her eyes. 'I thought you were with Peter on the Ruthwell theory.'

'Was!' Gary let his head loll again. 'Was yesterday. Might be tomorrow. Today I think it's crap.' Back went his head, hard enough to make Laura shudder. 'This article; where's it going to get us? Who's going to say sorry, we shouldn't have let these leaks happen, only we didn't know what we were doing at the time?'

'But isn't it best for people to know?'

'Don't ask me. I never went to college. I haven't got a degree in thinking.' He held up his hands to her face. 'I use these to build houses for a living. I do it because I've got a wife and kid to support, and that's all I know.' He swallowed the last words and shook his head. 'Only now I don't have them, do I? I built a bungalow for them that I don't even live in any more. Hannah doesn't want to know me, and my kid . . . Elliot . . .' Tears trickled from one eye, down the side of his nose. 'Tell me the truth. Has he had it?'

Laura glanced away towards the cliffs and the skyline. In that half-second she realised she had probably destroyed the last shred of Gary Wood's respect for her. 'We're doing all we can.'

'Says you!' He launched himself savagely from the entrance porch, across the car park, flinging his arms wide and yelling out across the field. 'You hear that? They're doing their best!'

Laura heard the echo bounce off Ravenscar and come faintly back.

'What if their best's not good enough?' Gary whirled round towards her. 'My little lad's lying in a hospital bed and I can't bring myself to visit him.' Lowering his voice, he stared at Laura. 'You know why not? Because I can't look him in the face and tell him he's going to be OK if that's not the way it is . . . So, tell me.'

'You're putting me in an impossible situation.' She struggled to explain. 'You want me to tell you Elliot's treatment will work.'

'Yes.' He was in agony, she knew, stripped bare.

'I can't, Gary. No one can.'

CHAPTER TWENTY

Luke drove slowly from the pub to Abbey Grange, realising that he would still arrive before Laura. He spent the time wondering why she'd refused the lift home, then checking and blaming himself for reading significance into her small and natural desire for breathing space after the prickly meeting.

He turned in through the gates, parked beside Laura's car and glanced through the driver's window. Then he tried the door.

The moment he opened it Laura hurried in through the side gate. 'I'm sure I left that locked.'

'Yes. It looks like someone broke in.' Luke pointed to the hole in the crazed, cracked glass, big enough for a hand to stretch through and release the lock. A classic piece of forced entry. He stood back to give himself time to think.

'I don't believe it! Why didn't the alarm go off?'

'Maybe it did.' Luke leaned forward again to check the damage. 'It's possible no one heard it. Or else the thieves were able to deactivate it.' He brushed beads of safety-glass from the driver's seat. 'The radio's missing.'

'They did all this just for a radio? Don't they realise it's no use to them?' Laura walked round the car and back again.

'Did you take the detachable unit out?' He examined the empty metal casing where the main carcase should sit and touched the tangle of raw-ended coloured wires.

'Of course I did. I always do.'

She seemed more upset by the incident than he would have

expected. 'Well, that's how stupid some people are.' Luke came across it daily during his work in the youth courts. 'They'll steal anything. You didn't have any other valuables inside the car, did you; like a camera or a lap-top?'

'No.' She opened the door and leaned in from the other side. Then she rummaged on the back seat and held up the journal containing Jim Conroy's article and a blue folder. 'Wait a second. These are Elliot's case notes from the hospital for Sheila to file tomorrow morning.' Laura flicked the folder open and took a sharp breath. She held it upside down to show him that it was empty. 'This is completely crazy! Why would a car thief want to steal case notes?'

Luke steadied his growing sense of alarm. 'More interestingly, why would anyone want both case notes and radio? It doesn't add up.' He took Laura's arm and led her into the house. Then he dialled the police station in Merton and waited.

'Because if it was stupid kids they would only want the radio,' Laura continued, thinking aloud. 'And if it was – well – more sinister and somebody was after these particular case notes, why would they take the radio?'

Luke interrupted her to report the theft to the officer on duty. He told him what was missing and that all they needed was a crime number for insurance purposes. 'It was my girlfriend's car. I'll hand you over.'

Laura took the phone and went through the formal procedure. She too played down the incident, laughing when the officer asked the routine question about whether or not she needed counselling as a result of the crime. 'Not unless you think it could be connected with some nuisance phone calls I've been getting lately.'

From the other end of the hallway Luke felt a jolt of anxiety. This was what had already alarmed him outside by the car.

'I was joking,' Laura protested when she put down the phone and saw his worried face.

'No, wait.' He walked to the open door. 'Maybe that's not as far-fetched as you think.' These seemingly isolated incidents were beginning to take on more sinister overtones and Luke was suddenly aware that, in his eagerness to involve himself and Laura in the Ruthwell case, he might have overlooked the attendant risks.

Laura sat down wearily beside him on the front doorstep. 'Are you telling me I've got secret enemies?'

Luke turned towards her. 'One step at a time. What if these aren't crank calls as I thought at first? How many have you had?'

'Three or four.' She paused. 'Four. And before you ask, yes the start of them did coincide with the early stage of us getting involved with the pressure group. But . . . if these phone calls are happening because someone mistakenly sees me as being at the forefront of an organised anti-nuclear pressure group, and they're supposed to deter me from pursuing the anti-nuclear case, all I can say is that it's not a particularly clever way of going about it.'

Luke thought this through. 'Maybe they're meant to intimidate you. Meanwhile, if this is an organised thing they would need more information to rebut the claims that we're making via Jim's article.'

'And they see me as the one with the information?'

He nodded. 'That's certainly true as regards the two leukaemia cases. Say this break-in started off as another generalised threat, but the case notes in the back of your car presented the thief with an unlooked-for opportunity.' Luke realised that his theory was beginning to fit together. 'For a start, the notes identify exactly what type of leukaemia Catherine and Elliot have contracted, which is not as straightforward as it seems, since, as we both know, there are dozens of different types and sub-types. That's the sort of thing a pro-nuclear group would need to know before they build their own argument.'

131

'You're sure you're not just being paranoid on my behalf?' Laura appealed to him, obviously hoping for a more acceptable explanation.

He sat down beside her. 'No. My problem is I should have thought about the possibility earlier. I should have taken better care of you.'

'How could you have known?'

'Listen, Laura, it wouldn't be unusual for a key figure in a pressure group to be targeted. We all know the stakes are pretty high.'

'That's what bothers me most – that they think I'm a key figure.' It was Laura's turn to stand up and walk away restlessly. 'They obviously don't know about the doubts I've had from the start!'

'You're the families' GP. You're very easy to identify. The rest of us have roles that aren't quite so clear.' Luke came out into the garden and put his arms round Laura's shoulders, encircling her.

'Who're "they"?' she protested. 'Are they the energy company who own Ruthwell? Are they workers there who think we're aiming to get the plant closed down?'

'I don't know,' he said gently. Guilt for setting Laura up in the front line subdued him and robbed him of his normally decisive reactions. 'Maybe Jim Conroy could dig up some information for us.'

'Why not the police?' Laura broke away and paced up and down the path.

'They don't have the resources; not locally at any rate. They won't go for grand conspiracy theories on the evidence of one break-in and a couple of abusive phone calls. I think Jim's a better bet.'

'Or we could let it drop.' Laura came and tugged at his sleeve. 'We could, Luke!'

'Let what drop? The break-in?' He was already shaking his

head, trying to put his arm round her again as she pulled away.

'Everything. We could back out of the whole Ruthwell investigation before it's too late.'

'Oh God, Laura, it's not that simple, is it?' He recognised that they were both too fully identified with the Woods and the Earles to pull out now. Yet he hated to see her so distressed. 'It's my fault. I should have realised what was going on earlier when you got the first phone call.'

'No.' She shook her head.

'But it is. I've been angry at you over this stupid Matthew business. It warped my judgement. I'm so sorry.'

She began to cry. 'I can't bear it when we pull in opposite directions.'

'We won't. Not any more.'

At last she stopped moving away and let him hold her. He breathed out as she put her head on his shoulder and closed his eyes. The tensions and misunderstandings had melted away the moment he'd confessed his jealousy. Maybe this was all it took to get them back together: a shared danger, a shouldering of responsibility.

But what if there's more, Luke thought. What if something else has happened that she's not telling me about? He tensed as the gap opened between them again and they stood, arms round each other, and the cool wind rustled through the trees.

CHAPTER TWENTY-ONE

To clear her head that evening Laura drove the car with its broken window along the road by the river, past Askby's two waterfalls, upper and lower, towards the source of the River Raven at the head of the Dale. Dusk was drawing in, and with it a mist that settled in the folds of the valleys, draining the land of its greens and yellows, letting the horizon float on a bed of thin, drifting cloud.

Luke had gone back to his house on Tan Hill and, alone, Laura's fears re-emerged. Although he had warned her not to draw any conclusions until they had found answers to some basic questions – such as who exactly had forewarning of the facts and figures contained in Jim's article – Laura felt sure that the phone calls and the break-in were more than coincidence.

She stopped the car on a high, clear ridge and gazed ahead at a ewe and her lamb trudging along the single-track road. What if she and Luke were wrong? The missing radio and case notes could have fallen into the hands of inept teenage thieves embarked on a mini-crime wave. If she rang the Merton police again, they would probably tell her that the theft from her car was one of a series in the Dale that day. And the phone calls could be as easily dismissed. Nutcase. Kids again. A cheap thrill.

The mist swirled up from behind and surrounded her. She lost sight of the sheep and the road ahead. Then again, if the link did exist between the phone calls and the theft, need it be Ruthwell? Might it not be Gary Wood?

Startled by the idea, she turned on the ignition and reversed on to a flat stretch of gravelly grass by the roadside. She turned the car and headed back the way she'd come, through the white mist, down into the valley.

Gary had blamed the doctors from the moment Elliot had been diagnosed. And to him, Laura was the most accessible target in the medical world. 'Stuck-up bitch' he'd called her earlier that day. And yes, it could be his voice on the line.

More significant still, when Laura had come across him outside the medical centre at lunch-time he'd been on foot and coming from the direction of the riverside walk that led to Abbey Grange. It would have been possible for him to have broken into her car at the time arranged for the meeting at the Falcon. What could he have been looking for? Her briefcase with letters and notes about Elliot? Well, he'd struck lucky and found the hospital file. Then, to cover his tracks, he'd taken the radio . . .

Laura drove faster than was wise down the winding hill. What she had to do now was to find out more about Gary Wood's movements that morning. And where should she begin except with Hawkshead Hall and Matthew?

She crossed the river over the old stone bridge by the Maskells' house as darkness set in and carried on up a gentler sweep of hillside until she came to the gates of the Hall. There were no lights on at the lodge and no pick-up truck was parked outside. Peering at her watch, Laura saw that it was ten o'clock.

She was still debating whether or not this was the right thing to do as she made her way slowly up the drive towards the big house.

It would be Matthew who came to the door and he wouldn't be able to hide his surprise at the unannounced visit. She would have to explain quickly why she was there and the reason would be bound to disappoint him. On the other hand, it still felt natural to turn to him for help.

She parked the car and walked up the wide stone steps to the main door, catching a glimpse of the oak-panelled hall through a tall window on the left-hand side. All the downstairs lights at the front of the house were on and the doors leading off from the entrance hall stood open.

Steps came to answer the bell: Matthew's, just as she'd supposed. She could see him crossing the hall under the artificial light, his face relaxed and unconcerned. But when he opened the door his expression tightened. His grey eyes narrowed into a worried frown.

'Laura. Is something the matter?' He urged her inside and shut the door.

'I'm sorry it's so late.' She glanced towards a sitting-room, half-expecting the small, upright figure of Maisie Aire to appear.

'Mother's out. Sunday's her bridge night.' Matthew read her thoughts. 'Come through.'

'No, I won't, thanks.' She still loved this house, with its low, carved ceilings and Maisie's collection of nineteenth-century paintings. 'Actually, it's Gary Wood I've come to talk about.'

'Ah.' The name transformed his manner from concealed agitation to open disappointment. He looked away.

'I'm sorry.' She gave a helpless shrug. 'I shouldn't have bothered you.'

She watched as he struggled to overcome his feelings and to become his considerate, well-mannered self. 'Tell me what the problem is. Have a drink at least.'

Laura stood in the middle of the polished oak floor. 'Has Gary said anything to you about me? Shown that he doesn't like the way I do my job, for instance.'

'Not specifically. I don't see much of him, except when I drive past the lodge and he happens to be outside. Then we stop and have a word.'

'How would you say he's been coping in the last week or so?'

'Since he went for you?' Matthew's frown deepened. 'I told him outright that was uncalled for.'

'What did he say?'

'He came out with some ferocious anti-female stuff. Not you specifically, but women in general. I took it that it was because of what's happened between him and Hannah.' Matthew looked directly at Laura. 'Why, what's he done now?'

'I'm not sure. I'm just trying to find out.' Reluctantly she confessed her suspicions about the phone calls and the break-in. 'What I really want to discover are Gary's movements this lunch-time. Was he at the lodge?'

'No. That's definite. His truck hasn't been here since early this morning. Laura, you shouldn't be dealing with this by yourself!' Matthew turned away.

'Listen, I'm either the random victim of mindless petty criminals, or on the receiving end of Gary's irrational but understandable grudge, or . . .' As she listed the possibilities on her fingers she felt her hands begin to tremble and tears well up. She paused to fight them back.

'Or what?' He held her shoulders, stared into her eyes, lifted a hand to stroke her hair.

'Matthew!' She stepped back.

'I can't bear it, Laura.'

'I'm sorry.' She brushed away her tears with her fingertips. 'Forget it, I shouldn't have come.'

She left without telling him the third and most frightening option: that an unknown observer was following her movements and was carefully, deliberately, creeping under her skin.

Abbey Grange was in darkness when she arrived after a wretched drive home from Hawkshead Hall. For once the

137

isolation of the house unnerved her and she felt the thick blackness of the starless sky envelop her on the short walk from car to front door. Flinging her keys on to the hall table, she went through to the kitchen to pick up any messages before heading straight for bed.

She pressed the play button on the answer-machine.

'. . . Hello, Laura. Luke. Just wanted to speak to you and check that you're OK. See you soon.'

End of first message. Laura closed her eyes and took a deep breath. She pressed again.

'. . . Bitch. Bloody interfering bitch . . .!'

She pressed the button to cut off the voice, then again to skip forward, touching the machine as if it were red hot.

'. . . Dr Grant?' This time a woman's voice, faint and tremulous. 'It's Hannah Wood here. I'm ringing from the hospital. They say Elliot isn't very well. How do they put it? His condition is deteriorating.' There was a pause, an ambulance siren faint in the background. 'I think he's dying, Dr Grant. My poor baby has given up.'

CHAPTER TWENTY-TWO

Elliot Wood was sleeping. His long fair lashes curved down over his pale cheeks, the veins in his lids showing blue through the translucent skin.

Laura sat to one side of his bed, the mother to the other. The little boy was peaceful, both arms flung back high against the pillow in sleep, his head turned to one side, his mouth moist. Leaning forward to stroke the hair from his high forehead and fold back the sheet more neatly, Hannah murmured his name.

Laura glimpsed the Hickman line inserted into a large vein in the boy's chest. Elliot's chemotherapy had been reassessed and adjusted, but there was no more talk of early surgery to tackle the metastases in the colon. Various scans earlier in the week had shown other secondaries in lymph nodes under the arms, and Rudi Grey's conclusion concurred with Hannah's view that the disease was progressing rapidly.

'Do you think he knows how ill he is?' Hannah asked in a low, defeated voice. Her long hair was tied at the nape of her neck, but lank strands straggled forward across her tired face. The shadows under her eyes were dark as bruises, her lip trembled as she spoke.

'Perhaps, but it means something different at this age. Very young children live for the day, almost for the moment. I expect Elliot knows he's ill, but he won't see the same significance as we do.'

'I hope not.' Hannah sat back, watching each breath.

'You're doing everything right, giving him lots of love.' Here at the bedside, it all seemed painfully simple. 'He's not frightened so long as you're here.'

'Mr Grey came to see him earlier today. He's really kind. He gave us this little side ward so I could stay with Elliot as much as I liked. He explained they would alter the drugs again tomorrow to try and get his blood count back up. He said there was always hope.'

Laura found that her own breathing had grown shallow, to match the sleeping child's. 'Are your parents coming in regularly to give you a break?'

Hannah nodded. 'My dad says Elliot's like me when I was little.'

Laura smiled at the odd, fierce pride in her voice. 'Is that good or bad?'

'Dad says I was stubborn. I think that's good, don't you? It makes Elliot a fighter.'

'Do you need any more help from us?' Laura could suggest a visit from Carole Fawcett to advise on special hardship grants to cover Hannah's travelling expenses, a link-up with a nurse specially trained in counselling cancer patients and their families.

'No.' Hannah watched anxiously as Elliot turned in his sleep.

Laura stood up. 'I'll go and find out what else Mr Grey has to say.' She couldn't get over how young and tired Hannah looked; a disturbing paradox. Young, like a bewildered, traumatised child, with her staring dark eyes: worn down by fear.

'Thanks for coming, Dr Grant.' She tore her gaze away from her son to tell her what else was on her mind. 'Gary still hasn't been to visit.'

'I know. I've seen him,' Laura confessed.

'Did you ask him to come to the hospital?'

'I told him what you said to me.'

140

Hannah sighed. 'Was it before or after Elliot got worse?'

'Before,' Laura murmured.

'What did he say?'

Laura shook her head. She broke the news as gently as she could, knowing how hard it was for her to bear. 'I'm sorry, Hannah. Gary just can't face it.'

Rudi Grey took Laura to the staff canteen to talk her through Elliot's case and describe the course of future treatment. 'I don't think we can pursue an agressive line for very much longer,' he stated. 'Ideally, we would have made the surgical intervention in early autumn and backed it up with the usual adjuvant therapy to put him into remission. But as you know, his red cell count is way down and we're discovering widespread mets.'

Laura stared at her coffee-cup. All around, the buzz of conversation and the clatter of crockery reminded her that individual tragedies took their place alongside the general mundanity of life's small, practical details. 'Is there any mileage in drastically altering the chemo?'

'You mean that since the present regime isn't having the desired effect, we might as well embark on something else, like Prednisone, for example?' The specialist considered the option. 'There's been a lot of discussion on it, but my opinion is that on balance the cytotoxic action would do too much damage to the normal cells.' He studied Laura's face across the table. 'Sorry, that's not what you wanted to hear.'

'How much have you told Hannah?'

'Pretty well everything. She asked me this morning how long I thought Elliot had got. She finds it hard to take in, but she's handling it well in the circumstances.'

Laura nodded. 'Do you know if anyone from the media has tried to get in touch with her since this cancer cluster article appeared?'

'Not that I know of. Perhaps even the tabloids have enough

tact to respect what she's going through.' Rudi Grey sniffed and rattled his spoon against the side of his cup before he drank. 'They have contacted me, though.'

Laura raised her eyebrows.

'They wanted a soundbite. Did I support the parents who were trying to lay the blame at Ruthwell's door? My answer was had they got two days to spare?' He smiled wryly.

'And do you?' she asked earnestly.

'Support the parents? Of course. I'd do exactly the same in their situation, and Peter Earle in particular has got what it takes to see something like this through. He's methodical and he channels his anger pretty effectively.' Rudi glanced up for a passing word with a colleague, then turned back to Laura.

'That didn't quite answer the question,' she persisted. 'I wanted to know what you thought about Ruthwell.'

'Have you got two days to spare?' He shrugged apologetically. 'I'm not joking; this is too complex for a yes or no.' Leaning across the table, he spoke confidentially. 'For what it's worth and in strict confidence, here's my stance on the Ruthwell theory, taking into account what I know about the pathology of the disease throughout North Yorkshire, plus what I learn from the local Health and Safety executive and all the reports since Gardner . . .' He paused, showing by his expression that the convolutions were immensely complicated. 'At the moment I'm bound to say that the incidence of childhood leukaemia in the area is more than a statistical blip. To that extent I think your pressure group is right.'

'But?' Laura felt the proviso coming.

'But I can't get past the multifactoral problem.'

'Diet, cosmic rays, occupational triggers?' she prompted.

'Yes. And radon and thoron,' he said emphatically. 'More than half the radiation released into the atmosphere comes from the rocks beneath our feet.'

'You think we should take a closer look at the geological factor?' Laura frowned.

'Maybe.' Rudi Grey pushed his cup away. 'Or a combination. But Laura, take it from me, don't overestimate what you can do. And don't drive yourself into the ground over it. Let me ask you something else. How good are you at conflict?'

'Pretty good if the cause is right.' The sudden personal turn of the conversation surprised her into a spontaneous response. 'Lousy if I'm not sure of my ground.'

Rudi nodded and stood up. 'Then be sure,' he said softly. 'Be as sure as you can possibly be.'

CHAPTER TWENTY-THREE

Laura left the hospital and drove towards the surgery feeling strained and exhausted. She had missed the eight-twenty, but still had to face Piers who had a patient with balance problems that he wanted to discuss; the father of a paraplegic car crash victim who had just moved into the Dale. The older man's carer role was in doubt due to spells of dizziness and ataxia. Laura had suggested possible MS or a tumour, and Piers had confirmed that the tests were to go ahead.

Then there were the Lawsons. As Laura walked in to reception she saw them talking to Philip. The results, it appeared, had not yet come through.

'I'll get Sheila to ring the lab and ask them to fax them,' he told Alison and Brian, as he picked up the intercom phone.

Laura sat beside them while they waited. 'How has Emma been?' she asked.

'Miserable.' Alison sat with the baby on her knee. 'Not herself at all.'

'But not really bad,' Brian insisted. 'Just a bit of crying now and then, nothing serious.' The landlord of the Falcon was incongruous in the surgery: a sportsman with a powerful physique, unused to coping with illness. Sitting with one foot pulled up and resting across his other knee, his large hand tapped at the side of his white trainer as he glanced at his baby daughter, then down at the blue carpet.

'Not long to wait.' Laura prayed for a good result.

'It's been awful,' Alison admitted. She cradled Emma in one

arm, stroking her soft brown curls. 'The waiting part. We've tried not to talk about it too much, but it's been hard.' Younger than her cricketing husband, with a strong and uninhibited maternal instinct, she made Laura acutely aware that the family's whole future rested on the news that came through from the lab.

'I've been telling her it'll be OK.' Brian filled the silence with his low, slow voice. 'Think positive; that's my philosophy.'

The baby began to whine and squirm, so Brian moved to take her from her mother. But Emma turned her face into Alison's chest and clung with her podgy fingers to her white T-shirt. As she did so, Laura saw how the fine hair at the back of the child's head had rubbed thin from lying in her cot, a detail that shook her carefully held equilibrium to the core.

Silently they watched as Sheila went through to Philip's office with fax paper, which rustled and curled awkwardly. She crossed the waiting area again without looking at the Lawsons and retreated quickly behind her glass panel.

Philip flattened the sheet of paper and beckoned them in. He read the figures, the bio-chemist's brief report.

Laura felt the fear grow tangible inside the room.

'Emma's blood count is normal,' he told Alison and Brian, his voice rough with emotion. 'Your daughter doesn't have leukaemia.'

'The amazing thing is that Piers can carry on with any semblance of normality.' Philip had suggested that Laura drop in to Bridge House for a drink after work. Juliet was out and he took Laura into the garden, under the beech trees that grew by the river bank. 'It takes enormous self-control to concentrate on your job with this going on.'

'Lack of self-control doesn't strike me as Piers's problem.' Laura gazed upstream through the arches of the old stone bridge. 'Once he got over the shock of Francesca being pregnant and had his bout of shouting, he composed himself within minutes. He was back in control and shutting her out, telling me that I should leave him to take care of it.'

'Shutting you out as well?'

'Very effectively. Not to mention his own emotions. Personally, I find that more frightening – the ability to cut off like that.'

'But we're neither of us concerned that he'll crack up at work, or that his concentration is so poor that he could make a bad diagnosis?'

'No,' Laura said slowly. It was a difficult judgement to make. 'He seems to respond well under pressure.'

'And he told me he didn't want to launch a full-scale search for Francesca, or bring in the police. We have to trust his instinct on that.'

'He spun me the same line.' Laura hunched her shoulders, then let them drop. 'But I can't help feeling that if I were in Francesca's position I'd want Piers to go to slightly greater lengths to try and find me.'

'I don't suppose we know the full story. Are we satisfied that the practice isn't being damaged by what must amount to quite a scandal in these parts?'

'You mean, doctor's pregnant wife vanishes shortly after said doctor's teenage son gets himself excluded from school?' Laura had little doubt that the situation would attract comment. Dick Metcalfe and Harry Braithwaite would soon make the Chandlers the main focus of bar-room gossip, she knew. And Piers hadn't helped himself by playing a leading role in the developing Ruthwell furore.

'Exactly.'

'We have to back Piers on that one,' Laura decided. 'After all, most of us live in glass houses. I wouldn't fancy casting the first stone.'

Philip stood up straight. 'You mean middle-aged married doctor has affair with young drama teacher.'

'I wasn't referring to you. I was thinking about myself.'

'Good God, Laura, people could chuck whole boulders at your house without doing any damage!'

'Tell that to Gary Wood.' She turned and wandered downstream. 'And to the person who keeps making abusive phone calls and the one who broke into my car. Or to Matthew Aire, for that matter.' The calm evening, the sound of running water made her want to share their troubles. 'You and I have never talked about Mary, have we?' Laura thought of her old friend, her passionate affair with Philip and her abrupt departure to the Midlands. She missed Mary's irreverent wit, her sense of fun and drama; longed to confide in her about her current problems with Luke and their campaign.

'No. Do you hear from her?'

Laura nodded. 'Do you?'

'No. How is she?'

'Busy working in rep. Running away.'

Philip drew a deep breath. 'One of the things I find so hard, apart from what I've done to Juliet, is trying to hang on to the quality of the relationship I had with Mary. That's such a fleeting thing and words don't capture it. I couldn't explain it to you now except in a trashy way like "special" or "life-changing". They don't get anywhere near the reality.'

'And that's difficult because if you can't express it, you begin to fear that the unique experience never really happened in the first place. Maybe you were kidding yourself all along.' Laura was describing things from her own perspective: the way emotions seldom seemed more than transitory.

'Yes.' Philip glanced up at her. 'And that would mean I put everything at risk for an illusion. I hurt my wife beyond repair for nothing.'

'And every word of endearment you ever spoke is hollow, every promise you made is broken.'

'Do you feel that?'

She smiled sadly. 'Don't look so surprised. I take it as part of the human condition.'

147

'I don't even have a photograph of Mary. And if I did, looking at it would be a self-indulgence. Even talking about her is a betrayal of a kind.'

'We can stop if you like.' Laura did what she'd been tempted to do for some time, which was to step out on to a series of steady rocks, leading like stepping-stones into the full flow of the river. She looked down at the swirling stream. 'We could talk about me and Matthew, me and Luke.'

'At least you keep your relationships in consecutive order.' He watched her balance on a slippery rock.

'I try to. It doesn't always work that way.'

'What's happened?'

'Nothing's happened. Or if it has, I'm like you: the words don't fit. I could say "Matthew won't let go", but that's not quite right. He hasn't made a definite move. I just know that he wants me back, or that he's never really released me.' She shook her head. 'You have to struggle with words to make them mean what you want them to. Yet they always win in the end.'

'How about you? Do you still want Matthew?' He studied her, the low rays of the sun cutting through the solid silver trunks of the trees on the bank behind her.

Laura knew that her face would be in shadow. 'Yes and no,' she confessed quietly. 'Part of the problem is with Luke and me. I love him, but I feel in danger of being overpowered by him – of letting him take control, like my ex-husband used to do.'

But that wasn't quite right either. Perhaps the problem lay with her? Perhaps she needed to ask herself whether she had the courage, after the failure of her marriage, to trust her emotions enough to commit herself to a man who reminded her so much of Tom.

CHAPTER TWENTY-FOUR

She breathed in the feel and smell of Luke's skin. It was Monday night and they lay in bed at Abbey Grange, listening to the sound of light rain gusting against the window-pane.

As Laura raised her head from his chest, her cheek brushed his chin and he kissed her. 'What's the matter?' he asked. 'Why are you sad?'

They'd made love, having come to bed before it grew dark, wanting to leave the day behind. Luke had watched Laura undress, hadn't taken his eyes off her as she slid under the sheet next to him.

'Not sad,' she answered.

'What then?' He kept his lips against hers, pulling her close, holding her there.

The conversation with Philip earlier that evening drifted through her head. He'd been sweet and compassionate, a sounding-board for her confusion.

'Please don't be sad. I want to help you.' Luke stroked her hair. Earlier, his passion had rocked her out of her self-possession, cast her into a rough sea. Now she hid her face against him.

'Keep talking to Luke about Matthew,' Philip had said. 'Don't have any secrets.'

'I'd like to talk,' she whispered.

'Go ahead.' He went on stroking her softly.

'About Matthew.'

He drew back a fraction, but went on cradling her.

Laura wrapped her arms round him so that he couldn't move away. 'It's so difficult.'

'He still loves you.'

'Yes.' The word disappeared beneath a drawn-out sigh.

'And how do you feel about that?'

Laura could sense him distancing himself from her, as he raised his head, studying her face.

'Every time I see him I remember that I loved him once. And I know I'm still hurting him.'

'And you feel sorry for him?' There was a flicker of fear behind Luke's eyes, though his soft voice disguised it well.

'No. But I understand what he's feeling. And I know he doesn't want my pity.'

The darkness seemed to deepen and the rain gusted more loudly against the window.

'If I were in his position, I might use it.' Luke's voice took on a harder edge. 'Pity and guilt can be clever cards to play.'

'You make it sound deliberate.' She loosened her hold.

His grey eyes held her gaze. 'We use what we can to hang on to someone we've lost.'

'Not you.' She was shocked by his certainty. 'You don't tie people down.'

'Not any more.' He turned slowly from her to lie on his back. 'But I know how it's done, believe me.'

'This is to do with honesty,' Laura said. She'd had time to work out what Luke might mean. If Matthew's tactic was to try to tie her down, might not Luke use this weapon himself?

It was two in the morning. Neither had slept.

'Surely you knew how Matthew felt.' Luke refused to move from first base. 'How can it have taken you by surprise?'

'But what difference does it make to us?'

Luke swung his legs over the side of the bed and sat up. 'Don't be so naive, Laura. You really want me to spell it out?'

Laura could feel the depth of his anger and frustration. 'This is . . .'

'Ridiculous? Childish? Yes.'

'Don't you trust me?' She panicked as she felt the wedge driven between them and resorted to what she felt were platitudes even as she spoke them.

'What do you want me to do? Say yes, and put myself at the mercy of the vagaries of your emotions?' He looked over his shoulder at her. 'Trusting you now that I know Matthew is still somewhere on the scene leaves me wide open.'

'He isn't on the scene.'

'But he's not off it either.' Luke raised his voice. 'You want honesty? Right then, this is me being angry about you not telling Matthew to piss off.'

'You want me to lie?' Laura demanded. 'If I say that I don't love Matthew, we'll be fine?' As in a child's story, everything would be simple. How could he behave so stupidly?

He reached for his clothes. 'Is it such a lot to ask?'

'You're jealous! That's what this boils down to. And I'm supposed to reassure you by promising never to see Matthew again?'

'No, obviously not.'

'Yes! You want me to obliterate Matthew from my mind, just as you wanted to push me into joining the campaign! Well, not this time, Luke.' She tried to grab his wrist and turn him round to face her.

He pulled free, deliberately misunderstanding her. 'Listen, I don't know what's going on, but whatever it is, I don't like it.'

'Then go,' she said, suddenly quiet and ice-cold. A hole seemed to open up beneath her.

'Are you throwing me out?' Luke rammed his shirt over his head, went to the door, then hesitated.

'Yes.' She felt dizzy.

He stared at her in disbelief. Then he came back at her, thrusting his face close to hers. 'You know your problem? You

151

don't know what or whom you want. You try to have things both ways!'

She recognised this as a variation of the accusation men made when they lost power in a relationship. Her husband's refrain had been 'Women are selfish. You think the world revolves around you'. 'And you,' she charged. 'You expect me to chop my past into little pieces and throw it all away!'

He groaned with exasperation, turned and left without another word.

His keys clinked as he lifted them from the bookshelf by the door. She heard his footsteps take the stairs two at a time, the dull click of the front door opening, then closing. His car engine started and the lights went on. Their beam raked across the bedroom ceiling as Luke's tyres squealed in the drive and he set off through the rain for Tan Hill.

Laura turned her face into the pillow and wept.

CHAPTER TWENTY-FIVE

Francesca stayed in her hotel room for days. She didn't know or care how many, but sat at her window and looked out over the stately Victorian spa town.

A town in aspic was how she thought of Wingate: with its domed and arched civic splendour, its acres of open parkland fringed by trees giving a glorious display of fresh green and bright, burnished copper.

Her hotel was called The Beeches. She'd chosen it at random, pulled up in the small car park at the front and checked in under her maiden name, Osborne.

'Room twenty-four,' the receptionist had told her. A well-groomed woman with almost black hair cut to chin length and an array of gold necklaces over a black silk blouse, she'd regarded Francesca with undisguised curiosity as she approached the desk so early on a Sunday morning.

Francesca had taken the key and gone up, impervious to the woman's stare. She'd taken off her clothes and put on a white towelling dressing-gown, which she tugged tightly across her chest. Then she'd pulled back her long, wavy, red-gold hair, leaving her face exposed to the harsh artificial light, and scrubbed off her make-up to show the shadows and lines, the dullness of her green eyes.

At some point during that first day the receptionist had spoken to her on the phone: would she want to take breakfast in the breakfast room or in her own room? Francesca had made it clear that she had no intention of going down and arranged to have a tray left outside the door.

With her mind as blank as the surroundings – cream walls and bedspread, pink floral-design curtains, veneered chest of drawers and bedside table – and her suitcase unzipped but not unpacked in one corner, she sat in a cane chair by the window.

The days were long and empty. The sun came up behind the hotel and cast long shadows across the dewy grass. Regiments of bright yellow and orange flowers stood to attention in their geometric terraced beds. People shopped, took tea, went to and from work. They had nothing to do with her. She was separate, isolated. The sun came round and shone in through her window, turned red, sank behind the beech trees. The time for her abortion had probably come and gone. Piers would be at work, as usual. Nothing mattered.

Her body felt heavy and leaden. A band tightened round her head and grew worse when she cried about the boys she'd left behind. She had to close her eyes to fight off waves of nausea, which became so bad that she drew the curtains and retreated to the bed.

'Mrs Osborne, are you all right?' A knock at the door penetrated the pain. The voice of the black-and-gold receptionist.

'I'm fine, thank you.'

'You're sure you're not ill? You've hardly touched the food on your tray.'

'I'm not ill.'

The woman went away and didn't return.

Francesca was glad. She'd come here to be left alone. It was people who pushed and pulled her, needed things from her, told her what to do, hurt her, said they were sorry and hurt her again. Alone, anonymous, she could escape.

Here, with the pressure inside her head tightening, she resented the days she had spent pleasing others.

She'd sought approval from the day she was born, it seemed, found it easy to win with her big eyes and halo of gold hair; then bewilderingly, cruelly, just as easy to lose. The reprimand, the smack, the kind face transformed to a harsh, hard mask, turning away. She'd been small; there were no recognisable reasons.

Then, having committed inexplicable wrongs at home, arriving at last in the outside world of school, with alphabets to learn and numbers to arrange in neat patterns on the page, she found once again that she was a winner. Races could be won. There was a row of gold stars against her name. At home it was all smiles again.

But there was always a dark, dangerous fear, a place in her mind like the cupboard under the stairs; a storage place for bad memories of affection withdrawn, the flat of a grown-up hand striking her child's leg, leaving the red, barred print of fingers on her pale flesh.

And Francesca as an adult, attuned to uncertainty, had fallen in love with Piers, had recreated in him the familiar demanding, authoritarian figure from her childhood. He had fitted the bill with his own exacting standards, his ambition, which was to drive him out from the foothills of his humble background into the mountains of medical research – until the birth of Harry had curtailed a career in the lab and sent him out footslogging around hospitals and general practice.

She had absorbed his disappointment; indeed, she had made it her fault, so that he was free to succeed along the new path. And her fear of his disapproval had taken residence in a dark corner of her mind, so that she kept to herself things that would displease him or that she thought would do so. She had become her own judge and jury; risked less; maintained a terrified silence.

Which had led to this: a decision to be made between life and death, with no one to talk to. She raised her head from the pillow and tasted water from the glass at her bedside. It was tepid and hard to swallow. Her swollen eyelids felt dry and hot, her hand fell back against her forehead and she stared up at the ceiling.

Three days after she'd cut loose and started to fall, when the anxious taps at the door were more frequent and it became obvious that the world would burst in on her again whether she liked it or not and the decision about the baby would have to be made, she forced herself to act. The name came into her head of someone who might listen after all. Or at least give her a pill that would put an end to the incessant round of self-doubt and self-pity, and bring her a few hours' rest. She leaned over and picked up the phone to ring the surgery.

'Please come,' she said faintly. 'If I don't talk to someone soon, I'll go out of my mind.'

'Mrs Osborne hasn't left her room once since she checked in.' Francesca heard the anxious voice of the receptionist approach along the corridor. 'She hasn't even come down to the restaurant. I've been up ever so many times to ask her if she was ill, but I never got a sensible answer out of her.'

There was a tap on the door, Laura's voice thanking the hotel woman and telling her not to worry, that she was a doctor and would take things in hand – as doctors did.

Francesca waited until she could be sure that the receptionist had gone, then crossed the room unsteadily to let Laura in. 'You came!' She sighed. It was like stretching out in the dark and finding that there was something to hold on to after all.

Laura looked at her swiftly, then glanced around the airless room. She couldn't hide a look of shocked dismay.

Francesca began to apologise for dragging Laura over, but was cut short.

'I won't ask how you are,' Laura began. 'I can see how bad it is for you. But your clinic appointment is held over until next week, if you decide you still want it.'

'I don't know what I want.' Francesca sat heavily on one

156

corner of the bed. 'I only know how I felt at the weekend: that I couldn't do it. I kept picturing myself parking in the car park and going in through revolving doors. I was having nightmares. I couldn't get the image out of my head even when I was awake.'

Sitting beside her, Laura drew a deep breath.

'It struck me that I was going to walk through the doors pregnant and come out again without the baby. I tried to tell myself that lots of woman do it; it's legal, it's my choice. I tried all that.'

'But?'

'For me there's a stumbling block.' Francesca ignored the stray strands of hair that had fallen across her face. 'It's melodramatic to talk about the baby's right to choose too, but I suppose that's what comes of having been brought up a Catholic.'

Laura gave a surprised murmur. 'I didn't know that.'

'Long lapsed. But you know what the Jesuits say: "Give me a child until he's five years old ..."'

'In the circumstances, I'm surprised you came as close to having the abortion as you did.'

'Sheer willpower.' Francesca glanced up. 'And the certainty that a new baby would destroy what's left of my relationship with Piers.'

'And you do want to stay together?'

'I don't know!' Francesca said again. 'I did want to. Now I'm not even sure of that. The more I struggle to sort things out in my own mind, the less certain I am.'

Laura put a hand over hers. 'And you've been in this room for three days without saying a word to anyone, with everyone at home going crazy with worry.'

Francesca groaned. 'I couldn't cope. I wanted not to be here. I wished the world would stop.' She bowed her head again, felt the tears begin to fall. 'Do you know what it's like, Laura? Have you ever had the feeling of struggling to break

157

free of a trap, only to find yourself falling through black space? That's all there is around you: space. You're falling and falling. You could fall for ever. Does that make sense?'

'I have some idea. Only for me it's not a fear of falling. It's the sensation that I'm hollow. Crumbling away from the inside.'

Francesca looked up sharply. 'You?'

'Sometimes I think I'm all hollow shell with nothing in the middle. It makes it very difficult for me to reach important decisions – not professionally, but personally. I think I must be a hard person to love.'

'Do you think we're crazy to feel this way? I mean, we have so many things in life that other people don't have.'

Laura smiled, but her eyes were earnest. 'Sometimes I think it's really the happy people who are mad. It seems to me that despair – whatever you call it – is the only sane reaction to living in this world.'

'You don't sound like a doctor, talking like this.' Francesca clasped her hands together.

'No diagnostic labels to stick on, I'm afraid. Life's pleasure and pain mixed. That's my experience. The trick is to find a balance in favour of pleasure if you possibly can.'

Restless, Francesca stood up and walked barefoot over the fawn carpet to pull back the curtain a fraction and gaze down on to the green park. A slice of sunlight fell across the darkened room. 'I haven't been able to sleep since I left. Joe and Harry – how are they?'

'Surviving.' Laura's answer was guarded. 'And Piers is coping.'

'What about Harry's school situation? Is there any change?'

Laura shook her head.

Francesca let the curtain fall. 'I've done a terrible thing.'

'Then change it. Get in touch with them.' Laura sounded more urgent. 'You know I can't leave here without at least a promise from you that you'll let them know where you are.'

'Then Piers would come to fetch me.' Francesca backed off in distress.

'Would that be so bad?' Laura urged. 'You will have to talk to him sooner or later.'

'Talk?' Suddenly Francesca snapped out of her hopelessness and self-reproach. She gave a faint laugh. 'You don't talk to Piers.'

'You mean, you listen? But that can't be the whole truth.'

Laura's insistence made Francesca rethink. 'He did used to listen,' she admitted. 'He was easier to be with when I first knew him. He was always ambitious, of course, but it wasn't such an impersonal thing. In those days he wanted to do ground-breaking research in order to help humanity. He was very idealistic. Now, his medical knowledge is just a way of setting himself apart.'

'You may be right,' Laura concurred. 'You know him better than I do. So why does he do it?'

That's obvious, Francesca implied with a shrug of her shoulders. 'He's scared too.'

'Of failing?' Laura looked surprised.

'Not in his job. The work's easy for Piers. What frightens him are the bits you can't control: parents dying, children growing up to be people in their own right.'

Still taken aback, Laura asked Francesca if Piers had told her as much.

'He doesn't have to,' she replied. She didn't falter or hold back now. 'I recognise it because I'm the same. Frightened by the chaos. Afraid of going under.'

'Then support each other,' Laura said gently. 'Let me tell him you're here.'

Francesca accepted the inevitable with a slight nod. 'I'll talk to him. But I won't go back until I feel stronger.'

'That's good enough. And, Francesca, try not to be so afraid. Lean on us and what we can offer you. Let us help, you, please.'

CHAPTER TWENTY-SIX

'We all are,' had been Laura's reply to Francesca's confession. Afraid of being alone. It was what made her almost pick up the phone to ring Luke a dozen times after their argument over Matthew. She realised that Luke had forced the situation through jealousy and also, if she were to be honest with herself, that she was partly to blame for this.

Once, since the row, Luke had rung her.

'You're putting too much pressure on me,' she told him.

'I thought by staying away I was taking the pressure off.' Luke sounded hurt and angry. 'You don't want me hanging around while you work out what you want to do.'

Intellectually he was right. Emotionally he was dead wrong.

Laura felt that her heart was being squeezed. When she had seen Luke at a meeting with Jim Conroy and Peter Earle in the Falcon on the Wednesday evening after she'd visited Francesca in Wingate they were cautious, considerate with one another, and kept their distance. Luke had gone home as soon as the meeting had ended.

She had stayed behind to talk to Piers about his wife. The message was that Francesca needed until the end of the week before she would feel strong enough to face her family. The job of convincing him that she was safe without giving away her whereabouts had been difficult, but she'd told Piers she was bound by her promise to Francesca. 'Above all,' she'd said, 'she wants Harry and Joe to understand that it wasn't anything to do with them: the reason why she disappeared.'

He'd nodded grimly. 'I expect she blames me?'

This had been much too complex a question for her to answer. 'You'll have to ask Francesca yourself. All I can tell you is she does plan to come back this weekend to talk things through.'

She'd left him in limbo and gone home alone.

On Friday she woke up to the sound of the phone ringing. Luke? A patient needing an emergency visit? She fumbled across her pillow to reach for the receiver, picked it up from the bedside table, still in the half-world between sleeping and waking. 'Laura Grant here.'

'I know who you are.'

She grasped the phone more tightly. 'Who is this?'

'Guess.'

Every nerve tensed. There was a jolt under her ribs, a rush of adrenalin.

As she moved to slam down the receiver, the voice spoke again. 'Don't do that. I want you to listen.'

She froze. It was as if there were eyes in the room, following every move. This was worse than insults and blunt, unspoken threats.

'I know who you are and what you are. You and your little group think you're clever going to the papers with your so-called facts and figures.'

'What do you want?' Amid her panic Laura reclaimed her common sense. She would make him talk, so that she could pick up intonation and speech patterns.

The man ignored her. 'You're not so bright. I watch you drive out on call in your car. Those are lonely roads.'

'I'll inform the police!'

He laughed. 'Easy to have an accident and come off the road up there in the hills.'

'They'll trace this call.'

'. . . It could be hours before anyone found you.'

'For God's sake!'

161

'. . . Too late to do anything to help.'

'Stop doing this!'

'I won't ring again. I'll be watching.'

The phone went dead. When Laura gave the police at Merton a description of the man's voice, she said it was thick and muffled, with a strong local accent. Whoever it was had enjoyed the sound of her fear.

After morning surgery Laura had arranged to drive up to Haresby Farm to see the Earles. The visit had been planned as part of a regular routine of drop-in calls to take blood samples and check Catherine's Hickman line.

She took the road past Hawkshead Hall, up the green hillside dotted with stone barns, criss-crossed with low, tumbledown walls, where white specks in the distance were sheep grazing, and peewits curved and called overhead.

Bright light shone steadily on the rugged horizon, but nearer to, clouds swept patches of shadow across the dips and hollows in the landscape. Where the road ran between tall sycamores and ash that blotted out the sun, she drove through a dark tunnel and only breathed again when she came out into sunlight.

Laura glanced in her windscreen mirror. There was a white car behind, coming too fast for the narrow, winding road. She saw the driver: a man in a dark suit, white shirt and tie. He sped up to her bumper, tailed her up the hill. She heard loud music through her open window, the impatient rev of his engine as he gathered speed after a sharp bend.

Heart thumping, hands gripping the wheel, she knew she had the choice of picking up speed and keeping the car firmly behind her, or of pulling in to let it pass: her normal way of handling such a situation. But what if this was the owner of the voice behind the phone calls? An invitation to overtake would be a chance for him to force her sideways off the road, across a narrow verge, through a hawthorn hedge and down a steep bank. She held her speed steady as she decided what to do.

The car behind veered out across the white line. The driver craned out of his window to see if there were any oncoming vehicles, saw another bend ahead and swerved back in behind her. In her mirror, Laura saw him pick up the carphone and speak.

This was a man in a hurry to get to his next appointment. Sales rep, surveyor – neat haircut, smart collar and tie. She signalled, slowed down and pulled into a lay-by. The white car shot past, throwing up a cloud of dust.

Laura relaxed her grip on the steering wheel. Was this what it was going to be like? Mike Jackson, the inspector at Merton station, had warned her to be sensible about when and how she drove. 'Always take your mobile phone with you. Let people at work know exactly where you're supposed to be. Avoid risky situations.' She must hope that the threat never materialised.

The scene fell quiet again. Haresby lay a mile up the road.

'I had to stay off school today to see you,' Catherine Earle complained when she greeted Laura. 'I'm missing a trip to a museum.'

'Lucky for you then.' Laura had regained her composure. 'Who wants to go to a museum on a day like this?'

Catherine sat quietly as Laura checked her tube. 'But it's not an ordinary museum. It's one where you dress up like in the olden days and pretend to be servants and lords and ladies in a big old house. You cook chickens over a fire and milk cows and make butter.'

'Any pigs?'

'No.' Catherine wrinkled her nose. 'But all my friends are going and I could have too.'

'I'm sorry about that.' Laura's next job was to take the blood samples. She was in Catherine's bedroom while Sonia

Earle made coffee downstairs. Hearing a car arrive in the yard at the back of the house, she glanced out to see Peter arrive with Adam.

Catherine submitted to the needle, then scrambled off the bed and over to the window. 'What's Adam doing here?'

She left Laura to pack her bag and ran downstairs. Laura heard Peter speak to Sonia and send Adam up to his room. She crossed paths with the boy as she came out on to the landing and made her way down to the kitchen. Adam scowled at her, went into his bedroom and slammed the door.

'I found him up by the Tarn,' Peter was telling Sonia. 'I'm driving back from Merton library, over the top way, and lo and behold, there he is, hanging about outside Ravenscar Hall.'

'By himself?' Sonia ushered Catherine out of the kitchen and told her to occupy herself elsewhere. But she invited Laura in with an apologetic gesture.

He nodded. 'Skiving. It's one thing if you do it with a load of mates. I remember risking it myself when there was a cricket match at Headingly I wanted to see. But you don't do it solo. Where's the fun in that?'

Laura sat at the table and listened quietly. She could see and hear the tension between the couple.

'I sent him off to school as normal. There was nothing to make me think he wasn't planning to go.' Sonia picked up Adam's schoolbag from the floor where he'd obviously dumped it.

'Well, he never made it. He did a detour up Ravenscar on his bike.'

Laura knew that Adam Earle would have had to cycle down into the valley from Haresby Farm, through Hawkshead and close by the gates of his school to reach the road that would take him up to the Tarn.

Sonia sighed. 'What did he do when he saw you?'

'Ran like hell, grabbed his bike and set off on a track through the bracken. I had to go off-road and drive after him.'

'And what did you say when you caught up with him?' Sonia's question carried an implication that Peter had probably been too hard on their son.

Peter took off his jacket and slung it over a chair. 'What do you think? I let him know it wasn't on.'

'And after you'd finished telling him off, did he say why he'd done it?'

'Not a word. Anyway, I've told him he's grounded until I can get some sense out of him.' He shook his head, then apologised to Laura. 'So, how's Catherine doing?'

'She seems very well. I'll send the samples off to the lab and give you the results as soon as they let me have them.'

'Did you ring the school?' Sonia dragged the subject back to Adam.

'I've only just walked into the house, haven't I?' He turned away, strode to the door and yelled upstairs, 'Adam, what's your group-tutor called?'

'Mrs Hathaway,' Sonia cut in in a distinct, clipped tone. 'Listen, Peter, if you'd given Adam a lift to school this morning like I asked, instead of haring over to Merton to catch the library as soon as it opened, this would never have happened. Better still, you could have dropped him off and come back up here to look after Catherine. Then I needn't have taken the day off work.'

Peter Earle came back into the kitchen, still fired up. 'I'm not reading these medical journals for my own amusement, you know. Ask Laura. She'll tell you that something fresh comes up every day since we set the ball rolling: new bits of research get reported, specialists write to the editors with similar case histories. It's all adding up nicely.'

'I know that. But what difference would a day make? You'd promised Adam that you'd take him to school today, remember.'

'Yes, and I forgot. And now you're saying it's my fault he decided to skive?'

'No. But let's ask Laura about something different for a change.' Sonia's voice rose. 'Laura, didn't you tell me we should keep an eye on Adam and ask the school how he was getting on?'

She nodded. 'I was concerned about him.'

Sonia turned on Peter. 'And what did you say when I told you? "Stop fussing"! Refused point blank to let me speak to Mrs Hathaway.'

Her husband cut her short. 'So, you were right.' His face was dark and scowling. 'I'll ring the woman now and pour out all our problems, since that's what you want!'

As he stormed from the room, Laura saw Sonia's aggressive stance drain away. She sat at the table, dropping her head into her hands. 'This isn't really about Adam playing truant,' she confessed.

'I know. Sonia, if you want someone to chat to, I do have time to listen.'

'It's about Catherine: about whether or not we should spend all our time trying to prove the cluster theory, or leave it to Luke, Jim Conroy and the Edwardses, now that they've got involved. Julia Edwards knows much more about Ruthwell and nuclear energy than we do. As it is, Peter has to read everything from scratch. It takes hours and hours to make sense of a single article.'

'And you'd rather he didn't?' Laura felt the weight of the practice's responsibility. If Piers hadn't been so ready with the early information, Peter Earle's own efforts might have fallen by the wayside.

Sonia shrugged. Her light-brown eyes looked defeated. 'I see what it's doing to him. At first I thought it would be good – give him something to focus on other than . . .' She faltered. 'I mean, I can understand why Peter has to follow up this Ruthwell thing. For the first few weeks after we had the

166

diagnosis he went completely to pieces, not sleeping, not eating. Catherine's always been a daddy's girl . . .'

Laura reached out and put a hand on Sonia's arm.

'Ruthwell gave him something to concentrate on. It was almost as if proving the link would actually help make Catherine better.' She stared at Laura. 'It's not logical, is it?'

'No. But channelling anger can be positive.'

Sonia moved her arm away. 'Can be,' she repeated. 'When Jim's article came out last week, Peter was almost . . . happy. We'd achieved the first step. But the days have gone by and he's finding stuff in the medical journals this week that completely reject Jim's piece. Someone at the Radiological Institute called it scaremongering. She said it played on the emotions of vulnerable families, meaning us and the Woods and the Edwardses. Just yesterday, a journalist from the *Yorkshire Post* rang us to get our response.'

Laura grimaced, realising that her fears about the effect on the families of a high-profile patient were becoming reality. 'Don't talk to them if you don't want to. And you can rest assured we won't pass on any information from the medical centre. Your privacy is very important.'

Sonia sat back and closed her eyes. 'You know what this feels like? It's like acid eating you away from the inside. You can feel it burning and you can't even let people know you're in pain. You have to suffer in silence for Catherine's sake.'

'Concentrate on the central thing if you can,' Laura advised gently. The image of acid had shocked her. 'Catherine is in remission and is doing well. Love her, make her feel safe. And if you can't keep the channels open between Adam and Peter, try not to worry too much. I'm sure it will all come right in the end.'

CHAPTER TWENTY-SEVEN

There were points in Laura's life where she'd had to accept that the only thing that would ease a problem was to do nothing. She had to let go of her tendency to analyse her way towards a solution; a string of fragile ifs and maybes that fell apart when others saw different reasons and answers.

'If I express my feelings, he will understand and because he loves me and doesn't want to hurt me, he will begin to behave differently,' she would tell herself when she'd been married to Tom.

'You use your feelings to control me,' he'd retaliated angrily on each occasion. 'You rehearse them to get me to react in a certain way, and you go away and cry in a corner if you don't achieve what you want.'

The accusation echoed down the years now as she compared the two men in her life at Ravensdale. Only, in this case, it seemed to be Luke who was forcing her into a corner and demanding a favourable reaction to his distress. Matthew, on the other hand, was the one who kept himself out of account and seemed to care only for her feelings.

Laura felt pulled out of shape by the constant dialogue inside her head. It was Friday evening, warm and clear, so she tried to weed out the rebellious debate by going into the garden to trim and dig: hebe, hosta, and horizontal cotoneaster; impatiens, recently planted out, and nasturtium seedlings just showing through after a winter in the frosty ground. Their flat round leaves collected beads of moisture as she showered water from the can.

A car came along the little-used lane; not Luke's powerful, smooth engine, but a sturdier, slower diesel. She saw the top of Matthew's Range Rover before he turned in at the gate.

She stood up slowly and watched him get out of the car. His straight dark hair was pushed back from his sunburned face, he wore an open-necked white sports shirt and dark-blue trousers. Laura frowned as the door clicked shut.

Matthew stood for a while, hands in pockets, studying the pale, heavy blossom of a white lilac tree above her head. 'Are you busy?'

She cast her trowel aside. 'No. Would you like coffee?' Do nothing. Show no reaction. She concentrated on the heavy, sweet scent of the lilac.

'No. I won't stop.' He came closer. 'I've brought some news that might interest you.'

'Come inside at least.' She led the way between the lavender borders, afraid to stand still under his gaze.

Matthew followed. 'I came to tell you that Gary Wood has left the lodge.'

Laura stopped on the doorstep. 'Do you know where he's gone?'

'No. As a matter of fact, Maisie had had enough. She gave him notice to quit.'

Laura stared. 'Your mother threw him out?'

'She does own the place,' he pointed out. 'I managed to keep a lid on his bad behaviour until a few days ago, because I knew what her reaction would be if she found out. But Gary isn't a quiet drunk. He's a rowdy one. Maisie drove by on Wednesday afternoon and heard him crashing about inside the house. She came up to find me working at Haresby with Peter Earle and told me Gary had to go.'

'And she wouldn't listen to any argument?'

He shook his head. 'She sympathises with his situation, but

not to the extent of letting him smash up the lodge. I went and told him yesterday morning and he was gone by tea-time.'

'And you don't know where to?'

'No idea. But I wanted to tell you in person.' Matthew stood on the gravel path, still staring intently at her. 'I'm worried about you.'

'Don't be.' She moved inside and away from his gaze.

'I can't help it. Have you had any more phone calls?'

'Yes. I notified the police this morning. It's in hand.' She intended to be brisk, but she couldn't stop her voice from shaking as she answered.

Matthew overtook her in the hall, 'Did you recognise the voice? Could it be Gary?'

'I don't think so . . . I don't know.' Laura turned her head away. 'Why? Did he say anything to you before he left?'

'Lots of incoherent stuff. He's permanently drunk these days, swearing at everybody under the sun. Bitch this and bitch that.'

She flinched.

'Bitch is the word your caller uses all the time, isn't it? Yesterday, when I told him to leave, first it was Maisie who was the bitch, then his wife, then you.'

Laura leaned back against the wall. Could it be Gary Wood who was watching her? What was his motive?

'Did you mention Gary to the police?' He moved in closer, took Laura's trembling arm.

'No. Don't, Matthew, please.'

'Let me help you.'

She searched his face, once more recalled the feel of his arms around her, strong and tender. It would be so easy to be there again: surrounded, protected, cared for.

The late news flickered on the TV screen as Laura sank into bed after a shower.

'No, Matthew.' She'd turned him away. His help came with too many conditions attached, his arms held defeat.

But the struggle had exhausted her and she paid little attention to the items attracting the world's attention until she noticed shots of a nuclear power station on the screen: the vast concrete-and-steel block, the giant white domes set on a moorland landscape. A journalist stood in the foreground talking of the hitherto unproven link between childhood cancers and the production of nuclear power, then of a significant new development. A so-called cancer cluster had recently been identified in a remote Yorkshire dale, the newsman told the nation, his voice high and strident against the background of the sinister-looking monolith.

There was a switch to the studio. A second broadcaster introduced an interview with an ex-worker at Ruthwell whose daughter had died of non-Hodgkin lymphoma three years before. It was only now, with the new alarm raised over the possible link between childhood leukaemia and the nuclear industry, that she had broken her silence.

'Julia Edwards,' Laura whispered.

The shot switched to a woman with short grey hair, a face with strong cheek-bones and jawline, and steady grey eyes.

'I'm talking about incidents which occurred during the time I was at the plant,' she insisted. 'On several occasions the management at Ruthwell received reports from the RSPCA and other concerned bodies of unusual fatalities among the native wildlife on the moor. Foxes and several different types of rodent had been found dead over a six-month period.'

Laura leaned forward. Her skin had begun to crawl.

'As a worker in the power station lab I was asked to examine tissue from the dead animals,' Julia continued.

'And is it true that you found higher than expected levels of radiation?' The journalist framed his question so that her answer could be unequivocal.

'We found extremely high levels that could only have been

the result of exposure to external radiation in dosages above 100 mSv. This suggested to us that the affected wildlife must have come into contact with unsafe levels of radiation within the immediate vicinity of the power station.' Julia gave the facts calmly.

'And after these results had been analysed, what further steps were taken?'

The camera lingered on the face of the interviewee as she paused before answering. 'Our results were forwarded to the management of the plant, who studied them and concluded that there was no possible risk to human health.'

'No risk to human health?' the journalist echoed. 'Are you saying that the decision was reached to keep this information out of the public domain?'

'Yes.'

'Were the RSPCA, the people who had drawn your attention to the potential problem, informed in detail of the results?'

'Not in detail, no.'

'Were Ruthwell workers outside the research laboratory or residents in the area informed?'

'No.' Julia was absolutely clear on every point.

The journalist sounded triumphant as the camera stayed on her and he signed off from the bulletin. 'Mrs Edwards, thank you very much!'

CHAPTER TWENTY-EIGHT

Saturday morning was a lousy time to have to visit a prisoner in the custody cells at Merton police station, but Luke answered the duty sergeant's call and went to sit in on an interview. The charge was GBH during a drunken brawl. The man was bruised about the eyes, with a small cut on his forehead, but his opponent had come off much worse on the receiving end of a broken beer glass and was currently in intensive care.

'Sorry about the timing.' The sergeant sealed the tapes inside brown envelopes and saw Luke down the corridor. 'Still, it could have been worse. We brought him in at three this morning, out of his skull. To look at him then, you wouldn't have thought he had two brain cells to rub together.

'He's still pretty confused. I doubt that he'll ever remember exactly what happened.' Luke had reached the sergeant's desk and noticed Mike Jackson in his office behind reception. The inspector nodded and stood up, as if he had something to tell him.

'Go through.' The sergeant lifted the desk flap.

'Luke.' Mike greeted him and reached for his hat. 'I'm on my way out, but I wanted to let you know that we've sent a form through to the Force Intelligence Bureau so we can get BT to monitor all Laura's calls in future.'

Luke frowned. It worried him that Laura was still getting those phone calls and that she had been sufficiently concerned about them to contact the police.

The inspector picked up his hesitation. 'She didn't tell you? Mind you, it was only yesterday. Anyway, can you tell her we'll have the system in place within twenty-four hours? After that, we'll be able to trace the caller, whoever he is.'

Slowly Luke followed Mike out into reception and downstairs to the car park. 'I'll let her know.'

'But don't raise her hopes. If they've got even half a brain, these guys ring from a call-box, a different one each time.'

'I'll explain.' As he got into his own car, Luke made the split-second decision to head for Abbey Grange. He didn't even know if it was Laura's weekend on call. If he'd thought about it, he would probably have passed on Mike's message over the phone, but he was on the Hawkshead road. He would arrive unannounced, then play it by ear.

Turning on the CD player, he left the town behind and rose up over the moor road, through Ginnersby, Waite and Oxtop. It was a day of brilliant sunshine. Perfect visibility gave a view of hills rolling on for ever, dale after dale. The sky was still and blue.

'Laura's favourite,' Luke murmured, noticing the Elgar cello concerto and finding himself stirred by the dipping then soaring notes. The music eased open the doors in his mind that he'd kept closed since the argument: getting up in the middle of the night, wanting her to stop him, angry that she didn't; too much pride to change his mind, taking his car keys, leaving the house, slamming doors.

Laura should have been more willing to make a distinction between how she felt about Matthew and him. She owed him that much. Yes, he was jealous, but Laura should have made allowances. Anyone would be unsettled in the circumstances. All it needed was one clear statement: 'I don't love Matthew Aire.'

But perhaps he wasn't thinking straight? Maybe he was simplifying, justifying, wanting to be right? Because jealousy was new to him. Sure, there'd been small pangs in the past, soon controlled. Nothing major. But jealousy big-time didn't feature among his normal tactics for dealing with uncomfortable feelings. Had he been mistaken, then, to immerse himself in work, or to pursue details of the Ruthwell scare?

Images of Laura smiling; Laura turning away hurt; Laura lying beside him; Laura walking into the room where he sat reading yet another research paper – hair around her slight shoulders, skin tanned after days in the sun – would float into his head, however tightly shut he kept those doors. And he would resent them and her, and begin again the never-ending cycle of telling himself she should have done this, said that; made it the way he wanted it to be – just him and Laura, and no one else in the world.

He found her sitting by the swift-flowing waters of Devil's Leap, a book lying open on her lap. He startled her, but she didn't stand up to greet him.

'I ran into Mike Jackson when I visited the police cells to see a client earlier today,' he explained. 'He mentioned the progress they'd made over your phone calls.'

She looked across the river at weekend walkers on the far bank. A chain of half a dozen brightly dressed, middle-aged people trod the steep, narrow path.

'Why didn't you tell me you'd decided to involve the police?' He stood up and flicked a small twig into the current. 'I might have been able to help.'

Staying in her patch of sunlight, the limestone rock warm against her back where she leaned against it, arms hugging her bent knees, she looked up at him without answering.

'I know we're supposed to be spending time thinking things over and not seeing each other, but this is different.' He could feel himself becoming impatient, angry at her silent reproach. 'I'm surprised you didn't let me know.'

'I would have next time we spoke.' Laura stood up with a sigh. 'Anyway, what did Mike say?'

'They'll monitor all future calls.'

'But they can't check on calls that have already been made, can they?' She sounded unimpressed. 'And on Friday morning my friendly alarm service told me that it was his last call, so there's not a lot of point, is there?'

'Maybe not, but at least the system will be in place.' He watched her walk away towards the path, then, heart beating fast, hating to see her like this, he caught her up. 'OK, you're right. The chances of detecting whoever's doing this are slim.'

Laura shrugged and walked on towards Abbey Grange.

'Anyway, what do you mean, he's not planning to ring again?'

'Change of tactic. Now it's traffic hazards I have to watch out for.'

'What are you saying?' Luke planted himself in front of her and stopped her in her tracks.

'He talked about an accident. All of a sudden I'm paranoid about getting into my car! I see shadows behind trees, imagine burst tyres, faulty steering, defective brakes.' Trying to move past him, she stumbled sideways against a rock and overbalanced towards the steep river bank.

He caught hold of her arm and pulled her upright, then didn't, couldn't let go of her hand.

'I'm OK.' Testing her ankle, regaining her balance, she insisted she was ready to walk on.

'No, you're not.' Luke couldn't bear another rejection.

'I am, I'm fine.' Her breath came short and shallow. She resisted as Luke pulled her towards him, then relaxed against him.

Overcome with relief, he kissed her. His lips were on her face, his hands stroking her. 'It's my fault. I let you down.' Giving up all attempts to analyse and control, he knew he wanted her and that nothing else mattered.

'Luke, I'm scared.'

'I know. But I'm here now. I'll stay with you until it's over. Nothing will happen, I promise.'

'His voice . . . it's as though he knows everything about me. It reduces me to . . . I don't know. I collapse when I hear it. I loathe the sound of it.'

Luke held her, his cheek against her hair. 'I shouldn't have left you.'

Laura closed her eyes. 'There's one thing.' She took a deep breath and struggled free. 'I need to say it. It's about Matthew again . . .'

Luke shook his head.

'Here I am, caught in the middle. I hate it.' She took him by the shoulders and held him at arm's length. 'Pulled this way and that. Hurting people.'

'It's not you. I hurt myself. When I'm alone at home, I imagine what Matthew's saying to you, see the way he looks at you, know exactly how he feels.'

'But don't you know that I won't do anything that would harm you?'

This was true. Laura's heart was warm and kind, not malicious. 'It's Matthew I don't trust. Anyone who wants someone as badly as he wants you will do anything to get you back.'

'But I'm not a possession.' She breathed unevenly. 'Oh Luke, why do we have to argue like this?'

'He's been back to see you, hasn't he?' He saw the defensive flicker in her eyes.

'Yes.' She broke away and set off under the canopy of trees, round the gradual bend in the river.

For a moment he was beaten. A tide of negative feelings engulfed him. Cursing Mattew Aire, he watched her go.

Luke took a deep breath. This couldn't be right: Laura walking away, him letting her. Over nothing. Over his inability to accept that she had a past that couldn't be neatly severed.

Knowing that he had to surface from under the wave of jealousy, he followed her to Abbey Grange.

He could see her running ahead of him to the house. It looked square and solid as the trees in the garden spread their arms towards her and their shade enveloped her. Then she was inside the white walls. She'd closed the door without waiting to see if he had followed.

Dismayed by how vulnerable she looked from a distance, Luke pursued her.

In the hall, the clock's tick was loud and hollow, an upstairs door clicked shut. He grew more uneasy, holding at bay the sensation that there were eyes in the house, watching him as he went into the kitchen. Everything's fine, he told himself. He turned on the kettle to make coffee.

Laura's handbag lay on the kitchen unit, its contents spilled across the surface.

'Luke!' Laura crept into the room, her face stiff with fear. 'The key to the side door is missing!'

He put down the cups and the milk, and walked back into the hall.

There was a second sound from upstairs. A footfall? The bottom edge of a door brushing over carpet pile?

'Someone's in the house,' she whispered.

They stood at the bottom of the stairs, looking up. Morning sunlight poured in through the landing window, down the corridor leading to bedrooms and bathroom. Turning his head to glance across the hall towards Laura's study, he saw files rummaged from her desk and scattered over the floor.

'I know!' Trembling visibly, she led him into the room.

Papers were everywhere, tipped from folders and drawers, fanning out across the polished boards. A computer screen was toppled sideways on the desk, wires trailing, a glass-shaded lamp was smashed.

As Luke investigated, Laura backed out of the room. There was a sudden rush of footsteps along as the landing as more

178

than one person thudded towards the stairs, stopped, then turned into a bedroom, still out of sight.

Luke guessed their intention. The bedroom at the back of the house overlooked an extension with a low roof. The intruders could climb out of the window on to the outbuilding and jump from there to the ground.

'Stay here,' he told Laura. Perhaps he could intercept them – at least catch a glimpse of them before they got away. He reached the landing window in time to see two shapes scrambling and sliding down the slate roof.

They balanced precariously at the edge, arms flailing, heads ducked low; slight figures in padded jackets and black baseball caps, seen from the back. They crouched, then jumped and disappeared in the yard below.

Luke ran downstairs, through the kitchen and out of the side door, closely followed by Laura. 'Stay back!' he warned. He wanted a better view, but they were lithe and fast, and had reached the back gate that led down to the river, were through it and in among the hazel bushes, trampling the undergrowth, shielding their faces with their arms.

'Let them go,' Laura pleaded.

Luke stayed to take care of her, knowing that to chase them through the thick woods would be hopeless now.

CHAPTER TWENTY-NINE

'This is where one of them broke in.' Luke pointed out the smashed window in Laura's study to the policewoman who had driven over from Merton. 'We've decided that he must have gone to the back door and let the second one in.'

After she'd glanced round the house, the officer had asked Laura for a list of stolen items.

'They hit upstairs pretty hard,' Laura told her. 'And this room. The kitchen and the lounge don't seem too bad.'

'And you think you interrupted them?'

'Yes. They must have heard us moving about downstairs.'

Luke had a flash of action-replay: of the two figures hunched at the edge of the outhouse roof, arms flung wide as they jumped.

'At least they didn't get away with much.' The policewoman had noted TV and video, the music-system still in place. 'Was there any cash around?'

Laura pointed across the hall to her bag on the kitchen surface. 'About thirty pounds. It's gone. Along with the door key.'

'And why the mess in here? Do you know what they were after?'

Laura glanced at Luke. 'That depends on who "they" were.'

'Laura's been having nuisance calls, possibly from someone with a vested interest in protecting the reputation of the Ruthwell processing plant,' Luke continued. 'If this break-in is connected with the calls we might be looking at an organised attempt both to intimidate her and to get hold of confidential information.'

'Patients' files; that sort of thing?'

'Yes. But why would they look for them here?' Laura objected. 'Wouldn't they break into the medical centre and try there instead?'

'Possibly.' Luke began to sift through some of the papers on the floor. 'But just suppose their aim is twofold: to scare you and pick up information at the same time. What better way than to break into Abbey Grange and take stuff from your study?' He picked up a thin A4 booklet and read the title. '"The National Registration for Radiation Workers". It wouldn't take them long to sort out the useful documents and scarper.'

'But what were they doing upstairs?' Laura demanded. 'I know I bring my work home with me, but I don't take it to bed!'

'Deliberately confusing the issue? Covering their tracks?' He shrugged and tidied the papers.

'Will you be OK?' the police officer asked.

Laura swallowed hard, then nodded. 'The worst thing is that I feel sickened by the idea of those two men having pried into every room. My underclothes have been tipped out of my bedroom drawers.' She turned away and walked out into the garden.

'I'll look after her,' Luke stated, following Laura and putting his arm round her shoulder.

'You know my main reason for moving out of the city to these beautiful, wide-open spaces?' she murmured.

'For the peace and quiet; I know.'

'And because it felt safe. Well, so much for that.'

'You're pretty isolated out here.' The woman officer had joined them. 'I'd advise you to have someone with you for a while until you get over the shock.'

Laura thanked her and turned to Luke.

'I'll stay,' he promised.

'And ring us when you've got a list of missing items together. I'll do the paperwork before I finish my shift and my sergeant or Inspector Jackson will take a look at it tomorrow.'

Like saw her to the gate, waited until the policewoman had driven away, then went to join Laura under the lilac tree.

'Abbey Grange.' She sighed.

'I know. You love the place. I'm sorry.'

'I was safe here, Luke.'

'And still will be.' He closed his arms round her. 'We'll get the window fixed, change the locks.'

He knew that the beauty of Abbey Grange for Laura had lain in her ability to walk out to Black Gill and up to Joan's Foss, leaving the doors open, as the previous owner, Lilian Rigg, had always done before her.

'Let me find out about installing a security system.' He took her hand and led her inside, avoiding the wrecked study, taking her quietly upstairs.

She hesitated at the door to her own room. The duvet had been pulled from the bed and left bundled in a corner, the sheet was thick with prints from an earth-covered shoe. Her underclothes were spilling out of their drawer, white lace and entangled straps, and on the mirror above the chest of drawers was a sickening mess of sticky sprays and creams, smears of lipstick.

'Come to the spare room,' Luke murmured. 'They didn't touch anything in there.'

She lay down on the white bed in the small, clean room with a sloping ceiling and a pale-cream jug of white lilac on the deep window-sill. Breathing in its scent, she began to weep.

Luke lay on his side beside her, his arm across her waist, silent until she wanted to speak.

'Matthew came on Friday to tell me that Gary Wood has

disappeared,' she told him. 'He thinks Gary might be behind this. He wanted to help me.'

'I want to help you too.' It was very important to Luke that she believed him. 'I love you, Laura.'

'I know.' She turned slowly to face him. 'But I needed help. You weren't there and Matthew is a kind man.'

'I love you.' Luke buried his face in her long dark hair.

She raised his head and traced her fingertip along his cheek, then smoothed his hair back from his forehead. 'On Friday he asked me to go back to him. I said I wouldn't.'

Luke's hold on her waist tightened. He kissed her wet face, her lips.

'Because I love you, Luke. Matthew understands that. He won't ask me again.'

CHAPTER THIRTY

Was it true, Francesca wondered? Laura had sat her down in the cane chair in the lonely hotel room and tried to convince her that every patient she met in her surgery and every friend she had was afraid of the unpredictable currents of life.

'Every one of us,' Laura had insisted. 'The sad thing is that it's the fear that drives us apart and leaves us lonely.'

They'd talked for another hour about Piers, and about Harry whose situation preyed on Francesca's mind and swayed her back towards her original decision to terminate her pregnancy. She'd admitted her fear of failure as a mother; her feeling that she had failed him in particular.

'It's my fault that the school excluded him. I'm not sure exactly what I did to make it happen, but I know it was me.' How familiar that sensation was: to have sought to do something right; to have misunderstood the unwritten rules; to have got it wrong.

'Sometimes, as a parent, you can take on too much rather than too little responsibility,' Laura told her.

'How can I not? And it goes on for years, never stops, not for twenty, thirty, forty years. Worrying about your kids, wishing they weren't hurting.'

'But at least it's life – living,' Laura had countered. 'That's what this struggle is all about.'

Slowly she had talked Francesca round into contacting Piers. She'd made her promise only to stay in Wingate until the weekend when she would have had time to pull herself round and prepare herself to meet him. In her own mind, Francesca gave herself this escape route; a few days in which to waver and if necessary to disappear again.

'Tell Harry and Joe I'm sorry I ran away,' she'd told Piers. When she talked to him, the receiver clasped tight.

'They need you,' he'd replied. Not 'I need you'.

Saturday came and she was still pale, still withdrawn. She chose a dark-green shirt and trousers, kept her hair drawn tightly back from her face, found that the practical details of checking out of The Beeches almost defeated her.

But she managed to get herself into her car and heading out of town towards Merton. Should she turn towards Hawkshead and Abbey Grange, talk to Laura again and phone Piers from there? No, she could only face the drive straight home and an unannounced arrival. For the half-hour journey she gripped the steering wheel and leaned forward in her seat.

I'm doing well, she told herself as she approached the market town. She passed the old castle on the hill with its round tower, the church at its foot and the long, straight main street where the stalls were set up. It was almost midday, with a crush of customers buying fresh fruit and vegetables, criss-crossing the street from one stall to another – not long now.

Francesca pulled up a hundred metres short of the house. Again she wondered whether to ring Laura and ask for more help, then decided that she must do this by herself. Pulling a paper tissue out of its pack, she wiped her damp forehead, then sat shredding the paper, taking deep breaths.

Hardly aware of what she was doing, she eased the car forward again, down the busy street and through the gate.

There was Piers's car, parked in its usual place. She hadn't given him a specific time, so he and the boys would probably have stayed in all morning awaiting her return. Her fingers fumbled in her bag for her front-door keys. She turned them in the lock and stepped into the house.

Instantly she knew it was empty. Tears sprang to her eyes, her heart ached. She wanted them to be here when she arrived. She stood in the hall like a stranger.

On automatic pilot she went down the long tiled corridor, down the steps to put the kettle on. The back door was standing open, she noticed.

Then Joe ran in – Joe, who was just like her with his thick red hair and pale skin, the look of confusion in his green eyes mirroring hers.

She dropped her keys and bag on the table.

'Dad, Mum's here!' he called over his shoulder, then turned back to stare at her again.

Francesca took a step towards him.

'Fran?' She heard Piers's voice.

At last, Joe seemed to realise she was real. His face crumpled and he cried out. Running towards her, he threw himself into her arms.

She bent forward to wrap her arms round him, picking him off his feet and sinking her head against his thin shoulder.

'Fran?' Piers stood in the doorway, waiting for her to lift her head and open her eyes.

She hugged Joe and sobbed. Looking up, she tried to read the look on Piers's face. He was shaking his head slightly, his eyelids flickering. His mouth worked, but he didn't speak.

As he came towards her, she gently put Joe to one side.

Piers stopped a few paces from her, still studying her face. 'Was it my fault?' he asked.

Francesca shook her head. 'Where's Harry?'

'Out. I couldn't get him to stay. He's handled the whole thing really badly.'

She sighed, recognising Harry's impulse to run away from the problems at home. 'Laura says we have to talk.'

'She's right.' Still, he held back from her.

Francesca glanced at Joe. 'My case is in the hall,' she said quietly to him. 'Take it upstairs for me, please.'

He ran off eagerly. Watching him, she realised that putting the bag in her room meant she was here to stay. This was the thing that mattered most to him in the world.

'I couldn't go ahead with the abortion,' she told Piers, once they had the kitchen to themselves.

He took a step nearer, reached out his arm, then let it drop: a gesture of defeat.

She needed a response. But then, she knew what it would be. Blankly, wearily, she turned away.

Piers pursued her. 'You want to know what I think?'

Without turning round, staring up into the stairwell, she shook her head. 'Not what you think. What you feel.'

'Confused,' he cried. 'Left out. Rejected. How do you think I feel?'

Francesca turned her head. 'Angry?'

He nodded. 'But I'm more hurt.' His eyes were narrowed, he breathed in fits and starts. 'God, Francesca!'

'I'm sorry.' Her foot was on the bottom stair.

He took hold of her and turned her round. 'Sorry doesn't do it. Sorry isn't what I'm interested in.' The words came in a rush, a jumble, as he held on to her arm. 'I'm sorry. We're all sorry. Let's kick the guilt into touch, shall we?'

Half afraid, she let herself be led back into the kitchen, out of Joe's hearing.

'If it's feelings you want, let me tell you. You cut me out!'

'I know.'

'And OK, I cut myself out!' He let her arm drop, walked swiftly around the table, the pent-up hurt exploding in small bursts as he ran a hand through his hair and paced up and down. 'I've been hard to get through to lately, I know that.'

'I used to say I'd like another baby, remember?' Years ago, when Joe was small, they'd considered it.

He gave a short, breathy sound, like someone taking a blow to the body.

'And you always said no.' It had been like talking to the

187

wall. For a second she imagined that Piers would set a condition on taking her back now. He would insist on the abortion after all. She wouldn't stand for it. She would leave again and this time she would take Joe.

'That was then.' He stopped, tilted his head back, looked out through the window.

'And now. You said no again. After Laura had seen us fighting, you listed all the reasons why not. You said we hadn't planned it, you were too busy at work, we were doing a lousy job with the boys.' She counted off his reasons on her fingers.

'That was me thinking, not feeling.'

'But the message came across loud and clear.' It hurt her again to recall it. With Piers, his negatives were so absolute.

'You didn't give me time to get used to the idea. You dumped it on me in public.'

'Not intentionally.'

Coming round the table, he stood facing her. 'I was scared,' he admitted. 'I lay awake all that night. I heard you go out and come back in. I wanted you to come to bed. You didn't. And I just lay there. I didn't know what to say.'

Francesca closed her eyes. She'd stood outside the bedroom door, desperately wanting to go in. She'd thought he was asleep.

'In the morning I was going to try and talk it through with you again. But you'd packed your bag and gone.'

'Didn't you hear me?'

'I heard a car.'

She took a deep breath. 'But you didn't follow it?' She'd looked back at the bedroom window, longing to see a light, wanting him to come after her.

'I was too bloody proud,' he admitted. 'Too shattered to move a muscle.'

'And now?' It was Francesca who reached out this time. She felt him shudder as she touched his shoulder.

188

Their eyes sought each other out.

'This time, let's get it right,' Piers murmured in response. 'Believe me, Fran, I want us to keep this baby.'

CHAPTER THIRTY-ONE

'Radon. Colourless, odourless, gaseous, radioactive, non-metallic element, symbol Rn, atomic number 86, relative atomic mass 222.'

Laura read an Internet entry and scribbled down notes. She'd restored order in her study at home, had her computer repaired and was spending a dull Monday evening doing what Rudi Grey had told her she must do more than a week before. If you want to survive this conflict, be sure of your ground.

'Formerly considered non-reactive, now known to form some compounds with fluorine.' Radon was one of twenty known isotopes, the densest gas known. Laura jotted this down, then turned back to the screen. 'Occurs in small amounts in spring water, streams and the air, being formed from the natural radioactive decay of radium.'

She looked up, pen suspended over the paper, and stared out of the window at the hulking horizon of Ravenscar swathed in blue-grey cloud.

'The National Radiological Protection Board sets a level of 200 Bequerels per cubic metre, above which removal of radon from homes is recommended. A level of 54,000 Bequerels per cubic metre has been recorded in limestone caves in the United States. The average radon radiation level found in forty British limestone caves was 2,900 Bequerels per cubic metre, the highest level being in the Giant's Hole in Derbyshire, with values of around 155,000 Bequerels per cubic metre during the summer months.'

From her window, Laura could see the trees clustered around the foot of Black Gill. The stream began high on Ravenscar and disappeared from view through layers of limestone until it reappeared in the gill and formed a series of small waterfalls into Joan's Foss, where the Hawkshead children played and swam.

The following morning, a Tuesday in early July, she was at the hospital when Elliot Wood died.

'What could we have done?' Hannah wept, holding the child's hand long after it was over.

Laura shook her head.

Hannah gazed down at the bed, cupping her hand and resting it against her son's pale, cold cheek. 'I love you, Elliot,' she crooned. 'You're Mummy's little boy.'

Laura drove to Askby that evening, relieved to see Hannah's parents' car outside the bungalow and a trickle of friends and neighbours calling to offer support.

'Hannah's in her room. She won't come out and see people, but she knows they've been and that's what matters.' Her mother, Jacqui Shepherd, a dry-eyed, small, sturdy woman in her mid-forties, welcomed Laura and showed her a living-room table loaded with sellophane-wrapped roses and carnations. 'The smell from those flowers!' She busied herself finding vases. 'We got a phone call from the hospital at ten o'clock. David answered it. I knew we were too late from the look on his face. We'd like to have been there when it happened, but it wasn't to be.' Jacqui paused, scissors poised over the stems of a bunch of deep-red roses, obviously picked from a neighbour's garden. 'From Alison Lawson,' she explained. 'She drove over from Hawkshead specially.'

'How's Hannah taking it?' Laura heard David Shepherd show the last visitors out of the front door. For a while they had the house to themselves.

191

'She doesn't know what's hit her. Neither does David, if you want to know.' Jacqui shook her head. 'He cried and cried at the hospital. I said to him in the end, "David, what good does it do?" But then, Elliot was our only grandchild.'

'Hello, Dr Grant.' Hannah's voice interrupted them from the door of her room. She wore a creased cream blouse and fawn trousers. Her hair was escaping in heavy, lifeless strands. 'Thanks for coming.'

Laura went to join her. Close to, she could see that Hannah's eyes were red and swollen, her body trembling.

'I heard your voice.' Taking Laura inside her room, she closed the door behind them. 'I'm worried about Dad,' she confided. 'Mum's coping OK, but he doesn't know what to do with himself. He keeps breaking down.'

'I'll have a word with him,' Laura promised. 'How about you? Is there anything I could do for you?'

'Elliot went peacefully in the end, didn't he? I was glad about that.' Hannah sat on the edge of her bed. 'And afterwards he looked perfect. Not wasted away so you could hardly tell who it was. I would've dreaded seeing him lying there, not recognising him, not being able to remember him how I wanted. And he hadn't woken up for forty-eight hours, not properly. He said my name a couple of times and sometimes I could see he was dreaming; his eyelids fluttered like they always did.'

Laura recognised the no man's land of the recently bereaved, after the drama of dying, before the grief kicked in.

'He asked for his daddy too. Just once.'

There was a silence that Laura didn't know how to fill; another wound that couldn't be healed.

Hannah sighed. 'I told him Daddy loved him too; we both did.'

Laura knew this was true.

'Gary can't have heard what's happened to our baby boy yet.' Perhaps the anxiety over her husband was the one thing that held Hannah together. She rubbed her face with both hands, then ran her fingers down her neck. 'It's not that he doesn't care.' She sounded as though she were trying to convince herself. 'It's that he cares too much . . .'

Laura knew that this was true too.

'The funeral's on Friday.'

Laura backed softly towards the door. As she left, she offered the only thing she could. 'I'll try to find him,' she said. 'I'll tell Gary that Elliot died peacefully in his sleep.'

CHAPTER THIRTY-TWO

Levels of radon up to 2.8 million Bequerels per cubic metre had been recorded in abandoned mines in south-west England. The ancient workings of Ginnersby lead mine lay in the tunnels beneath Luke's feet.

Luke did a rapid calculation: 2.8 million. Dividing and crossing off noughts, he came up with the figure of 14,000 times the NRPB recommended level for action for homes.

'That's unbelievable,' he told Laura on the phone after he'd read the paper she'd handed on to him. 'And you say that it's especially in limestone where it occurs in such huge quantities?'

'Yes. It's been extensively studied during the last ten years. And wouldn't you think that Julia above all people would have these figures at her fingertips?'

Laura sounded worried and exhausted. She'd been to Askby to see Hannah Wood, then spent the early evening searching for Gary to pass on news of Elliot's death. 'I'll go up to Ginnersby and have a word with Julia,' he told her. 'You forget about it. Leave this to me.'

He glanced at the *Yorkshire Evening Post* before he left home. The Ruthwell scare had slipped down the front page, but still commanded space, still provoked a furious war of words. There was a piece by Jim Conroy in an inside Comment column in response to an earlier article by the chief scientist from the Radiation Institute. Conroy was calling for openness over the RSPCA-led investigation of years before and demanded full publication of the lab-test results on the animal tissue.

The Institute asserted in turn that all figures were available for scrutiny. They defended Ruthwell's decision not to alarm the general public unnecessarily, but insisted that the evidence was much too complex to be interpreted by non-experts.

'It overwhelms me,' Laura had confessed before she rang off. 'How do we fix on the most significant factor among all these possibilities?'

Feeling similarly bemused, Luke drove up to Ginnersby, past the track leading to the tunnel entrances to the old mines and through roughly worked stone gateposts into the Edwardses' isolated house.

Frank answered, neat and spruce as usual in a dark-blue checked shirt, his posture upright, his face giving nothing away. 'No need to ask what you've come about,' he said without surprise. 'I'm making coffee. Would you like some?'

Luke succumbed to the smell of freshly ground beans and joined the Edwardses in a conservatory at the back of the house.

'Actually, you might not have guessed exactly what it is I wanted to talk about,' he began uncomfortably. 'Laura and I have been throwing an idea around . . . Well, it was Rudi Grey who put it into our minds when he reminded us that radon is an important source of exposure to radiation.' Watching Julia's reaction in particular, he saw her stiffen and focus her gaze on the valley below. 'Of course, you'd know that,' he prodded gently.

'What are you implying?' Frank spoke for his wife.

'I'm not implying anything. I was curious. So this morning I read up about the geology of Ruthwell and the surrounding area. The bands of limestone that form outcrops like Ravenscar in this dale stretch north-east across the North Yorkshire moors well beyond the site of the nuclear plant.'

He watched, waiting for a reaction. When he got none he

pushed on. 'Limestone apparently provides ideal conditions for the production of radon . . .'

'It's all right, Luke. There's no need to go on with your chemistry lesson.' There was no scorn in Julia's voice, though the content might have suggested it. 'But you are implying a criticism of me. You're saying that I must have considered the radon factor in these children's illnesses and that I deliberately suppressed it in presenting the anti-Ruthwell case to the press.'

Her calmness took him aback. 'I wouldn't put it quite like that.'

'I would.' She stood up and went to look out over the rocky slope leading down to Ginnersby mine. 'Strange, isn't it? Who would believe these beautiful dales were once home to thriving mining communities?'

Luke went to stand beside her. 'Lead mining round here goes way back to Roman times. In the twelfth century, lead from Ravensdale was sent to France for the roofs of the great abbeys. My own grandfather remembered miners in the twenties coming across discarded pigs of lead dating back to the second century. They used to say "t'owd man" had been there before them.' He shrugged. 'Sorry, another lesson. History this time.'

Julia smiled. 'Can you imagine leaving this bracing air every day of your life and burrowing four hundred feet into the earth?'

'And dying of lead poisoning and chest diseases.'

'Cancer?' she added quietly. 'They say gangs of miners used to sing as they trudged along the fell tracks to work. And they could find their way through miles of tunnel. But it's not romantic, not really, is it?'

'I wouldn't have liked it.' He looked sideways at her strong profile; the long, straight nose, the prominent cheek-bones. 'Now that I've got this radon business straight in my mind, I have to admit that I'm less certain about Ruthwell.'

'And you weren't sure before?' Julia didn't flinch. 'Come on, Luke, I want to know whether you ever fully subscribed. Piers Chandler does and, of course, Peter Earle; they do. But were you and Laura ever convinced?'

'Laura wasn't,' Luke conceded. 'But up till now I've been one hundred per cent in the Jim Conroy camp. So, why did you make your statement?' He was aware of Frank hovering protectively in the background. 'Why sound so certain?'

Julia swept a thick lock of greying hair from her face, but it fell and curved back over her cheek. 'We're families fighting for the truth about our children against organisations who don't know the meaning of the concept, against an industry that promotes its processing plants on TV adverts as squeaky clean entertainment centres. What's a little bit of distortion on our part going to do except redress the balance?'

'Right,' Luke agreed. 'But what about the Woods and the Earles? Sooner rather than later the media people are going to latch on to the radon factor, helped along no doubt by spokesmen from the nuclear industry. What's Peter going to do then?'

'Keep on fighting, like the rest of us.' She didn't give an inch, gazing down impassively on the landscape that could have been responsible for her daughter's death.

'Any sign of Gary Wood?' Luke asked Laura. It was late the same evening and, glad of the chance to be together, they'd taken to the shadow of the beech trees by the river, on the quiet bend by the footbridge and stepping-stones.

'No, and the funeral's on Friday. I spoke to one of his mates in the building trade earlier today and he reckons Gary might be in Leeds.'

'Leeds is a big place.' He knew Laura had many other things on her mind and in their new-found contentment together he wished to protect her from difficult topics, yet still wanted to work round to discussing his visit to Julia Edwards with her.

197

'I know. But I promised Hannah. Anyway, imagine him missing his own son's funeral.'

Luke paused and listened to the water running over the pebbles, gurgling and splashing around the larger rocks midstream.

'I've been thinking that Gary's disappearance does throw my own pet theory into doubt, of him being behind those phone calls and break-ins, rather than make some Ruthwell connection.'

'It's still possible though, isn't it?'

She glanced up at him. 'But less likely. It may be easy to go to ground in a city like Leeds, but if Gary had been hanging around Hawkshead in an unbalanced state of mind, waiting to pounce, surely someone would have spotted him?' Idly she picked up small pebbles and began to turn them over in her palm.

'I'm worried about Julia and Frank Edwards,' Luke confessed. 'Her especially. She seems so absolutely determined to hold Ruthwell to account.'

'It's her way of coping, that's all. When we have something dreadful to face up to, we resort to a particular manner. With Julia it's the don't-argue-with-me, I-have-scientific-proof routine. Really, she's still devastated by Louise's death.'

'And with Gary Wood it's drink,' Luke agreed. He was pleased to see a heron standing ankle-deep on the opposite bank; a bird which Laura had told him was a regular visitor both winter and summer. 'What is it with Peter Earle?'

'Don't-let-the-bastards-grind-you-down.' Laura kicked off her shoes and waded into the cool water. Her hair shone with copper and auburn glints in the dappled light.

Summer suits her, Luke thought. 'What's mine?' he asked. 'My way of coping?'

'Barricades of facts and figures.'

To prove my own point of view, he thought with a sinking heart.

'And mine is keeping the emotional doors tight shut,' Laura told him. 'It means neither of us has been absolutely honest with the other.'

'You've often kept me at arm's length,' he said quietly. 'And I don't want to be.'

'Me neither.' Laura turned and waded back towards him. 'But you're going to have to make allowances. I haven't had much practice at coming out from behind the barricades.'

Luke met her and embraced her. 'Things have been pretty complicated.'

'"Have been". Past tense,' she murmured.

He kissed her, then moved his arm round her waist to walk back to the Grange. Through the warm peace, above the rippling river and the gentle evening bird-song, Laura said, 'I love you, Luke.'

He absorbed the words as they walked, welcomed them like sunshine on his skin.

CHAPTER THIRTY-THREE

Not out of the woods yet, by any means. Francesca told Harry to stay where he was in the car, not to move a muscle while she went into the medical centre to talk to Laura.

He hunched down inside his jacket, staring at the dashboard as if he hated the round dials.

'Harry, I mean it. If I find you gone when I come back out, that's the end as far as I'm concerned. You hear?' She'd got out and slammed the door, then thrust her head back inside to issue the final warning.

His clenched teeth had made nerves in his jaw flicker, his face was pale, his eyes screwed up and looking straight ahead.

Giving up on getting any reply, Francesca left him and marched into reception. This was not the time for self-doubt and recriminations. She thrust open the door and glanced around the empty waiting area.

Sheila Knowles looked up in surprise. 'Piers is out on a home visit.'

'Is Laura in?'

'Just back from the hospital. Shall I page her?'

'No, thanks. I need to see her right away. Keep an eye on Harry out in the car for me, will you? If he makes a move, give me a shout.' She was half-way across the room when Laura, apparently having heard the interruption, came to her door and invited her in.

'It's OK, this is nothing to do with the pregnancy,'

Francesca reassured her, refusing a seat. 'We're planning to go ahead after all and I feel fine.'

'You don't look or sound fine,' Laura commented. 'Are you sure Piers and you have worked things out?'

'We're getting there. You've no idea how grateful I am to you, Laura.' She thought of Harry and how long it would be before he took off. Yet it was so difficult to come out with it cold.

'What about the depression? Do you need to discuss treatment?' Laura looked puzzled.

Francesca shook her head. 'Thanks, but no. I seem to be through the worst, but it's still close enough to know that I never want to feel like that again.' She shook her head at the recent memory. 'It was like being paralysed, waking up each morning, trying to pull myself together just enough to get through the day and being really frightened that I wasn't going to be able to.'

'It's very common,' Laura reassured her. 'And it does respond to treatment if you should ever feel you needed it. We're linked up with a counselling service based in Wingate.'

'Thanks.' She paused. How was she going to tell Laura the real reason for her visit?

'Piers has seemed a lot better since you came back,' Laura said, to fill the silence.

Francesca nodded. 'He's being considerate, more easy-going.' She bit her lip. 'That's what makes it so hard. We get over one crisis and now here's another.'

'Is this to do with Harry?'

'Yes. I've got him waiting outside.' She slumped back, her resolution draining away. 'I know I shouldn't be taking up your time.'

'No, no, it's fine.'

Francesca stood up and glanced out of the window. Sure enough, Harry still sat sullenly in the car.

'Look, if you want me to talk to Harry and offer him some

counselling we'll have to make a proper appointment, I'm afraid.'

'There's something I have to show you!' Agitatedly, Francesca turned towards her. 'I can't tell Piers. It'll finish him, I know it will.'

'Steady on. That's what you thought last time, remember? It was not including Piers in your decision about the baby that was at the root of the problem. And you should know this time that you don't have to protect him, whatever it is.'

Francesca stooped to pick a bundle of untidy papers held together by an elastic band out of her bag. 'I found these in Harry's room.'

'What are they?'

'Case notes.' Francesca swallowed, frightened of the storm that was about to break. 'And letters to you from Rudi Grey.'

'About Catherine Earle and Elliot Wood?'

She nodded again. 'Harry stole them from your car – and your radio and the cash from your house.'

'Harry?'

'He's admitted it. He forced another boy to join in. I'm telling you the truth, Laura. After everything you've done for us, I'm here to tell you that Harry is the thief.'

It was like tipping over the first domino in a standing row. Francesca told Laura, who went straight to Philip for advice, who inevitably said Piers should be told. Philip brought them all together as soon as Piers got back from his home visit, having persuaded Harry Chandler to come in from the car.

'You can lay off the "how-could-you" and "why-did-you-do-it" stuff,' Harry told Piers. 'I already got all that from Mum. Just report me to the police and get it over with.'

'No way!' Laura was the first to speak. She went up to Harry and forced him to look at her. 'You're the one who's stolen from me and wrecked my house. I need to get you to face that fact.'

Harry stared back.

'I'm not going to let you walk off without telling me why. Why me?'

He shrugged. 'Why not?'

'Harry!' Francesca longed for him to break down and say he was sorry.

Piers stood by the door, looking on helplessly.

'That's just not good enough.' Laura stood over Harry. 'OK, so the car radio's gone – so what? I get it back on the insurance. But why the letters and case notes?'

He glared back at her, mouth curling into a sneer, shoulders slouched.

'No one sees them,' she cried. 'They're private. Don't you think those two families had enough on their plate without you getting your hands on what no one but they should have known?'

'I never even looked at the poxy notes. I only took them to make you think one of that Ruthwell mob had done it.'

'So, you just shoved the papers under your bed. And the radio wasn't any use to you, was it?' She shook with rage. 'You couldn't sell it, so you came back to the house to see what else you could lay your hands on.'

'Dead easy. No one was around.'

'Listen.' She pressed him back towards the window. 'You want to know what it's like to have someone break into your house and pore over your stuff? It's not the money that gets stolen or the broken window that matters. It's the sick feeling you get when you know a stranger has pried and poked into every corner of your life.

'A place that felt safe for me isn't any more. So where do I go now when I want peace and quiet? When do I stop looking over my shoulder wondering who's hiding in the next room, waiting for me at the top of the stairs?'

Harry was at the window, leaning against the pane. 'I only took thirty stupid quid!'

'Fool! Stupid little fool!' Piers lunged forward to grab his son, pushing Laura out of the way and clutching the neck of Harry's T-shirt.

Francesca cried out but couldn't stop him.

Harry pushed him off and slid sideways, wrenching his T-shirt free. 'Lay off me!' He stood up straight and tried to regain his sneer.

Piers lunged again. This time he forced Harry back to the wall, pinning his forearm against the boy's chest. 'This is bullying, see? This is what you did to the little kids at school feels like. This is how Joe felt when you kicked him.'

'Let go!' The cry was high and scared.

Piers released his grip and watched Harry sink and tilt sideways, his tough front shattered. He was gasping for breath.

'This is down to me,' Piers told the others. 'I should have done that when it all first started, instead of letting it get out of hand.'

'Yeah, that's right. It's your fault!' Harry hit out at his father, his voice cracked, punctuated by sobs. '"Do this, do that, don't waste my time!"'

Francesca saw Piers freeze. She felt sick with the sudden swings of accusation and counter-accusation.

'"Yes, sir, no, sir!"' Harry yelled. He went round behind Laura towards the door. 'We had to do everything you said, didn't we? You were always right. But it doesn't work like that, not any more.' Harry's hand was on the doorknob, his face white with fury. 'Ask Mum!' he yelled. 'Ask her what it's like living with someone like you!'

'Let him go,' Francesca insisted. 'We'll find him later. He'll soon realise that now it's all come out there's nowhere for him to run.'

'There's the whole of Ravensdale for a start.' Once he'd

recovered from his shock, Piers had arranged for Laura and Philip to cover his evening surgery, then set off in the direction of the river with Francesca.

'He's on foot and he hasn't any money with him. He can't get far.' It was mid-afternoon; a cool, grey day after several gloriously sunny ones. Though her face was still burning with shame over the public row, and she was desperately praying that Harry wouldn't do anything foolish or dangerous, she began to work out their son's options. 'He could walk things out of his system. In which case he'll head somewhere remote where no one will see him.'

'Or he could try hitching a lift out of the valley.' Piers's voice was strained. 'It could be that he's planning to get right away.'

'But where?' As they drove slowly along the riverside and down the lane past Abbey Grange, Francesca's sense of alarm heightened. What would happen to Harry if he cut loose without money? 'You don't think he doubled back home to collect some cash, do you?' she said suddenly.

'It's worth a try.' Piers turned the car in the narrow road. They took the back way to Merton, past Hawkshead Hall, up to Haresby Farm and over the top. 'Was he right about me?' Piers asked, once they were on their way home. He'd been unexpectedly subdued since his son's outburst.

'Partly. You were always a bit heavy-handed.'

'But you didn't stop me?' He glanced at her. 'No, I don't suppose there was any point.'

As they climbed out of the valley she glimpsed two figures striking out along a bridle path, one on a bike, the other walking. Straight away she recognised Harry's loose, loping stride. She yelled at Piers to stop and, as he braked, the boys heard the car. The one on the bike jerked it round and cut across the rough grass towards Haresby Farm, while Harry kept going, breaking into a run to get away.

Swearing, Piers swung round to the left on to the bridle

path. The car crunched over gravel and lurched from side to side, quickly catching up with Harry, who swerved across the grass, stumbling as he went. Piers stopped, jumped out and yelled his name.

Francesca watched him give chase, then began to run after them. Fit and strong, fuelled by the outrage of what Harry had done to Laura, Piers soon caught him. Harry stopped, turned and sagged forward.

'What the ... what is this?' Piers demanded. He was gasping for breath, gesturing angrily towards the other fleeing figure. 'Is that the Earle boy?'

Harry sobbed through grating breaths. 'Leave me alone!'

'What's Adam Earle got to do with this?'

Over at the farmhouse, Francesca saw Peter Earle come out of the barn to intercept Adam. The boy looked startled, then sullen and defeated. Within seconds they set off towards Piers, Harry and Francesca.

'For God's sake!' Francesca breathed.

'I only came up to warn him,' Harry gabbled. 'I promised Adam I wouldn't dob him in.'

The schoolboy phrase shook Francesca. 'What do you mean?'

'I'm saying it was just me – no one else.'

'Adam was with you?' Piers turned from one to the other. He strode to meet the Earles. 'Do you know what's going on?' he asked the father.

'Not a clue. Except I'm aware that Adam's been skiving again.' Peter Earle's face was dark and angry.

'It was me. I made him do it. I can get him to do anything I say.' Harry was suddenly cool and full of bravado.

Adam Earle was white with fear. He seemed much smaller than Harry, who had drawn himself up defiantly.

'Adam, did you break into Dr Grant's house with Harry?' Piers demanded.

'Shut up,' Harry warned. He went up to Peter Earle and

206

spelled it out once more. 'I forced him to do it. Take me to the police, I don't care,' he told Francesca. 'But leave Adam out of it. He doesn't count.'

'Will they press charges?' Philip asked Francesca on the phone. He'd heard the latest news about the break-ins via Laura and rung to find out how things were.

'I don't know. They took full statements from both Adam and Harry. The sergeant says he'll have to file a report with the DPP. It's likely the case will go before a juvenile court.' Saying the words made her feel hopeless.

'I'm sorry,' Philip said quietly. 'But Harry will learn from this, believe me.'

'Let's hope we all will.' She let Piers take the phone from her and listened as he took up the conversation.

'What about Laura?' he asked. 'How is she?'

'You know. Quiet. It came as a shock. But Luke's with her.'

'Philip, since we got back from the police station I've been thinking about the practice. There's no getting away from it, Harry's behaviour puts us in a bad light.'

Francesca guessed what was coming.

As Philip evidently made conciliatory noises on the other end of the line, Piers pushed on. 'No. It's good of you to call this a temporary blip. But it's not so much the fact that it lays us open to gossip. It's more Laura I'm thinking of. If Harry had chosen someone else's car and house it might have been different. But you saw how she was and I can hardly blame her.'

Francesca had to turn away, to go outside into the garden. Still, she heard Piers's voice pressing on with what he'd planned to say. 'Yes, Fran feels the same as me about it. We won't be able to hold up our heads after this. It's too humiliating.'

Turning back, reaching the doorway as Piers delivered the news, Francesca closed her eyes and held on to the doorpost.

'I want to hand in my resignation, Philip. That's it. No argument. I want out.'

CHAPTER THIRTY-FOUR

When Laura had overcome the anger she felt over Harry Chandler, her thoughts turned to the Earles. 'How are they going to cope with this?' she asked Luke, who had come to Abbey Grange straight from prosecuting a case that afternoon in Leeds Crown Court.

'Let's go and see,' he suggested.

'We can't barge in.' She was reluctant to leave the garden and its cool evening shadows to face another trouble-torn situation.

'What makes you suppose you'd be barging in?'

Laura looked at her house, set in the flat valley bottom against the sheer rise of the scar. It appeared strong enough, square and solid, with its shallow Georgian roof and heavy cornerstones. But would she ever feel the same about it, she wondered. 'I don't suppose they want to see me right now.'

'Peter rang me at the office. He asked me to tell you he was sorry.' Luke interrupted her thoughts. 'Aren't you relieved to find out who did it?'

'A little bit.' But part of her wished the break-ins had in fact been one fragment of a big cover-up by faceless men who ran the country's nuclear industry, instead of this focus on two small domestic tragedies. Then she could have been justifiably angry instead of sorry for the perpetrators.

'At least it won't happen again.' Luke drew her to him. 'Even if it does weaken our conspiracy theory.'

She smiled at him. 'It could easily have been the Ruthwell

people. Do you remember that elderly woman who played a big part in the peace movement years ago? She was found murdered in her country home, and for years and years the CND people tried to prove it was linked to the weapons industry.'

'Were you afraid the same thing would happen to you?' Luke held her tight.

'It did cross my mind.'

'And the phone calls didn't help.' He leaned his face against her hair, swaying with her and looking up at Ravenscar. 'You don't think Harry Chandler could be behind those too?'

'No.' She was certain. 'The phone calls are different. There's absolutely no way that voice belongs to a kid.'

'He hasn't made any more since he threatened you with an accident?'

Laura shook her head. 'But I'm still wary when I see cars lurking round bends or parked in farm gates.'

Luke hugged her more tightly. 'What about Gary Wood? Do you still think he's in the picture?'

'I just don't know any more.' She'd been so wrong about her burglars that she'd lost all sense of who might have made the threats. 'Why? What have you heard?'

'Nothing. Well, something that Mike Jackson mentioned when I had to call in at the station this morning. Not about Gary, but about some character who used to work at Ruthwell.'

'A suspect?' Laura moved away. 'Why didn't you tell me?'

'Suspect is too strong a word. They're investigating a letter written to the editor of the *Yorkshire Post*. It comes across as pretty unbalanced, condemning our pressure group as interfering busybodies, identifying himself as Geoffrey Whittaker, a worker at the Ruthwell plant when Julia Edwards and co. carried out the lab tests on the dead animals. The editor couldn't print it because it was so defamatory. He handed it over to the police instead.'

'And now they think he's behind the calls?'

'His choice of insult is similar. They've checked his phone calls via BT, but of course he wouldn't have been stupid enough to use his own phone.' Luke held her hand as they walked towards the house. 'As far as the police are aware, Whittaker could be a one-off nutcase who's got the whole thing out of perspective. He must imagine we're out to destroy the entire industry and his job along with it.'

'Aren't we?' Laura could fell the gap opening between them again.

Luke frowned. 'No. What we're after is accountability.'

'Accountability.' She repeated it slowly and nodded once.

He swung towards her, put an arm round her shoulder and steered her towards his car. 'Come on, let Mike Jackson work on his new line of enquiry and get back to us if there's anything in it. We'll drive up to Haresby and tell Adam Earle you've let him off the hook.'

'It's really shaken us,' Peter Earle admitted. 'Just when you think nothing worse can happen, along it comes and flattens you.'

He spoke to them in the barn where tractors and farm implements were stored, out of hearing of the rest of the family. Swifts swooped and darted in and out of the wide barn entrance, then soared up into a pink-gold mackerel sky.

'Here comes Adam now.' Luke had spotted him crossing the yard. In the background, Sonia Earle looked out from a side window with Catherine.

'Mum says I've to say sorry.' Adam stopped a few yards from where they stood and spoke in a toneless voice. He tried but failed to look Laura in the eye.

'Say it as if you mean it,' his father urged. 'I'm sorry . . . you're sorry . . . your mother's sorry. It doesn't alter the fact of what you've done.'

'What you did was upsetting,' Laura agreed. She felt none

211

of the surge of anger she'd let loose on Harry Chandler. 'But I'll get over it pretty soon. On the other hand, it might take you and your mum and dad a bit longer.'

Adam's lip trembled and he kicked at a loose stone. 'I never meant to do it. I thought Harry was joking when we first talked about it, so I went along with it for a laugh. That was on the Saturday. I'd met him up at the tarn.'

'And when I caught you skiving and you said you were alone, you were really with Harry?' Peter seemed shocked that the boys had preplanned it all.

Adam nodded. 'I couldn't dob Harry in.' His face coloured a deep, troubled red. 'I never thought he'd do the break-in. Then, when we met up and went to Abbey Grange I found out he was serious.'

'Pathetic.' Peter Earle was still furious. 'What did Harry do? Press a button to program you?'

Laura could see Adam struggling to keep control. He took a deep breath and plunged on. 'He kind of dared me.'

'And in spite of everything your mother and I taught you, you went along with it?' His father turned away.

'I won't do it again. I only did it because I was stupid. I'm not blaming Harry. In a funny kind of way, I knew he was daring me. And I said yeah as a dare back, just to see . . . to find out . . .'

'What?' Laura asked.

'If he's as tough as he reckons. We dared each other and it just got out of hand.' Adam paused, then managed to meet her eye. 'I'm sorry, Dr Grant.'

'Thanks, Adam.' She smiled back and drew Luke forward. 'Count yourself lucky. Here's a good solicitor to give you some advice.'

Luke took Adam into the house to talk through what would happen when the case came to court. Sonia crossed paths with them on their way out, while Catherine remained alone at the window, a puzzled spectator.

212

'I don't know what to say.' Sonia was on the verge of tears as she approached Laura.

'Nothing. It's fine.' Laura grasped her hand. 'Adam's explained. I'm sure he won't do anything like it ever again.'

'We should have paid more attention,' Sonia murmured. 'We didn't give him enough of our time. We will in future.'

Peter Earle hadn't spoken for a while, but now it seemed he'd come to a decision. 'Funny how you ignore what's going on under your nose when you're caught up in something big.'

Like Ruthwell, burning him up from the inside, taking over his life so that he didn't have to contemplate the possibility of Catherine dying. But now it looked to Laura as if there was a change.

'What are you saying?' Sonia's face began to clear.

'I don't feel we're getting anywhere with this nuclear stuff. Oh yes, we caused a fuss with Jim's article and started people thinking. Then Julia came out with her story and you'd think that would be it; something would have to be done.

'But no. Look what they came back with. No risk to public health. They investigate our Catherine's and poor little Elliot's cases, and what do they call them? A coincidence.' Peter's voice was flat with disgust. 'And soon they'll find all sorts of other reasons why our kids have cancer ...'

Radon, Laura thought.

'. . . But the fact is, we'll probably never know.' He looked at Sonia. 'You were right. I'm going to leave it to others to fight for us.'

'Don't give up completely.' Sonia grasped his hand. 'We'll keep on fighting!'

He raised his head and nodded. 'For Catherine?'

'And for Adam,' Sonia added. 'We'll help her to get well, see him through this bad patch, then we'll all be a family again.'

'You're shocked. You're not expecting another call from me.'

Tuesday evening. A message on Laura's answer-machine. Her heart jolted as she gripped the receiver.

'You've been getting too cosy with that boyfriend of yours staying over.'

Whose voice? Whose eyes following her?

'This is just so you don't rest easy in your nice double bed.'

'Stop!' she pleaded, powerless to turn off the machine.

'Too cosy; too easy for an interfering, stuck-up bitch. But you know your boyfriend can't save you, or the police. I can get to you whenever I want. They can't stop me.'

A click, a discordant tone, three sharp pips.

Luke came in as the message ended. He saw Laura standing hunched over the phone, punched the playback button and listened again.

'Shocked . . . cosy . . . nice double bed.'

'That's it!' Luke held on to her, his voice implying that this was one phone call too many. 'We'll get him this time if it's the last thing I do!'

CHAPTER THIRTY-FIVE

The tiny white coffin stood in the nave of St Michael and All Angels. Fluted stone columns supported soaring arches, bright light filtered in through rose windows to either side. Behind the coffin, a brass crucifix above the altar glinted and reflected red and blue beams on to the white altar cloth.

The big church in the grounds of the abbey was full. Mourners had come over from Askby, and down from the hilltop villages of Ginnersby and Waite. The families most closely involved in Ravensdale's cancer scare – the Edwardses and the Earles – were represented, as were members of the pressure group such as Luke and Jim Conroy. Laura stood with them, two pews behind Hannah Wood.

Piers was missing, she noticed, but Philip was here with Juliet, beside Gerald Scott and his wife, Janet.

And most of Hawkshead seemed to have chosen to pay their last respects to a little boy whom they'd scarcely known, but who represented a significant loss within the community. The death of a child always called forth strong emotions, and in Elliot's case the tragedy had been heightened by controversy and blame.

'Suffer little children' was the vicar's theme.

Laura scanned the faces in the church as the last hymn played. There were many tears. She gazed again at the coffin. It had one spray of white lilies from Hannah. The rest of the flowers were banked against the altar step and by the church door.

215

'The Lord's my shepherd . . . He layeth me down to die . . .'

The coffin was lifted from its rest and carried shoulder-high down the aisle. 'In death's dark vale . . .' Laura saw Hannah stumble as she stepped out to follow her son. Her mother and father supported her, then she straightened up and walked alone. As she passed Laura her gaze flickered. She bowed her head and went on.

Outside, the grave was prepared. A sheltered spot had been chosen, close to the west wall of the abbey, on a slope overlooking the river. People gathered round, hands clasped, anticipating the moment when the white casket would disappear from sight. A strong breeze buffeted them and there was a sprinkling of cold, light rain.

Hannah moved to her position at the foot of the grave. She watched every detail as the undertaker's men took the lilies from the coffin, put straps in place and swung it over the deep, smooth-sided hole, lowering it to the sound of the Lord's Prayer. She swayed forward.

'Ashes to ashes.' Black soil fell on to the pure white box. 'Dust to dust.'

Hannah trembled and cried. She trickled a handful of earth on Elliot's coffin, then stepped back into her mother's arms.

At the close of the sad, dignified ritual the ranks of mourners broke up. People dispersed in different directions, murmuring sorrowfully. Jacqui Shepherd clung on to her daughter and accepted condolences, but her husband, David, made his way towards Laura.

'Hannah would like a word,' he told her quietly. Grief seemed to have stripped his voice of expression, his face was blank.

Laura nodded and followed him, picking her way against the flow of mourners who were heading away from the graveside towards the church gate. As she reached the mother and grandmother, she grew aware of a solitary figure, instantly recognisable as Gary Wood, standing on the wooden footbridge about a hundred metres downstream from the abbey.

'Hannah?' Laura spoke softly, touching her on the shoulder.

She pulled away from her mother's arms. 'Gary's on the bridge,' she told Laura.

'Yes. I've just seen him.' He seemed to be staring at Hannah and her parents while the mourners trailed away between the ancient gravestones.

Raindrops spattered on to the green canvas sheet that covered the mound of earth at the graveside. 'Did you tell him?' Hannah whispered to Laura.

'No. I couldn't find out where he was. But he must have heard.'

'Did he come into the church?'

'I don't think so.' Laura imagined Gary Wood watching the arrival of the funeral cortège from the far river bank, from the cover of beech trees clinging to the steep slope. He must have stayed there during the funeral service and only emerged after the interment, as mourners began to leave. 'But he's here now.'

'Where he's not wanted,' David Shepherd said suddenly. 'The man doesn't deserve to be allowed anywhere near.' He set off across the worn mounds, towards a side gate in the low churchyard wall, obviously intending to confront his son-in-law.

Laura saw Luke run to cut him off and reason with him. Hannah, still gazing at her son's coffin in the ground, seemed not to have noticed.

'Hannah?' The vicar offered his hand. He appeared to Laura to want to move her away from any possible trouble.

'Come on, love, it's all over.' Gently her mother led her back towards the church porch.

Laura could see Luke remonstrating with Hannah's father. Suddenly Gary turned and began to run towards the church.

Crossing the graveyard to intercept him, she met him at the side entrance.

He shoved roughly at the kissing-gate, which Laura refused to open for him.

'Gary!' Close to, she had the full impact of his unshaven face, his frantic eyes.

'Let me through. I want to talk to her.' He shoved again, then collapsed sobbing on to the wooden railings.

It was Laura's first sight of him since their argument outside the medical centre. He was thinner and more unkempt, his dark-brown hair fell forward over his forehead and his clothes were filthy. Glancing over her shoulder, she saw Luke still trying to deal with David Shepherd.

'They buried my little boy!' Gary cried, raising his head and shaking it.

She reached out her hand, but he thrust it away.

'I never even saw him.'

'He died peacefully.'

Gary stared at her, tears trickling down his face. 'A baby! Let me see him!' He pushed against her, but more feebly this time.

'Later.' She wanted Hannah and the Shepherds to be gone before she let him in.

'Let me talk to Hannah.'

'Not now.' Laura stood firm. 'She couldn't cope. The funeral's been too much for her.'

'Is that what she told you to say?'

'No. It's what I'm telling you, Gary. Why not wait until everyone's gone, then spend some time by the grave? After that, if you still want to see Hannah, you can sort out a time and a place.' She became more insistent as she heard the father-in-law's remonstrations grow louder. 'Shall I tell her that's what you want?'

Banging the gate against the post, Gary swore. He let go of

it, turned and set off at a ragged run across the rough grass as David Shepherd arrived.

'It's OK.' Laura took a deep breath of relief. Up by the church porch the vicar was still comforting Hannah.

'But it wasn't OK,' she told Luke later, as he drove her back to the medical centre after the brief gathering at Jacqui and David Shepherd's house at Town End. 'Gary Wood looked dreadful. Goodness knows where he's been living since he quit the lodge. He's not been eating or sleeping by the look of him. And in terms of mental stability I'd say he's right on the very edge. One more thing and he'll tip over.'

'And do what?' Luke leaned out of the car window as Laura stooped to kiss him goodbye. 'He can't change what's happened.'

'No, but it's what happens next that I'm worried about. What if Hannah goes on refusing to see him?'

'Which is quite likely, if she stops to listen to what her parents are telling her.'

'Exactly. That could be the thing that plunges him into the next desperate act.' She straightened up and braced herelf to face an afternoon at work, gazing up at Ravenscar. 'The fact is, I'm worried he might be suicidal.' She could imagine Gary Wood being pushed to that, now that Elliot was dead and he had nothing left to live for.

CHAPTER THIRTY-SIX

'Laura? It's Luke. I'm at Merton police station. Give me a ring when you get back.'

It was late on Saturday afternoon, the day after Elliot Wood's funeral. A misty rain covered the window in fine droplets and had kept market trade in the High Street to a minimum.

His voice must have conveyed an urgency that Laura couldn't ignore. Five minutes later she was on the line. 'Hi, it's me. I just got in.'

'Listen.' Luke took a deep breath. 'I was called over to see a client who's been pulled in for a break-in at a chemist's on the High Street last night. We're waiting for him to be interviewed any time now. But that's not what I want to tell you.'

'What then?' She sounded tired and unsettled, was probably still feeling low after the funeral. The rain didn't help; it pulled down the mist, which settled over the horizon and slid down the sides of the valley.

'Mike Jackson was here when I arrived. He told me the Ruthwell police have interviewed this Geoffrey Whittaker character.' He picked up the hesitation on her part and pressed on. 'Don't panic. Just listen. They asked him about the phone calls.'

'And?'

'As they thought, he's an oddball. Apparently writes dozens of letters to the local paper about anything from dogs fouling the pavement to rhyming couplets on ideas for celebrating the millennium.'

'So, he's not the one?'

'They were fairly sure he wasn't. Then they got BT to trace that last call you had.' Luke hesitated, waiting for a response. 'Laura?'

'I'm still here. Did they come up with a number?'

'Yes. It was from a call-box, as you'd expect.'

'Whereabouts?'

'In Ginnersby.' Luke pictured her reaction, alone in the house. He wished he'd driven over to tell her face to face. 'Laura, are you there?'

'Yes. Go on.'

'Mike's pretty sure the caller has to be a local man ... Laura?'

'I'm still here. What do I do now?'

'Stay put. Mike's been called out on another job, and I have to deal with this joker's not-guilty stand on the chemist break-in. But Mike wants to come and see you later tonight.'

'To ask more questions?'

'Yes. So don't go out until one or the other of us gets back, OK? Just sit tight.' The rain drifted in fine drops against the window, obscuring his view.

'But I won't be able to tell Mike anything new. What's the point?' Laura's voice sounded strained.

'The point is the threats are coming from within the area. I'm back to thinking it could be Gary Wood.' He didn't want to panic her more than she already was, but on the other hand he had to make sure she stayed inside the house. 'Lock the doors, OK? I'll be on my way as soon as I can.'

'But he's in Leeds.'

'Not yesterday, he wasn't. Anyway, I've told Mike about him and his precarious state of mind. He thinks we should make him a definite possibility.'

There was a frightened pause. 'How long will you be?'

'Two hours maximum. Stay inside. Don't go out.' Six-thirty. He would be there well before dark.

'I won't move,' she promised. 'And Luke . . . be as quick as you can.'

Outside, the rain smothered the crumbling abbey walls and mist gathered damply around the crosses and stone angels of St Michaels and All Angels churchyard.

But even in this dismal weather, if Laura climbed the stairs and stood at the landing window, she could look down to the western wall of the church and see there the yellow, white and red wreaths stacked high against the newly filled grave of Elliot Wood.

After Luke's phone call she tried to close her mind to all suppositions. She turned on the radio in one room, the TV in another. When the phone rang again she answered it normally and spoke to Francesca Chandler. Piers and she had been talking non-stop, she told Laura. Harry's suspension from school had come before the governors for review and the vicar, Marsden Barraclough, had spoken up on his behalf. He'd persuaded the board to interview the boy in person and a date had been set for two weeks hence. And now Francesca wanted to thank Laura properly for being so understanding over Harry.

'We want Piers to stay with the practice,' Laura insisted. 'If you, he and Harry can ride the storm of a court case, which will be a seven-day wonder and then no doubt forgotten, I'm absolutely sure we'll gain a lot from keeping him with us.'

'That's wonderful, Laura.'

'Well, you both know that's how we feel. Let's all talk about it again on Monday.'

'And, Laura – I want to say thank you for, well, everything! For being such a good friend to me.'

Laura closed her eyes and took a deep breath. 'I'm just glad things are getting better.'

Typically, she put the phone down without giving away her own problem. In the lane outside a car approached.

It slowed by the gate, then stopped. It couldn't be Luke; it was too soon and he would have brought his car straight into the drive. Perhaps it was Mike Jackson. Laura went upstairs to look out of the bedroom window.

She caught sight of a red roof beyond the high stone wall. A van roof or the top of a pick-up truck. She leaned forward against the sill to steady herself.

There was a jolt of adrenalin, then she clicked into action, running down the stairs to check that the side door was locked. She waited in the kitchen, listening for the crunch of footsteps on the gravel drive, not hearing any.

Instead, the catch on the kitchen door eased and clicked. Laura turned to look, realising that the intruder must have cut across the front lawn and round the side of the house, hoping to slip in. She tried to remember the Merton station number, was flicking through to the back page of her diary by the phone when the window smashed and shards of glass flew across the room.

Gary Wood was hauling himself up on to the sill and through the jagged frame, carrying a shotgun, his face desperate and haggard.

She picked up the receiver and began to dial 999.

He lunged, tore the phone from her hand and swiped the diary to the floor with the butt of his gun. Then he swung it at her, catching her in the ribs. She doubled over and fell to the floor.

He grabbed her arm, dripping blood on to the shoulder of her white shirt from a cut on his forearm made by the glass. He dragged her to her feet, kept hold of her wrist and dragged her towards him.

Laura twisted and pulled back. She used her free hand to push him away, but he was stronger. She felt his blood soak through to her skin.

And his face was close to hers, his right hand clamped round her wrist, the shotgun held loose in the left. He drew it up and brought it through the narrow gap between them until the cold metal met her jaw.

'You carry on like this and I'll blow your head off.'

She felt the barrel press against the underside of her chin and froze.

'Back off,' he yelled. 'That's right, towards the door.'

She stumbled against a chair and knocked it over. Her feet crunched on broken glass. Then, when her back was against the door, he let go of her wrist and, keeping the gun in position, he turned the latch and opened the door.

'Luke's on his way. He could be here any moment.'

'You'd better hope not, for your own sake.' He shoved the gun more firmly into position, still making her walk backwards along the side of the house. 'And for his.'

'Where are you taking me?'

No answer this time. No hurry as he backed her across the lawn. He didn't even check to see whether the coast was clear.

'They'll find you, Gary. Stop now, please!' She felt herself edged through the gate and up against the parked pick-up truck.

'Get in.' He flung open the door and forced her inside, keeping the long barrel of the gun aimed at her head. 'And don't talk.'

She sank against the seat with a gasp. In a world that wasn't making sense, there was blood on her shirt, a man with a shotgun, a car engine starting, the horizon of Ravenscar beginning to slide away.

'Don't try to get out,' he warned, the gun across his knees. His wheels skidded and churned up the grass verge, then he shot on to the road. He looked straight ahead, leaning forward, building up speed.

'If you move I'll drive us off the road and we're both dead.'

It was the last thing he said. No explanations, no reasons.

An oncoming car braked and veered to get out of his way. He headed past the abbey and the churchyard with its new, flower-banked grave, through the square and, climbing steeply along Town Head, towards open country via Hawk Fell, Oxtop and the wild moors of Ginnersby beyond.

CHAPTER THIRTY-SEVEN

'An abduction usually has one of two motives behind it,' Mike Jackson explained to Luke. They stood in the wrecked kitchen at Abbey Grange, waiting for the CID inspector to arrive from Wingate. 'It's sometimes for financial gain, in which case we treat it as a grade-one emergency and put a secret operational response into play.'

'For God's sake!' Luke turned away and walked out into the rain. It had happened and he'd not done enough to prevent it. Why hadn't he left the client at the police station and moved to protect Laura the moment alarm bells had begun to sound? One feeble phone call to tell her to lock the doors; not enough!

'Or it has a sexual motive,' the inspector continued. He'd shown no reaction to the broken glass, the drops of dark-red blood on the flagged floor.

Luke shook his head. He knew all this only too well. How many cases of serial killings had he read up as a student? Didn't he know the criminal mind better than the next man, better even than Mike Jackson who pontificated now? 'How long before we can do something?'

'Back off, Luke. It's already happening. I've got two uniformed officers looking for witnesses in town and one at the station checking the registration details of Gary Wood's pick-up.' Jackson trod carefully over the pieces of glass and looked down at the smashed phone in the far corner of the room. 'The sexual motive can be mixed with revenge. Does Wood have a specific grudge against Dr Grant?'

Luke ran a hand over his face. 'She treated his son who's just died of leukaemia. Look, are we sure it is Gary Wood?' No one had seen the actual abduction. Luke had raced over to protect Laura, found the broken window and rung the police.

'Hang on.' The policeman turned his attention to his pager to pick up a crackling message. 'Witness in town saw a red pick-up drive through the square at speed just after five,' he relayed to Luke. 'My man's taken a statement, including the information that there was a woman passenger with long dark hair in the truck. The driver was thickset, dark-haired, wearing a navy-blue fleece jacket ... Ring any bells?'

'Gary Wood,' Luke groaned. 'Where was the truck heading?'

'Witness gave the direction as Town Head. After that, it's anybody's guess.'

'There's only one road you can take after Town Head,' Luke reminded him.

Hearing a car arrive, the inspector beckoned him along and went to the door to greet his boss. 'The Ginnersby road?'

Luke nodded and pulled out his own phone. He rang Directory Enquiries for Dick Metcalfe's number at Highfield Farm, dialled it and asked the old farmer if he'd noticed a red pick-up drive by an hour or so earlier.

The conversation was short and to the point. 'Yes,' he told Mike Jackson, clicking the off-button. 'Dick heard the truck coming up Hawk Fell, going like the clappers and kicking up a cloud of smoke. He recognised Gary's truck and guessed something was up.'

'You didn't tell him what?' the policeman checked. 'I don't want it to get around just yet – not before I've spoken to Wood's wife. It won't look good if she hears this from someone else.'

'I gather she's been staying in Town Head with her parents since the funeral. Gary probably drove past the house with Laura.' He stared with glazed eyes at the chaos in the kitchen, trying not to imagine what had got into Gary Wood's head. Absent-mindedly he stooped to pick up a chair that had tipped over in the struggle.

'Leave that where it is, if you don't mind,' Mike Jackson reminded him as he ushered in a short, white-haired man with strikingly sharp features.

They'd crossed paths often enough in court for Luke to recognise James Walton, the CID man from Wingate. He let the chair clatter back on to the flagstones, then passed on the information from Dick, which confirmed the town witness's sighting of the red pick-up. 'What now?' he demanded, staring at the blood on the floor and picturing, in spite of his efforts to keep his imagination in check, Laura's reaction as the kitchen window had shattered.

'Now we're sure who we're after, which makes life a lot easier for us,' the new, older man answered. 'Listen, Luke, you know Laura better than anyone. I need you to tell me how you think she'll stand up to an abduction situation. Might she try to talk Wood out of it if she gets the chance? Or is she likely to panic and do something stupid?'

Luke closed his eyes on the blood, the shattered glass, the overturned furniture. But the images in the darkness inside his head were too dangerous, too gruesome to bear. He opened them again and stared at the grey mist outside. 'Please God,' he breathed. 'Let her be safe.'

'I can't believe Gary will harm her.' Hannah Wood had reacted to the news with tears.

'This is the first time she's cried since Elliot died,' Jacqui Shepherd told Luke and Mike Jackson. 'Her world has fallen apart, yet she's done nothing except visit the bungalow once to stuff Gary's belongings into binliners and dump them in the front garden. She didn't touch a thing of little Elliot's. The rest of the time she just sits here and stares at the wall.'

'We've got to work out what's going on in his mind.' Mike

Jackson leaned towards the distraught younger woman and spoke slowly. 'You must have seen him upset at times. What does he do? Does he get violent?'

'He never hit me, if that's what you mean. Once or twice he gave Elliot a tap on the leg. I said he was too little to be smacked.' Hannah stared at the policeman. Her voice was a dead monotone punctuated by sighs.

'Was he out of control when he hit him?'

She looked blank. 'How do you mean?'

'Did he lose his temper?'

'No. It was a gentle tap. Gary loved Elliot.'

It was Jacqui Shepherd's turn to sigh and shake her head.

'He did,' Hannah insisted. 'He just wasn't strong enough to cope.'

'And if he didn't hit you when he was angry, what did he do?' Mike Jackson held to his line.

'He would shout.'

'Did he frighten you?'

'Sometimes. I knew to keep quiet then, until he calmed down. He would soon come round and say he was sorry.'

'So he isn't a violent man, but he can lose control. Would you say frequently or not?'

Luke saw Hannah shift uneasily in her seat under the pressure of the insistent questions. This time she shrugged and refused to answer.

'OK. We're trying to build up a profile of your husband that will assist us when we find him and Dr Grant. The other thing you can help us with is where he might have taken her.'

Hannah blinked and glanced at Luke, then at her mother. 'Have you tried the bungalow?'

'I've sent a general duties vehicle to take a look,' Jackson replied. 'But it's unlikely. For one thing, it's far too obvious. For another, Askby is by the river and Gary's truck was seen heading out of the Dale towards Ginnersby. What reason might he have to drive Dr Grant in that direction?'

She shifted again and appealed to Luke. 'Mr Altham, I don't know what's going on.'

'We know that, Hannah.' He sat across the small, prettily furnished front room, trying hard to hang on to his own sanity.

'I don't want to answer any more questions.'

'I understand. But please think about Laura for a moment. We're sure Gary's broken into Abbey Grange and kidnapped her. Imagine how terrified she must be.' He heard his voice crack, paused, then continued. 'So, if you can think of anywhere they might be ... anywhere at all ... or anything else that could possibly help us, tell us now.'

'I don't know!' She dropped her head and hid her face behind her long hair. 'Gary sometimes goes up on to Hawk Fell ...'

'What for?' Luke caught at the hesitation.

'He goes to Waite, to the rifle range. They do target practice there.'

Luke watched as Mike Jackson froze. 'Does Gary own a gun?' he asked.

Hannah kept her head down and nodded. 'A shotgun.'

'What kind?'

'I don't know. An assault rifle. It fires cartridges.'

'Does he have a licence?'

Luke stood up, his heart thumping. 'What difference ...?'

Jackson warned him to be quiet. 'I need to check the licence and make sure that the gun is where it should be, under lock and key. Hannah, you know that the new law introduced after Dunblane means that Gary should have handed the firearm over to a rifle club for safekeeping? Well, did he?'

'It was his father's gun.' She began to sob again. 'He's had it for years. There's never been any licence.'

'And he didn't hand it over when he should have?' The inspector had stood up and made his way to the door.

'No. He kept it in the wardrobe. I did nag him about it. I

230

asked him what would happen if Elliot got hold of it by mistake. He said it wasn't dangerous because he never kept it loaded. The cartridges were in our bedroom drawer.'

The details were a diversion, Luke realised, as if Hannah was still holding something back. He also knew through Jacqui Shepherd that Hannah had recently been home. 'Is the gun there now?' he asked.

Hannah moaned and covered her face with her hand. She bent forward almost double and began to rock her whole body. 'No. It's gone.'

'Come on.' Mike Jackson was out of the room, of the small terraced house and on to the street before Hannah had finished speaking. He ran to his car and talked rapidly into the phone. 'Serious Crime Unit, Inspector Walton, please. Sir, we have an armed abductor. Level 4 Emergency. Whereabouts of abductor not yet known.'

CHAPTER THIRTY-EIGHT

Laura felt the truck sway as Gary Wood swung it off the road at the top of Hawk Fell. He pulled at the wheel, swerving on to a shale track beyond the Edwardses' isolated house, half a mile or so before the village of Ginnersby. She recognised the rugged lie of the land despite the low clouds: the deep grooves in the hillside and the rough mounds of ugly stone debris ditched at arched entrances to shafts that led underground.

He drove hard down the track, throwing her violently from her seat so that she had to clutch at the door handle to save herself from slamming against the windscreen. The shotgun on his knee slid to the floor, barrel-first, the wooden butt lodged close up to the gear-stick, the trigger within reach.

He swerved again and the gun tipped against his leg. The new, green track was out of sight of the Edwardses' house, dipping down towards the lead mines and the ruins of the smelt mill. Rabbits started up from the cover of heather and bilberry bushes to either side of the track, zigzagged in front of the careering truck, then vanished into the undergrowth.

Laura hung on. She braced one arm against the dashboard and watched the crumbling walls and tall, square chimney loom up through the mist.

'Get out!' Gary slammed on the brakes, leaned across her lap and shoved her door open. 'Go on, get out!'

Shaking and dizzy, she did as she was told. She looked around at the hills, brownish in the fine rain, folding into one another, intersected by low stone walls. This could be her chance to escape.

He was backing the pick-up through an entrance into a nearby derelict shed. She stood on a low, flat mound covered in scrub, in the shadow of the tall chimney. There were two hundred metres of track and open space before she could climb a wall, duck down the other side and run under cover back to the road. The opposite direction took her along the green track deep into the valley. Off the track, the hillside was steep, with stretches of loose scree.

She heard the careless scrape of metal against stone as Gary backed the truck out of sight. Then the engine cut out and a door slammed. She began to run for the shelter of the wall.

He saw her and followed, his feet thudding on the compacted ground. Now was when he might use the gun. She forced herself to run faster as she heard him gain on her.

He came at her with his shoulder, charging from behind, bringing her down with his full weight on top of her. He recovered first, pointing the long barrel at her, ordering her up and back towards the mine.

'Where are you taking me?' He hadn't used the gun to stop her after all, though there was nothing except ruined mine buildings and open countryside for miles.

'Keep going.' He directed Laura back past the old shed where he'd hidden the truck, picked up a rucksack from the ground, then pushed her along the track deep into the valley. 'Now turn left.'

Her feet hit rough ground. There was a boarded-up, narrow arched entrance ahead that must lead to one of dozens of steeply sloping shafts once used by gangs of miners to reach the levels below.

'Stop,' he said.

The entrance was low, set into the hill. He went forward and kicked at the wood with his heavy boot, which splintered and split. Beyond was a pitch-black tunnel.

'Gary, please!' She resisted as he came back and grabbed her by the arm. 'It's not safe!' Decades had passed since the lead mine had been worked. There would be roof-falls, floods, crumbling edges to unseen, vertical shafts.

He kept hold of her and pulled her close as he had done at the house. She could feel his breath on her face. 'Get one thing straight: safe or not, I don't care. This is where we're going.'

Laura struggled to stay in the light. Being in the dark with Gary Wood terrified her even more than his gun. Once more, she felt the warm trickle of blood from the cut on his arm.

He dragged her towards the tunnel. The old arched entrance was mossy, dripping and oozing soot. She fought hard, kicking at his legs, wrenching her wrist as she twisted and pulled away. It made no difference. The dank atmosphere hit her as she stumbled against rusting iron debris at the mouth of the tunnel and fell to her knees. Daylight faded. They were inside the shaft.

Rusting iron tracks curved ahead in the yellow beam of a torch which Gary Wood had taken from the rucksack. The floor of the tunnel was strewn with stones and pieces of metal, the rough surface of the vaulted walls wet to the touch. There were muddy puddles between the rails, a steady drip of water from the roof.

They walked a hundred paces, stooping forward through the low shaft. Laura counted each one. A hundred paces out of sight, away from the sounds of the outside world. Then the level changed and they began to climb a gradual slope; fifty more paces, stumbling against an ancient metal cart that had been derailed and tipped on to its side.

'How much further?' Laura had hurt her leg on the edge of the cart.

Gary flashed the torch up the slope. The beam picked out more upturned carts, a twist in the rails where the rock floor had subsided. Then there was a right-hand turning and beyond that, only dimly visible, one to the left.

'We'll take the left,' he ordered.

A hundred and fifty paces from the entrance, then the carts; fifty more paces, then left. Laura desperately made a map in her mind. She repeated the numbers as he shoved her forward, tried to pick out memorable features; the carts, the twisted section of track, two giant iron hooks hammered into the wall as they turned out of the main shaft into a side tunnel.

'What's wrong?' Gary noticed her limping and leaning against the wall for support. He brought the torch beam down on to her legs and feet, flashed it up the length of her body to her face.

'I've hurt my ankle.' She knew she'd gashed it against the rusty metal.

'It's bleeding.' He held the beam steady.

'So is your arm.' The forearm that held the shotgun was streaked crimson.

'OK, we stop here.' The decision was sudden, an erratic change of mind. Gary had obviously intended to take her much deeper into the mine. He dumped the rucksack on the damp ground. 'Sit,' he ordered.

She slumped down, sickened by the fetid air, trying to ignore the pain of her ankle. Her damp hair fell forward across her cheek. Her hands, as she pushed it back, were trembling. She must try to clear her head, think what tactic to use.

Gary propped the shotgun against the wall and sat opposite. 'I'm turning the torch off,' he warned.

'No, please!' A flare-up of dread at the thought of total, dank darkness.

He shone it on her face. 'To save the batteries.'

She shielded her eyes. 'No. Leave it on. Tell me what you want.'

'I've got what I want. You.' Behind the glare of the torch, his voice was thick with contempt.

'It won't take them long to find us.' The truck was badly hidden in the roofless stone shed, someone must have seen which way they were headed.

'Good.' He kept the torch aimed directly into her eyes. 'You still want this torch kept on?'

'Yes. Point it away from my face, Gary.'

He did as she asked, letting the light linger on her mouth, her neck, her breasts.

'Why is it good if they find us?' Laura sat perfectly still, hardly breathing.

'Because there's no point making it too hard, is there?'

'Why not?'

'I might want to talk to them, or I might not.' He slanted the beam at her face again. 'It depends.'

This time she closed her eyes.

She heard him shift position, opened them and saw the beam waver above her head and along the wall.

It was strange how quickly she'd adjusted to the lurch from normality into nightmare. After the terror of Gary bursting through the kitchen window, the reckless drive through town and the sickening realisation that he planned to keep her prisoner in the disused mine, Laura had managed to steady herself. 'How long do we have to stay here?'

'As long as it takes.'

'To do what?'

Gary laughed. 'To bring Elliot back.'

Laura turned her head away. There was no point in trying to reason with him after all; no way through the distorted maze of Gary Wood's mind. She felt the fragile hold on her panic begin to slip.

'You can't do that for me, can you?' The yellow beam fluttered across the ceiling as he cast the torch to one side and dug deep into the rucksack.

'No.' Her eyes followed every shadowy movement, her ears took in each echoing drip.

He pulled a hurricane lamp from the bag and set it on the floor. Once lit, it gave a steadier, stronger light. Strangely, the action intensified Laura's fear. It meant that Gary had planned carefully and probably intended to keep her here for a long time. She watched as he delved deep into the bag a second time.

'See this photo?' He offered her a glimpse of a small framed picture of Hannah and Elliot. Hannah was dressed in a smart blue suit and wide-brimmed hat, as if for a wedding. The baby was smiling. Gary balanced the frame on top of the rucksack. 'I took it from our bedroom when I went back for the gun.' He gazed at the picture. 'This is as close as I can get to Elliot from now on.'

'I'm sorry, Gary . . .'

He lunged and knocked her back against the wall. 'Don't say that to me! Sorry . . . sorry . . . sorry!' He shook her savagely three times. 'Were you sorry when you lied to me about Elliot getting better?'

'I didn't!' She struggled for breath, tried to push him off. 'When did I do that?'

'Outside the surgery. I asked you was he going to die? You came out with what you lot always say: "We're doing our best." It was crap and you knew it.' He let her go and watched her sag. 'All I was asking for was the truth.'

Laura bent forward, hands resting on the filthy floor, arms braced to support her.

'I needed to know. I never asked you to cover it up. It was Hannah who was living the lie, telling me Elliot would make it. He would fight back, we would help him, Mr Grey was the best cancer doctor in the country . . .' He mimicked an optimistic tone, his face twisted into a sneer. 'I knew it wouldn't make a blind bit of difference.'

'But Hannah was dealing with it in her own way. She couldn't give up hope.'

'It was a lie!' He hunched back against the opposite wall and, tucking the gun closer to his side, studied Laura in silence for several minutes.

'You know what it's like to lose everything?' he asked suddenly. 'One day you have a future, the next thing, nothing. Everything you were living for has gone.'

'Yes,' she said quietly. The world tilted and you lost your bearings; you were alone. 'I'm divorced.'

She had gone to bed one night still married and miserable. She had got up the following day and decided to end it. She had shaped her statement. And her life had disintegrated.

Gary turned his head towards the photograph, then looked sideways back at her. 'Was that down to you?'

'I made the break, if that's what you mean. But it was the last thing I wanted. It was a question of survival.' Laura was aware that she was confessing to Gary things that she had been determined never to speak about. Because she too had nothing to lose.

'Did he slap you about?'

'No. He acted as if I was invisible. It felt worse than being hit.'

'I don't get that.'

'He cared about everyone and everything else on this planet, but not about me. He said he did, but he didn't. It took me years to realise that he didn't love me, even longer to get out of the mess.'

'How come?'

'He was working for the good of others. But I was the needy one. Maybe I wasn't worth loving. Once you let that idea get to you it's hard to make decisions. Anyway, I'd said for better, for worse.'

'What did he do, this husband of yours?' Gary rested his head against the wall, looked at her through narrowed eyes.

'He was a journalist.' She closed her own eyes and saw Tom. They'd just gone to bed for the first time and he was telling her he loved her.

'Like Jim Conroy?'

'In a way.' She flicked through the years. Tom was berating her. He called her narrow-minded, predictable, boring. Opening her eyes and sighing, she stared at her abductor. 'I finally gathered the strength to leave. So, yes, like you, I did once have everything. And I lost it all.'

CHAPTER THIRTY-NINE

Hawk Fell was where Luke came when he needed solitude. It was high on Ravenscar; a wind-swept ridge too steep and inhospitable even for the hardy sheep farmers of the upper Dale, aptly named home to kestrels which would hover over the heather, catch an air current, whirl away, dip and hover again.

Brutal in winter, its icy winds cut through the thickest jacket and it remained dramatic with every season. Winter snow lay on the horizon long after it had melted in the valley, summer rain clouds gathered there and gusted across the bare hills. In spring it was a haze of purple heather, in autumn a blaze of red and orange ferns.

Luke waited with Philip and Piers. Laura's fellow GPs had picked up the news that had spread rapidly from the Shepherds' house on Town Head around the village. They'd worked out Luke's whereabouts from the rumours and counter-rumours and now, late on this Saturday evening in July, they stood in silence at the roadside, looking out over the gloomy hill where the rifle club had its ranges. Meanwhile Mike Jackson and his CID colleague had driven the further mile to Waite, intending to interview the secretary of the village rifle club. A patrol car was parked nearby, outside the door of the Miners Arms.

Luke watched the colours drain from the landscape as dusk fell and the last patches of daylight on the rolling hills were swallowed by fast-creeping shadow. 'Don't worry, we'll find her.' He heard Mike Jackson's comforting words echo faintly in his mind. But the wild sweep of the land and the deepening dusk made any such reassurance futile.

'Come into the bar,' Philip suggested. He and Piers seemed out of their depth but anxious to help.

Luke nodded and followed.

Inside the Miners a police officer was picking up scraps of information. The landlord, Terry Rowson, and his wife, Pat, had run the small hilltop pub for ten years and knew the comings and goings of most people in Ginnersby village. But they seemed mystified by reports that Gary Wood had driven his truck up the one-in-six gradient at reckless speed earlier that evening.

'I swear he didn't come past here,' Terry told the uniformed woman officer, aware of all eyes turned in his direction. 'Our windows face straight out on to the road. We'd have noticed if he had.'

'Maybe he slipped by?'

'No way.' The landlord shook his head, casting a sympathetic look at Luke.

'Well, he definitely came past my place,' Dick Metcalfe cut in. Having spied the congregation of police cars from his hillside farm, he had given up his warm corner at the Falcon for a windy drive up to his second-string local pub. 'I'd stake my life it was him ... and your young lady doctor,' he added, for Philip's and Piers's benefit.

'Is there another road he could have turned on to?' The policewoman had her notebook open.

'There's no junction until you come into Ginnersby, then you can take the top way over to Merton. But he'd have to go past here first.' Dick was adamant. He turned to the newcomers. 'What's up?'

Luke stiffened.

'Dick doesn't mean any harm,' Philip murmured, leading

241

him to an out-of-the-way corner, then going to order whisky from the bar.

'I should never have let this happen.' Luke found that he could hardly speak. 'I talked to Laura less than an hour before. I was telling her not to leave the house until I got back.'

'There's nothing you could have done.'

'Why didn't Wood's wife tell the police straight away that he'd taken the gun? She must have known he was in a dangerous frame of mind.'

'Probably because in spite of everything she didn't want to get him into trouble.'

Luke was aware of Piers trying to calm him down. He looked at his watch, wondering whether the inspectors would gain anything from their visit to the rifle club. He'd just decided that Gary must have driven the truck past the Miners, and that the best thing to do when Jackson and Walton got back was to spread the search further afield, when he noticed Frank Edwards come through the door.

'What's with the police car?' Frank walked straight across to Luke's table. 'We don't get many of those stopping in this corner of the Dale. Julia and I were on our way back from Merton when we spotted it. What's going on?'

As he carried the drinks from the bar, Philip explained about the search for Gary and Laura. 'I don't suppose you were at home earlier this evening?'

'You mean, when Gary Wood drove up the fell?'

'Did you see him?' Impatiently, Luke pressed for an answer. Frank nodded and Philip called the woman officer over.

'With Laura?'

'I think so. I was in the conservatory at the back of the house, but I heard a car coming way too fast. I looked out and I was pretty sure it was Gary driving. Then, when he turned off the road, I got a better look.'

'Where? Where did he turn off?' Luke stood up, almost pinning Frank against the bar.

'Down the track – the track to the smelt mill. It runs by the side of our house. It struck me as odd at the time. No one takes a car down there as a rule, because it doesn't lead anywhere. It's a dead end.'

Inside the tunnel, Laura had no way of knowing if night had fallen. They would already be looking for her, she was sure. But would anyone know where they had gone? And, once dark, would they call off the search until dawn? She thought of Luke, and how he must have arrived at Abbey Grange and discovered that she was missing. By now the police would be involved. And yes, she thought, Luke would carry on looking all through the night. He wouldn't sleep or rest until he'd found her.

She shivered. The damp and cold had crept into her bones. In the dim light of the hurricane lamp she saw that Gary Wood's face was a picture of misery, his mouth drawn down by deep lines of grief, his eyes hooded and swollen. And he had begun to drink.

There was a bottle of whisky in the rucksack. He'd reached for it, even offered her some after she'd told him about her divorce. She'd said no and pleaded with him to let her go. 'Not in a million years.' He'd silenced her by quietly tapping the barrel of the shotgun. 'All the talking in the world won't make any difference. We sit tight.'

'Why?' she asked him now, huddled against the wall. They were back to square one.

'Will you stop asking me that.'

'I deserve a reason.' Her body was shaking with cold, the blood on her ankle had congealed around the bottom of her trouser leg and she was terrified.

'Wrong place, wrong time. And you happen to get on my nerves.' He drank from the bottle, letting the top fall and roll away. 'Your type thinks they have rights, like you were born better than the rest. We don't have rights, we just come into this piss-awful world, some of us live longer than others, then we all die. No one has any rights. No one deserves reasons.'

'You're wrong,' she protested.

'OK, give me one reason why my boy had to die. You can't, can you? Yeah, you can give me the stuff about bone marrow and blood cells. You can pretend he got it because I worked on a farm near Ruthwell. What kind of reason is that, when no one really knows?' Gary tilted sideways, then steadied himself. 'That's what I hate: the way you pretend you've got the answers and we look up to you. Then you let us down.'

'I tried not to.' Laura moved out of his way as he struggled to stand up. 'I'm sorry if that's how it came across.'

'Here's a reason. I wanted to get my own back. This and the phone calls. I knew they'd upset you.'

She hated him for towering over her with the gun and gloating. He was hurting and drunk, sadistic, cruel. She turned her head away.

'Look at me!' He lunged and seized her hair, wrenching her head round and pressing the cold gun barrel against it. 'Reasons? Number one, my little boy died. Two, my wife won't let me near. Three, you're a stuck-up bitch.'

Laura held her breath. This would pass, she told herself. In seconds, the pain, the anger would fade.

He released his hold, the gun dropped. Her head sank forward. 'Have you heard of radon gas?' she whispered. 'You can't see it, you can't smell it, it's radioactive.'

'You mean it gives you cancer?'

'In high doses, yes. It's not the waste produced by the power stations. It's a natural gas found in spring water and in the air.'

He vanished into the dark a few paces down the tunnel, deeper into the side shaft, then strode back. 'What are you saying?'

244

She went on in a low, almost mechanical voice, staring at the glow of the lamp. 'You find a lot of it in limestone; in caves and streams – sometimes hundreds of times higher than the safety level set by the Radiological Protection Board.'

'Limestone,' he repeated. 'Radon? I've never heard of it. This gas – you'd find it around here?'

'On Ravenscar. Around the tarn. In Black Gill.'

'Could it have given Elliot leukaemia?'

'It's possible.'

Gary flung the shotgun to the ground and dropped on to his knees in front of her, forcing her to look him in the eye. 'Yes or no?'

'I can't say for sure. It's as likely as the Ruthwell thing. Maybe more likely.'

She saw the confused flickering of his eyes, smelled the whisky, felt him fall against her and begin to cry.

'Why him? Why did he get ill and die, and not someone else's kid? He was a little boy, my boy – mine! You can't believe it's happening. You say no, this isn't true, at first. Then he falls really sick and you have to stand by watching him get worse.

'You pray, and the stupid thing is you don't even believe in God. You look at your kid's eyes and you know he knows. He wants to come home with you from the hospital and you say no, the nice doctors will make you better. His eyes tell you you're lying. You're lying to protect him and he looks at you as if you've let him down. In the end, you can't stand that look any more.'

Laura let him lean against her, his head on her shoulder, her own pressed back against the wall. Her hands hung by her side as grief swept over him.

'You stay away from the cancer ward, you let him down big time. You hate yourself for ever.'

Luke ran in the dark down the winding gravel track towards

the lead mine, ignoring Philip's shouts and Piers's attempts to hold him back.

The police officer at the pub was paging Mike Jackson and his CID boss to get back to Ginnersby as soon as they could. They were ordering more immediate vehicles over from Merton and Wingate, promising a response time of twenty minutes. 'Armed abductor has been located,' he'd heard the policewoman repeat. 'Emergency. We need armed officers, an ambulance, a hostage negotiator.'

Breaks in the cloud gave him enough moon- and starlight to make out the tall chimney of the smelt mill, the skeleton framework of derelict sheds in a flat-bottomed dip below. It was the end of the track, surrounded by ugly slag heaps as high as the pointed gables of the old sheds.

'The truck! Look for the truck!' Luke heard footsteps and turned to see Philip and Piers sprinting down the track. 'If we can find where Gary hid the truck, we can pin-point where he's got Laura before the emergency vehicles arrive.'

'In here!' Piers ran from shed to shed and quickly found the red pick-up. He vaulted into the back and peered through the window. 'He left the keys in the ignition.'

Philip was looking back the way they'd come, picking up the noise of more cars arriving, blue lights flashing. They hadn't sounded their sirens, thank God. 'You know this area is riddled with old mine shafts,' he told them from the shed doorway. 'They're boarded up, so we need to find one that's been broken into.'

'And that'll be where he's taken her?'

Luke ran out to join him. His breath was jagged. He felt as if he were being ripped apart with every second that passed. 'Can you find your way around here?'

'I know most of the tunnel entrances into the main levels from when we used to walk with the boys. But watch your step – some of the minor shafts drop straight down.'

'Come on, Philip!' Luke ignored the caution and ran ahead, along a worn grass track.

'He's got a gun, remember. If he hears us we don't know what he'll do.' Philip too stuck to the track, closely followed by Piers.

Back on the brow of the hill, headlights turned off the road and headed slowly towards the smelt mill. Help crept across the moor: three white patrol cars, a police Land Rover and an ambulance.

'What was that?' Gary Wood leaped to his feet and grabbed the shotgun. He caught the lamp with the wooden butt and sent it rolling between the rails.

Laura started back as he raised the gun. She stood up and pressed herself against the wall.

'Don't move. Did you hear something?'

She heard the sound of her own heart thumping, the rocking and clicking of the lamp against the metal rail.

'From outside. Did you?'

She listened and waited.

'Stay here.' Keeping the gun aimed at her, he backed out of the side tunnel, disappearing beyond the reach of the lamplight.

As she leaned forward to set the lamp upright, she knocked the framed picture of Hannah and Elliot on to the ground. The glass cracked and splintered.

'There! Did you hear that?' Gary was calling back to her from the main level, his voice muffled.

Left alone in the narrow shaft, she fingered the broken picture. Then, filled with fresh panic, she seized the lamp and set off down the side tunnel, not knowing where it led, fleeing with nothing in her mind except escape.

He heard her go. Within seconds he was coming after her, stumbling and swearing. She ran, swinging the lamp wildly at

247

arm's length to pick out a way, until she came to a wall of solid rock.

Laura put out her hand. Her fingers felt the rough, wet surface and she began to cry.

He caught up, grabbed the lamp and smashed it against the wall. In the pitch dark he hooked his arm around her neck and dragged her back until they stumbled against his rucksack. Then they knew they'd reached the junction with the main shaft. There was cooler, drier air, and more of the sounds that Gary had first heard.

'Laura!' called a distant, muffled voice, as footsteps came nearer.

She cried out, 'Luke! Go back!'

Gary shoved her to the ground and fired the gun. Laura rolled, curled up and put her hands to her head. Another shot.

'Go back!' she pleaded.

'Do it!' Gary yelled. 'Get out of here or she's dead!'

CHAPTER FORTY

The police sealed off the area. They stopped traffic from coming up Hawk Fell and put a road-block across the junction in Ginnersby. Only official vehicles were allowed through.

From the sheds by the derelict smelt mill James Walton directed a cautious operation to send a field telephone into the shaft where Wood held Laura hostage. 'We'll need to take it very, very slowly,' he warned Luke and the rest. 'We leave the cars and the bulk of officers here, and we offer him the phone ... We arrange to do that in a way that doesn't threaten him.'

Two gunshots had been heard from up on the road, as Walton and Mike Jackson had arrived. An officer had been detailed to hold customers from the Miners Arms at bay.

Luke was aware of Philip and Piers keeping a close eye on him. Once they'd discovered the broken door to the shaft they'd been unable to stop him running into the tunnel, but the blast of gunfire and Laura's voice pleading with him to go back had shocked him into retreat.

'She's still alive!' Piers reminded him. 'Hang on to that.'

But Wood's threat to kill Laura had sounded genuine. Luke listened out for more gunshots, his heart lacerated.

'From now on, you do exactly as we tell you.' Mike Jackson instructed two armed officers to accompany him and the CID inspector to the tunnel with the phone. The men were fully kitted out with handcuffs and telescopic truncheons belted round their waists. They took guns from their holsters and waited for their next order.

'Where's the negotiator?' Walton asked. He was systematic and calm, his white hair marking him out from the group of a dozen or so police officers gathered by the mill.

'Still on his way over from Leeds, sir.' The woman officer who had raised the alarm was keeping track.

Walton looked at his watch in the beam of a headlight. 'Let's get the phone in anyway.'

'I'll come.' Philip stepped forward, warning Piers to keep hold of Luke. 'I've been the family's GP for years. Gary knows my voice.'

'I have to come too.' It was more than Luke could stand to watch Philip and the two senior policemen try without him. He wrenched himself free of Piers and squared up to Walton.

Mike Jackson nodded at his fellow inspector, who gave Philip and Luke the go-ahead. 'We go as far as the entrance with the armed men. You two keep to one side. Philip, you speak to him through the loudhailer.'

Carefully Philip took in the instructions as they set off towards the shaft. Car headlights were brought into position to light up the track and, overhead, the night sky was clearing.

'Have we any idea how far inside the tunnel they are?' Walton asked. He was the one who carried the field phone and the hailer.

'I must have run about fifty metres in before he fired the shots.' Luke tried to judge the distance accurately.

'We couldn't see a thing,' Philip added. 'But Gary obviously heard us. They can't be too much further back than that.'

'We won't take lights in,' Jackson warned. 'That's bound to upset him. We have to do this in the dark.'

With every sense straining and his whole body tingling, Luke arrived with the group at the tunnel entrance.

Walton handed Philip the hailer and nodded. 'Just tell him we want to give him a phone. Nothing else.'

Philip stared into the darkness. Luke willed himself to stay calm and listen as he spoke into the mouthpiece.

'Gary, it's me, Philip Maskell.'

His voice, unfamiliar through the hailer, met deep, long silence.

Laura raised her head. Gary had fired the gun twice and the shots had echoed down the tunnel. He'd pulled her up from the ground and bundled her back down the main shaft until they'd crashed against the upturned metal carts. Then he'd stopped. He'd forced her down on to her knees close to one of the carts, which she'd grasped for support. Then they'd endured a long, tense silence.

Now she felt the barrel of the gun in her back.

'. . . Gary, it's me, Philip Maskell.'

He dug the gun between her ribs.

'. . . We've brought a phone. We want to talk.'

Gary didn't reply. Laura clung to the cart, her cheek pressed against the rusty metal.

'We'll leave the phone switched on by the tunnel entrance and go back to the mill,' Philip went on slowly, evenly. 'All you have to do is come and pick it up. We'll stay well back.'

Who was 'we'? Was Luke with them? Laura felt the pressure from the gun barrel lessen as Gary bent to pull her to her feet.

'Gary? It's OK, you don't have to answer. We're going to leave the phone exactly where I said and you can fetch it in your own time. We'll wait until you're ready.'

Laura fell against him, her legs stiff from crouching. He put his arm round her neck in the same stranglehold as before.

'When you do want to talk, remember we lose the signal if you go back down the shaft. Stay near the entrance, OK?'

Gary moved her forward, shielding himself behind her. He was saying nothing, breathing hard, crying.

*

251

'Good.' Walton was satisfied. He put down the phone inside the tunnel entrance and ordered everyone back to the mill.

Philip let the loudhailer drop. 'How are you doing?' he asked Luke quietly.

Ignoring the question, Luke retreated up the track. 'She's alive. She has to be,' he muttered, brushing the tears from his cheeks with the back of his hand. A glare of headlights silhouetted the tight knot of people waiting at the mill for news.

'We got over the first hurdle,' Mike Jackson reported.

Now all eyes were on the tunnel entrance, only dimly visible beyond the reach of the car lights.

'You did well,' Luke heard Walton tell Philip. 'If things move fast and Wood makes contact before our trained officer gets here I want you to carry on talking.' Seeing that Luke was about to interrupt, he held up a warning hand. 'I know what you want to say, but this isn't one for you,' he insisted. 'If Wood and Laura so much as know you're here, it turns up the heat too high for us to handle.'

'What do I say next?' Philip asked.

'Stick to the approach you just used, nice and calm. Play on the fact that you know him and want to sort things out. Whatever you do, don't ask him what he wants. Much better to go in low-key with "We've got a problem".'

Philip nodded several times.

'Remember, this is an unusual abduction,' the inspector went on. 'As yet, Wood hasn't made any demands. And we don't want to offer him any opportunities to do that. It would only lock him into a position he can't back down from.'

'Jim!' Mike Jackson interrupted with a gesture towards the tunnel. 'Looks like we've got action.'

Sure enough, there was movement. Two figures stumbled into view. Laura's white blouse showed up in the dark. Luke's heart thumped so hard it almost broke through his ribs. The armed officers stood ready.

Walton warned everyone to stay where they were, thrusting his own phone into Philip's hand. 'The hostage is being used as a shield. Let's take this carefully, shall we.'

The fresh night air hit Laura as she and Gary reached the exit from the tunnel. Her eyes, accustomed to the pitch black of the interior, soon made out the long sweep of hills, the line of the horizon, the stars. Nearer, her gaze was met by the glare of headlights, dark figures standing still, watching and waiting. Was Luke among them, she wondered?

'Gary, it's Philip again.'

She heard the voice speak through the phone where it lay on the ground. Philip holding steady in a crisis; a flood of gratitude washed over her.

'Let's try and sort this out. Pick up the phone and talk to me.'

Once more she felt the gun in her back as Gary reached for the phone. He grasped it clumsily and held it between them, allowing her to hear and studying her reaction.

'I want to help,' Philip insisted. 'Let's talk about what we can do.'

'I've got your Dr Grant right here with me.' Gary wanted to warn them not to make a move.

'Yes. How are you both?'

'She hurt her ankle.'

'How bad?'

'She's bleeding from a cut, but she can still walk on it.'

'I'm OK!' Laura tried to reassure them, but the phone was pulled sharply away.

There was a pause. 'And how about you, Gary?'

'Fine!' he mocked. 'I want Hannah. Bring her here.'

The dialogue had swung in the wrong direction. Philip tried to put it back on course. 'We'll talk about that later. First I need to know what you need; blankets, food, first-aid equipment.'

'Get me Hannah,' Gary repeated stubbornly.

'Get the wife!' Luke hissed, ready to accede to any demand. 'For Christ's sake fetch her!'

'If you don't bring her up here, I've got nothing to say to you. We go back down the tunnel.' Gary retreated a couple of paces, weakening the signal.

The CID inspector nodded and motioned an officer to stand by.

'OK, Gary, listen to me!' Philip pressed on. 'I saw Hannah a couple of hours ago, at Town Head. They'll send someone to fetch her. If you come to the entrance of the tunnel, you'll see him go.'

Luke watched as the figures came back into view and a uniformed man jumped into a car and drove up the track.

'She'll be here within half an hour,' Philip assured him. 'Now, next thing: are you cold in there? Do you need blankets?'

'Just tell me when she gets here.' Gary flung the phone to the ground, sending it skidding against a rock.

'They think I'm thick – trying to get me to waste time talking to them,' he told Laura. He pointed the gun at her to get her to back off into the tunnel again. 'They don't understand – the only person I want to talk to is my wife.'

'Sorry.' Philip handed the phone back to Walton.

'We made good contact. If fetching his wife solves it, we could soon be out of here without anyone getting hurt.' Walton took his armed men to one side to talk tactics.

Luke tilted back his head to look at the night sky, trying to fix himself in time and space, and to get rid of the feeling that he was living a nightmare. It was impossible. Unable to stand still, he began to walk urgently up and down, striding into the derelict shed. Seeing the parked pick-up, he crashed his fist against its side.

'How are we going to get her out of there in one piece?' he asked Piers, who had followed.

'By keeping our heads. Listen, Luke, if Gary really wanted to harm her he would have done it by now. At least we know what he's up to. Once we get Hannah here, we're giving him what he wants. And Walton won't let him talk to Hannah until he's let Laura go.'

'What if he refuses?' Luke imagined what he would do in Gary's situation. 'If he's got any sense, he'll hang on to Laura. She's his safe passage out.'

Luke looked up the road at the cluster of police cars. He noticed the tall figure of Matthew Aire, recently arrived, standing there in silent reproach. He wished uselessly, with sickening futility, that he had followed Matthew's instinct to protect Laura and that he'd never dragged her into the Ruthwell fiasco. When it came down to it, it was he, Luke, who had made her a target for Wood's twisted revenge.

'Hannah, we're going to try and set Gary up with another telephone.' Luke watched as Mike Jackson explained what was going to happen now. 'They'll use a loudhailer to tell him you're here and after that they'll take the phone to the entrance of the tunnel. You have to stay here by the smelt mill, out of sight.'

She'd arrived in an Immediate Response Vehicle, surprisingly calm, but looking small and lost among the uniforms and glaring headlights. 'Why out of sight?' She watched carefully as Walton briefed Alan Morley, the newly arrived negotiator, and the two men approached the mouth of the tunnel.

'For your own safety.' Philip stepped in, took off his jacket and offered it as an extra layer for Hannah, who was shivering on the windy hillside.

'And what do I say to him?' She turned to Philip for support.

'Basically, we want to get Laura out. You have to make it clear you will speak to him, but not until he lets her go. He just has to know you're here and willing to talk. Leave it to the police to arrange the details.'

She nodded. 'Thank you, Dr Maskell.'

He put his arm round her. 'This must be terrible for you.'

'I have to help get Dr Grant out. As for Gary, there isn't a thing he could say to me that's going to make any difference to the way I feel.'

'OK!' Gary was back at the tunnel entrance with Laura. He'd heard the negotiator's voice on the loudhailer announcing Hannah's arrival and retraced his steps. 'But no phones this time!'

Laura stood between him and the police marksmen, the shotgun rammed into her back.

'Give Hannah the hailer. Let her talk into it!'

They waited, the wind blowing strongly against them, dazzled by the lights.

'Gary, it's me. I'm here!'

'Hannah!' His voice cracked and broke.

'Yes . . .'

'Gary, this is Alan Morley. I've just arrived. I'm here to help sort things out.'

'Where's Dr Maskell?' he yelled, disorientated by the new voice.

'He's still here, Gary. But listen, we can't get very far until you let Dr Grant go . . . Gary, can you hear me?'

'Don't mess me around. I'll use the gun!'

Laura raised both hands to Gary's arm to try and relieve the pressure of his hold round her neck. She felt her knees sag as she struggled to breathe.

Luke shouted out and sprang forward. Piers stood in his way, other pairs of hands grabbed him and held him back.

'Hannah!' Gary yelled.

'She's here, Gary, waiting to speak to you. But we've got to sort out a few things first.'

He swore and stood his ground.

'Let me speak to him!' Hannah pleaded.

Mike Jackson held her back. 'Not yet. Wait until he releases the hostage.'

'Please!' She strained towards the tunnel, sobbing loudly.

'Hannah, I'm sorry!' The words disappeared into the night sky. It was as if the wind had caught them and torn them away. Then the gun went off.

Laura turned to see the long barrel slip from under Gary's chin. She heard the butt thud to the ground, then he swayed back, arms spreadeagled.

Gary twisted as he fell, face shot away, toppling full length, flinging one arm across his head to shield them from what he'd done.

CHAPTER FORTY-ONE

Luke ran forward at the sound of the shot. He swerved past Piers, then Walton and the negotiator, who both stepped across his path.

'Wait!' Walton spun round to follow him.

Luke kept going towards the tunnel.

'Move the cars in! Bring the paramedics down!' Jackson bellowed orders. Suddenly everyone was running.

'Laura!' Luke shouted her name.

She was crouched over Gary Wood, her white shirt covered with blood. When she saw Luke, she leaped up and ran into his arms.

He held her sobbing, trembling body, kissed her, cried with relief.

Philip arrived close on Luke's heels. He responded to yelled instructions from the paramedics. 'Turn him on to his back. Try to find an airway, check his pulse!'

Over Laura's shoulder, Luke saw Philip examine the destroyed face, then tear open Gary's shirt before the paramedics and Hannah crowded round.

'We need to get air into his lungs,' Philip muttered. 'We have to get at the windpipe. We need instruments, catheters . . .' He looked up to see the traumatised face of Gary's wife.

Hannah came and crouched by her husband, resisting attempts to hold her back. 'Leave him,' she said quietly, recognising that it was hopeless. She reached out and gently touched the hand that had held the gun.

'There wasn't a chance,' Walton told them. 'There was nothing anyone could have done.'

They were using the Miners Arms as a refuge while the paramedics and police cleared the scene. Philip, Luke, Laura and Hannah had waited almost silently in the bar.

'I know.' Hannah had accepted what Laura was still struggling with. She moved into a strange calm. 'He'd suffered enough.'

Laura had taken a blanket from the landlord's wife and wrapped it round her shoulders. She sat in her bloodied clothes, waiting to be allowed to go home. She ached with cold and shock, resting against Luke's sheltering arm.

'Poor Gary,' Hannah murmured quietly. 'There was no need to say sorry.'

'Do you think that's what he planned all along?' Luke asked Laura. 'To take his own life?'

She shook her head, unable to express the purposelessness of it. 'I don't think so.'

'Would it have made any difference if they'd let me talk to him properly?' Hannah asked.

'No. He told me a lot of things while we were in there. There was no way through this for him. He was lost.' Laura held Luke tightly, drawing strength from his warm body. 'But I do know this,' she told Hannah. 'Gary loved Elliot and he loved you. He would have wanted me to tell you that.'

Breathing again after the harrowing night, Luke and Laura sat at dawn under the lilac tree in the garden at Abbey Grange. It was Sunday. The rooks used the air currents to soar above the green trees of Black Gill.

'You need some sleep,' Luke told her. He had spent the night awake, bathed in relief and a sense that he was the recipient of a blessing he hardly deserved.

The air was pure, growing warm with the rising sun. There

was a mist over Ravenscar that would soon burn off and leave the day clear, the sky eggshell-blue. 'Later,' she murmured. First, she had told Luke, she wanted the scent of roses, the feel of the sun's rays on her skin.

Luke hovered over her. 'I thought I was going to lose you.'

She stood up and leaned her head against his shoulder, felt his arms round her waist.

'I couldn't bear it.' He kissed her warm, soft hair and stroked it. 'I've never felt so helpless . . . so desperate.'

'I'm here now,' she whispered. She lifted her face to his.

He kissed her softly, held her.

'Don't let me go.' Her cheek was against his, her arms round his neck.

'I won't. I love you.'

Slowly she moved her head to look at him. They were so close that his face was blurred, his grey, half-closed eyes searching hers.

'I love you, Luke.'

Above their heads the leaves were green against the dappled blue sky.

CHAPTER FORTY-TWO

'Catherine looks well, doesn't she?' Peter Earle asked. He and Sonia had heard about Laura's involvement in the events leading to Gary Wood's death, and they'd called with Catherine and Adam at Abbey Grange. It was Sunday evening. The busy working week lay ahead.

'She looks great,' Laura could genuinely agree. Her patient had just run out of the gate with her brother, across the field towards Black Gill. The girl's bobbed black hair shone in the sun, her limbs were brown.

'We saw Mr Grey on Friday for her regular check-up. He says she's in full remission.' Sonia sat with the others on the lawn drinking red wine. 'We don't need to take her back to the hospital for another three months.'

'That's wonderful.' Laura lost sight of Catherine among the trees. 'You must both be relieved.'

'And, to tell you the truth, a bit guilty.' Peter opened up now that Catherine and Adam were out of hearing.

'Comparing ourselves with what Hannah has to cope with.' Sonia stared into her wineglass.

'She's an amazing woman,' Laura said. 'Really stoical.'

'And young enough to make a new start, eventually.' Peter looked at Laura. 'Still, it makes Sonia and me wonder what would have happened if Catherine hadn't made such good progress.'

'But you two stuck together.' Laura looked back over the last few weeks.

'Only just.' Sonia smiled wryly. She turned to Luke. 'To be honest, the pressure group was the thing that nearly split us up.' Realising she might have been too outspoken she rushed on. 'Not that it was the group's fault. It just . . . drove me mad.'

'Me too,' Peter confessed. 'I was like a rat in a maze. But I'm still glad that you and Jim were there to do it, Luke . . . Are still there,' he corrected himself.

'Plugging away.' Luke cleared his throat. 'Has Laura told you we might have to change direction a bit? There's the radon gas business and the fact that Ravenscar is limestone.'

Peter nodded. 'Mr Grey mentioned it. He says he wants to write a paper on it. Does that mean you'll let up on Ruthwell?'

Laura listened to talk of the new and old avenues, letting it wash over her. She shrugged at Sonia, who gave the same wry smile as before. The two of them stood up and wandered among the rose bushes.

'Will they?' Sonia asked, stopping underneath a trellis arch.

'Let up on Ruthwell?' Laura considered it. 'If I know Luke, I doubt it. They've got Julia and Frank Edwards on board, and a long way to go before they've finished with the whole nuclear industry.'

'I suppose I'm glad.' Sonia sighed.

'You mean, someone ought to hold the power plants accountable?'

'As long as it's not me and Peter,' she agreed. 'Is that spineless of me?'

'No. It's called recognising your limits.' Laura picked a rose, then another. Soon she had a bunch of the velvety creamy pink flowers to give to Hannah Wood when she visited her at her parents' house in half an hour's time. 'It's something I've been working on for the past few months, and it's a very difficult lesson to learn.'

'Ready, everyone?' Philip gave the go-ahead for the morning meeting. 'Take a few days off,' he'd told Laura. 'Give yourself time to get over the shock.' But here she was, a day later, in her cream summer dress, her dark hair tied back, a new ring on the third finger of her left hand.

'Luke's grandmother's,' she'd confided with a smile before the others had gathered for the eight-twenty. 'Rubies and diamonds. He gave it to me yesterday.'

And now she was looking with concern across the room, as Piers signalled that he had something important to say. Sheila had come out from behind reception to listen too.

'This won't take long,' he began. 'No big speeches. You all know that Harry, my son, is being prosecuted for burgling Laura's house.'

Laura gazed steadily at Piers. Sheila stared down at the papers in front of her.

'Which is about as bad a start as anyone can have in a new work situation,' Piers went on. 'Not to mention the way I went about making myself unpopular in my own right.

'Anyway, to cut a long story, which you all know, short, I handed in my notice to Philip.'

Sheila frowned. 'Not for our sakes, I hope,' she said brusquely. 'We're just beginning to get used to you.'

'And not for mine, either,' Laura added.

Piers paused. 'Francesca and I have spent a lot of time talking things over in the last few days. We both know we want to see Harry through this.

'The Merton police and Luke say that it being a first offence should make a difference, plus the fact that Harry will plead guilty. And the way Francesca and I see it, there's something to be gained from making him stick it out and trying to get himself reinstated at the school here . . . not taking the easy way out by moving him on to another place.'

'Yes,' Sheila agreed. 'That takes a lot more doing.'

'Well, if that's true for Harry, we saw that it must hold good for us too.' Piers took a deep breath, turning to the head of the table. He spoke quietly, his eyes narrowed by nervous tension.

'I don't know if it's too late, Philip, but I want to withdraw my resignation. If you'll have me, I'd like to stay here in Hawkshead.'

Laura's round of morning visits took her up Hawk Fell and through Ginnersby over to Waite. Passing the Miners Arms and the glimpse of green track down to the old lead mine, there was no reminder for her of Gary Wood's suicide except the scenes that played out inside her head.

She drove on. Here, on the ridge of the hill, there were no roadside walls to pen in the wandering sheep, no trees growing in the thin covering of soil. The rocks beneath showed through in places, white as bone.

'Don't lose your human face,' was what her old teacher had instilled into her. 'In the end, we're all in the same boat.'

We breathe the same air, tread the same beautiful earth, run the same risks. And the earth round here was lovely as she drove along the ridge of Ravenscar, the tarn to her left, the drop to her right into the valley where Hawkshead sat at the foot of the cliff and the abbey nestled in the bend of the river.

For how long would she remember Gary's voice as he'd told Hannah he was sorry, she wondered? For ever. As long as she lived – and the look on Luke's face when he said he loved her.